#follo

Tower Bri

It is two in the morning, ̣ ̣ ̣ ̣ ̣ ̣ ̣ ̣ ̣ ̣ ̣ ̣ is seen diving off the bridge into the dark, icy waters below. When his body is recovered from the river, it is found to contain high levels of the drug Ecstasy.

The dead student shared a house with the niece of investigative newspaper reporter Jack Richardson, who decides to retrace the student's last few days to establish the true story behind his death.

However, as Jack follows this trail, he encounters dark forces, and a perilous outcome for both himself and his niece…

Philip Cox was born and raised in the UK seaside town of Southend on Sea, which lies forty miles east of London. After graduating from High School, he began a career in UK Banking and Financial Services, and spent the next decades working his way through the ranks, finally becoming a Branch Manager of a major UK bank.

Philip left banking after the birth of his first child to be a stay-at-home father, and it was during this time that, in between changing diapers/nappies, he began to write his first novel, 'After the Rain'.

Now having written thirteen books, he is based in Hertfordshire, some twenty miles north of London, with his wife and two daughters.

During his spare time (what spare time there is between school runs and writing!), Philip enjoys indulging his interest in Model Railroading/Railways.

He is tall and slim, has a few grey hairs, and wishes he could get to the gym more often.

Philip's website is www.philipcoxbooks.com, and he can be followed on twitter @philipcoxbooks, on Instagram https://www.instagram.com/philipcoxbooks, and Facebook https://www.facebook.com/philipcoxbooks.

Also by Philip Cox

Jack Richardson
The Value of Nothing
The Angel
The Coyote

Detective Sam Leroy
Last to Die
Wrong Time to Die
No Place to Die
Another Way to Die
Ready to Die

Standalone thrillers
After the Rain
Dark Eyes of London
She's Not Coming Home
Should Have Looked Away

THE
TRAIL

PHILIP COX

This book is a work of fiction. Names and characters are the product of the author's imagination and any resemblance to actual persons, living or dead, is entirely coincidental.

www.philipcoxbooks.com

ISBN 979-8422972159

FOR CHASE MCGUIRE

Taken from us far too soon

ACKNOWLEDGEMENTS

All I did was write the book! Thanks are also due to (as ever) Anne Poole; Kendal University; London Underground; *Café Rouge*; SpitalfieldsLife; DrugFacts; House of Commons Library; *Town of Ramsgate*. Tower Bridge is owned, funded, and managed by the City of London.

Cover photograph by Andrew Murdock

.

The use of Kendal University is arbitrary and references *The Coyote*. No inference should be made concerning that establishment and the events in this book.

CHAPTER ONE

HE FELT LIKE he could do anything.

When he had heard people talking about it before, they used the word *euphoria*.

Was this what *euphoria* meant?

He couldn't remember how it started. He could vaguely recall, somewhere in the back of his mind, being in a pub. He had no recollection where the pub was, or what it was called. Or much about it, except that on one wall, just by the door to the bathroom, there was a TV screen on the wall. A football match was playing. No idea who was playing. Some of the players were wearing red.

The pub...

Or was it a club? Now he recalled music, loud music. A loud beat. Lights. Like searchlights.

Or was it a pub *and* a club? He had a recollection of going to the gents, of walking past that TV screen. As he came out, he was met with a loud cry from some of the people by the TV. Not because he had emerged from the gents, but because one of the teams had scored.

Yes, it was a pub, first of all, anyway. He must have arrived on his own. He did that a lot. But he could remember, vaguely and faintly, talking to some people there, people he didn't know. A guy and a girl. Or was there a third there? Two guys and a girl. Or a guy with two girls: he couldn't remember. It was all too hazy, and too tiring to stretch his memory.

He could recollect talking to them, no idea about what. Then they were on the street, walking together. Then sitting somewhere else, something moving. That was it: they were on a bus. Then those bright searchlights and the thudding beat, like drums beating inside his head. Drums, dubstep, bass.

He was sitting in this other place. They had just got back from the bar, and he was talking to the girl. She gave him something. He was tired then, and had had a few drinks.

He shook his head. It was fuzzy. It was strange his memories were so vague, but it didn't really matter. He was so happy now. He had found new friends, and they were such wonderful people. It was as if he had known them all his life. As if they were brothers and sisters. He remembered the girl hugging him, and that felt so good. She held him tight, he held her tight. He could feel the warmth from her body, and she smelt so good.

Now he felt on top of the world. He was no longer sat in his bedroom, gaming or chatting. He felt weightless, like he was in the sky, looking down at all those tiny people scurrying around, doing whatever tiny people did.

Where had she gone? He could no longer see her in the throng. Couldn't see the guy either. He hadn't been paying attention – they had probably left.

He was sure he was outside now. The music had stopped, or had it? Somewhere in the back of his mind, he could still hear it, beating away, somewhere behind the other sounds. There were lights now, not the searchlights but white, and red. The sounds were like cars, and buses, so he had to be outside, but he couldn't feel the air against his skin.

But he was deliriously happy.

And he felt strong. Stronger than he had ever felt before. So strong he could do anything.

And the lights were so bright. Not blindingly so, but clearer, in a much higher definition. And he could hear everything. He realised now it was traffic he could hear, so he must be outside. But not merging into one piece of background noise: he could hear every single vehicle. Cars, a bus, a van, a dustcart, another bus. The distinctive sound of a taxi.

He yawned. Not because he was tired: the opposite in fact – he had never felt so alive, so awake, so full of energy. His jaw felt tight, and he yawned to exercise it, also grinding his teeth. He had a strange sensation in his mouth.

Another sound. A horn, but not coming from the traffic. It was coming from below. He looked to his side. A long, wide, winding stretch of water. Along this water, by the side, he could see lights from buildings, a large wheel-like structure on the left. Across the water, lights were travelling in either direction. More bridges.

He looked down at his feet. His toes were tingling. He could see that he was standing on pavement, but it felt as if he was shuffling on gravel. What was telling him the truth: his eyes or his head? There was a stone pillar nearby, and he sat on that and removed his trainers. He stood up, shivered as it was getting cold, and looked back down at his feet again. Wiggled his toes. Yes, it still felt like he was on gravel, although his eyes told him clearly he was not.

He set off, with no idea where he was headed.

Now he wanted to fly. He climbed another pillar and began walking again. Then stopped. A bus went by, and he noticed two faces looking directly at him from the upper deck. He waved back at them; he wanted to hug them too.

He lifted his head and held out his arms. He was higher up now, and could feel the breeze blowing through his shirtsleeves.

He was at one with nature. He studied the river, as it curved one way and the next into the distance, the moonlight reflected from its dark surface. He had never felt so much at peace before; no conflicts, no fights, no arguments, no problems. He was at peace with the world, and with himself, and had never felt stronger and more in control.

He was on top of the world at last, and he really could fly.

The woman on the top deck of the night bus saw him as the bus passed by. She screamed as he left the ledge and plummeted the one hundred and fifty feet to the water below.

CHAPTER TWO

JACK RICHARDSON STARED at his reflection. He moved his head around so he could see his face from all angles. Then looked at his electric shaver. He rubbed his hand over the three days' growth.

It was down to his daughter. She was now at the age where she was beginning to notice things about people. Their looks, their hair – colour, cut and washed or not – their clothes and fashion sense.

Jack had always been clean shaven, apart from some experimentation in his early twenties with various styles and lengths of facial hair.   His daughter had never seen him unshaven.   She had obviously seen somebody with a beard, maybe somebody online, or a singer; maybe a teacher or a classmate's father.   God forbid a boyfriend.

'Why don't you grow one, Dad?' she asked one weekend, when she was staying with him. Monday to Friday, Cathy lived with her mother, Mel – Jack's ex-wife.

Jack was reluctant. 'I don't think it's me,' he protested.

'I think you ought to try. You can always shave it off if it doesn't work,' she replied, sounding three times her age of twelve.

Jack gave in.

That was three days ago. He had always felt that beards, and, to a lesser extent, moustaches, could look smart, if you had the kind of face that suits them. But not in the first few days. There was a distinct difference, he felt, between having a beard and not having shaved for a few days; and in the early stages, every beard looked scruffy and as if the owner had neglected to shave.

Jack was at that stage; but to try to mitigate the unshaven look, he had taken care to carry out some rudimentary form of styling: attention to under the chin and to the neck, making a clear division between beard and non-beard; also the sides of his face, keeping the beard growth to sideburns and around his mouth.

What did concern him, however, was not the untidy appearance: the last couple of days he had noticed a few grey flecks appearing on his chin, around the sides of his mouth. He was not sure if he wanted any grey hairs yet.

Jack nodded at his reflection once he had done what little bit of shaving he had planned on doing. It was getting there: looked better than yesterday, although he was still not sold on the idea. He would give it a few more days, maybe until next weekend.

Jack was preparing to go out on an assignment. It was a job, handed to him the day before by Mike Smith, his News Editor.

'I expect you'll consider this a BSA,' Mike had said, 'after all your other illustrious work, but you can't be Charles Foster Kane all the time.'

Mike Smith's uncharacteristically erudite remark made reference to some previous assignments Jack had been on, where he had uncovered a network of modern-day Fagins exploiting homeless kids, getting them dependant on drugs, then forcing them to carry out robberies or offer sex to feed their habits. His last scoop was more tragic for Jack on a personal level as it cost the life of his brother-in-law: a ring of sex trade traffickers bringing in girls from Eastern Europe. The Charles Foster Kane comment was a reference to the 1941 movie *Citizen Kane*, starring Orson Welles as the titular newspaper tycoon. Jack was sure Mike Smith had never seen the movie, and was just repeating a throwaway remark he had heard somebody else use, as it sounded good.

The BSA was shorthand for bullshit assignment, which in this case was taking Jack over to the North London suburb of Cricklewood, not a million miles away from where he lived, to gather facts about a dispute that had arisen regarding rights of way.

The dispute centred around a small park, mainly frequented by dog walkers. The park was surrounded by housing, one side of which comprised houses built around the turn of the century. There was a path leading from the park, through these houses, to the main road. On one side of the path was a block of garages; the other a high fence acting as the boundary of the garden of the adjacent house. There was also a wooden gate halfway along the fence. The owner of this adjacent house, clearly fed up with dog walkers passing her living room window, got a fence put up, blocking the path, with a sign stating PRIVATE PROPERTY NO TRESPASSING. Her justification for this was that when she bought the house as new, there was a codicil in her contract which stated that this path was not a public right of way. She was unable to answer why it took her over twenty years to realise this. Many of the dog walkers complained to the local council, who advised that notwithstanding this codicil, the path had been used as a public right of way for so long, it was in fact now, a public right of way, and she should remove the fence. She refused, and the council's dispute mechanism was in process. Somebody made an anonymous call to the *London Daily News*; hence Jack was being sent over to talk to the occupant, the neighbours, a sample of dog walkers, and hopefully a spokesman for the council.

'It's not like we're drowning in more newsworthy or interesting stories at the moment,' Mike had said. Jack had to reluctantly agree: there was a dearth of what he called proper news items right now.

CHAPTER THREE

AS THE LOCATION was not far from where Jack lived, and still in a residential neighbourhood, Jack drove there. Once he was on the street in question, he could see the house and footpath in question. He found a space not on the actual street, but just around the corner, and parked there. Walking up to the end of the road, he noticed the houses were all well-maintained semi-detached properties. Around twenty years old, he guessed, in contrast to those across the road, which were older, but equally well maintained. A respectable neighbourhood, his mother would have said.

At the end of the street was a small garage block, with two freshly painted corrugated metal doors. Then came the path in question. Around twelve feet along the path was a metal chain, painted bright yellow, affixed to a hook on the side of the garage block, and the same on the side of the first house, number one.

A metal sign hung from the middle of the chain, reading:

PRIVATE PROPERTY
NO TRESPASSING

Jack looked around and walked up to the chain. Without stepping over it he could see the fence the occupant of number one had erected. There was a slight dogleg in the configuration of the path, but by leaning over, Jack could see a standard wooden fence panel. Now he needed to see the other side. He would check it out, park-side, then talk to some of the locals.

Not being able to use the path, he had to walk to the end of the road, and round the block to get to the park. The park was surrounded by a row of high trees and bushes, with a bridle path running through the bushes. He turned left and walked along this path, stepping to one side to let a couple of women with buggies pass by. He soon reached the spot. He was at the corner of the park. The bridle path bore round to the right, with a small stub heading to the left and the disputed right of way. If this had been a road, it would have been classified a T-junction.

At the beginning of this stub, tied between two large tree trunks, was a length of tape. Like police tape, but not. Maybe meant to look like it. The tape seemed new, and another length of tape, screwed into an untidy ball, lay on the ground at the foot of one of the trees. A sheet of A4 was stapled onto each of the two trunks. Jack walked up and read them. Each A4 sheet was a photocopy of a letter from a house building firm, stating that the path was not a dedicated right of way and never had been. It was redacted in places, including the addressee and date.

Jack stepped back and took a photograph on his phone of the letter and the taped off path. This was a sign of the times: it was not that long ago that he would have gone to something like this, accompanied by a photographer, with a proper camera.

The taping off of the path was only a gesture: Jack was easily able to walk round the tree and up to the other side of the fence. Again, it was a standard fence panel, cut to size, but amateurishly erected. There was a large square of black paint on this side of the fence: Jack guessed this was to cover up some graffiti.

The fence around the perimeter of the garden of number one was constructed of standard fence panels, seven, eight feet high, and this seemed to be consistent with the other houses in this row. Probably been there since the houses were built. There was an alleyway along the back of the row of houses, each with a gate. Except number one, which had a gate at the side, the street side of the obstruction. Jack reflected that all the other occupants in the street would have to take the same hundred yard walk to access their gardens, apart from through the house.

He took another dozen pictures, and now it was time to carry out some interviews. He walked back to the bridleway and came across a woman in a headscarf, and walking a white poodle.

'Excuse me,' said Jack, as he approached and introduced himself.

'I'm sorry, I don't live around here,' the woman said, and scurried off.

'Okay,' said Jack to nobody in particular. He noticed a couple, probably in their seventies walking from the other direction. They were with two larger dogs, probably Labradors.

They paused as Jack approached them, showed them his identification, and told them why he was here.

The man gripped the lead he was holding tightly to get his dog to heel, then said angrily, 'You're bloody right there's a dispute. It's an inconvenience, to put it mildly. That woman has no right to block the path.'

'Apparently it's not a public right of way,' said Jack.

'Rubbish. Crap,' the man barked.

'George,' his wife gently chided him. She turned to Jack. 'It's always been a right of way. We've been using it for ten, twelve years now, without any problem.'

'That path had been there since the houses were built.

If that damned woman doesn't like the fact that there's a path running alongside her house, she shouldn't have moved there in the first place.'

'Are you going to do something about it?' the woman asked Jack.

'I'm just reporting on it. My understanding, though, is that the council is taking enforcement action.'

'What does that mean?' she asked.

'According to my sources, the council are investigating. If they decide what she's done is illegal, then they'll tell her to take it down. If she refuses, then they'll dismantle it themselves.'

'So they bleeding well should. And quickly!' the man barked again.

Jack thanked them for their time, took their names, and walked in the other direction. He soon came across a woman with a little terrier. The conversation was similar.

Next was a man with a dachshund. The conversation was going in a similar direction, when they were interrupted by a woman walking a husky.

'You talking about that fence?' she asked.

Jack nodded thank you to the dachshund man who slipped away, and turned to the husky woman. 'Yes, I am. Did you use that path yourself?' He explained why he was asking.

The fact that Jack was from the Press seemed to embolden her. 'You're damn right I did. For years. Then she puts up that fence. I went round to her front door to ask what was going on, but she wouldn't talk about it. Just threatened to call the police.'

'Everybody talks about a woman putting it up. Why's that?'

'Because it was a woman who put it up. Sure, there's a husband there too, and their kids – have you seen how many cars there are outside the place? But you hardly see him – maybe he works away, or she keeps him locked up somewhere. Wouldn't surprise me, the bitch. She's a nutter. See that tape over there? It started a few weeks back. I noticed a sign stuck to the tree. It said something like she wanted to politely remind everybody that the path is private property. Signed it, Karen. That's about right, isn't it? Karen. Put some of that tape up too. But one evening, my husband, he was walking Toby here, and he tore her sign off the tree and tore down that tape. And you know what? Next evening, there was more tape up there, plus that letter you see from the builders. My old man, he said we ought to leave it as it looks sort of official, but me, I told him I don't think it's genuine. I mean, she's a psycho. But my friend, she said it doesn't matter if it's a genuine letter. She said if the builders are saying that, then they're full of shit. Pardon my French. My friend says that if the path's been in use by the public for as long as that one has, then it automatically becomes a public right of way, never mind what the builders or that stupid woman say.'

That was Jack's understanding too. He thanked the woman, took her details and let her get on her way. He had enough information from the local dog walking community; now it was time to speak with the neighbours, to 'Karen' from number one, then the council.

There were six houses this side: one to eleven. He knocked at number eleven first. There was no answer. No answer at number nine. That was hardly surprising: it was late morning, the driveways were empty, and all the windows were shut. Most likely, the occupants were at work.

An Indian lady answered number seven. Jack showed her his ID, and explained why he was calling.

'I have nothing to say on the matter,' the woman said, closing the door on him. Great, he thought, let's try next door.

A younger, Caucasian woman answered number five. She looked in her early thirties, had blonde hair tied back in a ponytail, and was wearing no make-up. She was wearing a green top and blue jeans. She listened while Jack introduced himself and explained why he was calling.

'Look, can you come in?' she said. 'I'm just in the middle of something.'

'Okay,' he nodded, and followed her through to the kitchen at the back of her house. By the door was a pair of black woman's shoes, a pair of white trainers, and a pair of blue children's trainers. Along the way to the kitchen, he noticed a number of coloured drawings blu-tacked to the wall.

She picked up a wire. 'I'm trying to change the fuse on this,' she said, 'but…'

'Let me,' Jack smiled. He took the opened plug from her. 'You got a screwdriver?' he asked.

'Here,' she said, handing him one. Fortunately it was flat bladed. He was able to prise the fuse from the plug with the screwdriver.

'You got a fuse?' he asked.

'Oh, yes, I think so.' She opened a drawer by the sink and passed one over to him. 'Try this.'

'That's the wrong kind. This is a three amp fuse; your kettle needs thirteen amps. Have you got any thirteen amp fuses, the brown ones?'

'Brown ones.' She looked in the drawer again and passed him another fuse.

'Perfect.' Jack replaced the fuse, screwed the plug back together and passed it to her. 'All done. Try it out.'

She took the plug, filled the kettle with water, plugged it in, and switched on.

'Geronimo,' she said as a blue light on the kettle illuminated. 'Thank you so much. I know I should be able to do it myself, but…'

'No problem. Glad to be of service.'

'It's just that my ex used to take case of all that stuff. But now…' Her words trailed off. 'Would you like a coffee? As my way of saying thanks.'

'Please. Just black.'

As the kettle boiled, she asked, 'What is it that you want to ask me about? Not about that fence?'

Jack nodded, and explained the story so far. She nodded as he spoke.

'Don't get me on about her at number one.'

'Oh, why?'

'We just don't get on. I don't think she gets on with anybody here, maybe the Singhs next door at number three.'

'Why's that, do you think?'

'She's so…. What's the word? Narcissistic. Everything has to be about her. Did you notice the cars on her drive?'

'Yes, I believe I did. Four black ones.'

'Yes, four huge, petrol guzzling monstrosities. My ex used to say it was like an FBI Convention. One's hers, the other her husbands, and she has two sons, eighteen, nineteen, something like that. The other two are theirs. She doesn't work, the husband's at home a lot. I think the boys work in Central London so go in by tube. But some mornings, at least two of them are left idling while they get ready to leave. It's even worse in the winter, while their cars are warming up and the ice is melting. No concern for the neighbours, or the environment. What about global warming? I'll give you an example. The other week, Kyle – my son – was playing with a friend on that trampoline,' - she pointed out into the garden - 'making some noise, obviously, but she knocked on my door, complaining. Said she was trying to sleep. At four in the afternoon.'

'Nice.'

'Kyle's father used to tell her to do one, but he's not here now. And now she's blocked the path. That's so *her*, doing something like that. Now Kyle and I have to walk miles to get to the park. Well, not *miles*, but…'

'I get the picture. Other people have said the same thing.'

'Sorry, here's your coffee.'

'Thanks. My understanding is that a complaint has been made to the council, who could well be taking action against her.'

'Really? I didn't know that. That's good. What does that mean, though?'

'It means,' said Jack as he sipped some coffee, 'that assuming the council decide she's in the wrong, and I'm certain she is, they'll tell her to take it down. If she refuses, then they will take it down for her.'

'Brilliant. Do you know how long that will be?'

'I don't know. I just know that local authorities have a statutory enforcement procedure, and things always take time.'

'And all this is going into the paper?'

'Probably. If my editor thinks it's newsworthy.'

'Do you need my name?'

'Yes, I was just coming to that.'

'Susan Farmer,' she said. 'Aged thirty-three. You always put a person's age, don't you? How can that be relevant?'

Jack laughed. 'Most of the time it's not. I guess it makes the person being quoted more real in the eyes of the reader. Industry practice. Well, I have all I need. Thanks. And for the coffee. Here's my card. My number's on there if you think of anything else.'

She took the card and read his name off it. 'Jack Richardson.'

'That's me. Forty-six.' They both laughed. 'Well, thanks again, I'll leave you to it.'

'It's my day off today. I have to pick Kyle up from school. Normally my mother does it.'

'What do you do?'

'I work in an Estate Agency. We're open weekends, so today is my Saturday day. I'm just pottering around, changing fuses and stuff.'

'How old is Kyle?' Jack asked as he made his way to the door.

'Seven. You got any kids… Jack?'

'A daughter. Cathy. She's twelve, going on forty-two. I have her every weekend.'

Susan Farmer nodded. 'My mother has him most weekends, just to give me a break. So I have every weekend free.' She put her hand to her mouth. 'That sounded so bad. Sorry. I didn't mean it that way. How embarrassing.'

'Don't worry,' Jack smiled. 'Thanks again.' He paused. 'In case I need to ask you anything else,' he asked slowly, 'to save me having to drive over, do you have a number?'

'I do,' she said. She looked around for something to write it on, then said, 'Can I text it to you?'

'That would be perfect,' said Jack. 'Thanks.'

'Are you going round to see her now?'

'I will, yes. Have to get both sides. Balanced picture, you know.'

'Well, good luck with that. Bye,' she said, slowly closing the door.

Jack waved goodbye and walked to the house next door. No answer. As with the other houses, he slipped a card through the letter box.

Then to number one. He squeezed his way through the four shiny black cars. Two were Range Rovers. He could see what Susan Farmer's ex had meant about the FBI. He rang the doorbell, and almost immediately it was answered. This must be Karen.

She was tiny, little more than four feet. Her hair was neatly permed, nothing out of place, and she was wearing a red dress. She waited for Jack to make his introductions, then said, 'I don't want to talk to any newspapers.'

'But you'd have the chance to put your -'

As Jack spoke, she was immediately joined by her husband. Taller than her, shorter than Jack. Grey hair, in shirtsleeves.

'You deaf or something, mate? You heard what she said? Get out of here.'

Jack put his hands up. 'Okay. Can I quote you on that?'

'You're trespassing, mate. Piss off.'

Then the door to number one slammed shut.

'Fine.' Jack turned, threaded his way through the FBI car park, and returned to his own car. He would leave here now, drive home, and call the local council from there. As he turned on the engine, he checked his phone screen. There was a text from a number he didn't recognise.

Heres my number. Tx 4 the kettle. Nice 2cu. S

He leafed through the notes he had made, and the images he had on his phone. Next stop: home and the council. He had got all he came for.

He looked at the text message once more.

Maybe more than he'd come for.

CHAPTER FOUR

Upon getting back home, Jack fixed himself a sandwich and a coffee, and sat at his table, where he booted up his laptop. He took a bite from his ham sandwich and leaned back in his chair.

Next, he checked his emails. Always a bad idea, as it was easy to get distracted by something in the inbox, rather than focus on the task at hand, namely filing this story. Bad idea or not, he always did it.

He groaned aloud when he read what was in the inbox. Two emails from Mike Smith, his news editor, sent earlier that morning, ten minutes apart. Both were assignments for him to cover.

Jack and his colleagues had always had the flexibility to work from home, the only expectation was that they attended the office in London's Docklands at least two days a week, plus when a meeting had been called. Some of his colleagues stuck to that rigidly, but Jack had always been of the view that by being physically present in the office, your chances of being handed a story were greater than if you were working remotely. The pandemic changed all that: working from home became the norm; only now were staff beginning to appear in the office, albeit for only one day a week. There was talk a while back of the newspaper closing the premises, and having one hundred percent remote working. Even the weekly editorial meetings were now held on Zoom. Stories were passed to the reporters by way of email now.

Of course, the cynic in Jack came to the conclusion that the management preferred to allocate assignments in this way. In the past, if Jack was given what he considered a bullshit assignment, a BSA, he would say so, and there would be some kind of discussion. Nowadays, it would be all on email, and Mike Smith's phone would always be on voicemail. Jack had come to not even bother arguing.

These two emails were no exception. The first was concerning a football club in Wanstead, East London, who had achieved promotion from the National League to England League Two. Not being a soccer fan, Jack had no idea what that meant, but the word promotion meant that it was a good thing. Mike would like Jack to visit the team in training, get a few interviews, and a few pictures. Dev Shah, who was the paper's Entertainment Correspondent, was away on holiday, otherwise he would have gone.

The second story was concerning a spate of thefts from garden sheds in Enfield.

'Wonderful,' Jack muttered as he tabbed through the details.

He pushed the laptop to one side. Something to look forward to later. A phone call to make first.

The call was to his sister, Madeline Glover, who lived the other side of London. She had been widowed two years earlier: her late husband Graham had somehow got involved with a ring of people traffickers, who were bringing in girls and boys from Eastern Europe to work as prostitutes or in the domestic slave trade. Foolishly, he interfered in the operation, and was murdered. Jack took up where his brother-in-law left off, from the point of view of an exposé rather than any personal revenge. The story was published over several editions, a few people were arrested, but the trafficking goes on.

'Hey Sis, how're you doing?' he asked.

'I'm doing fine, thanks. I just got off the phone from Amanda.' Amanda was Madeline's only child, Jack's niece. She was living away from home at Kendal University, reading sociology. She had just begun the course at the time of her father's murder, and now she was in her final year.

'Oh, how is she?'

'Oh, she seems okay. You know Amanda.'

'It's good that she calls you regularly.'

'Once a week.'

'Once a week. I thought she used to call every few days.'

'Once a week now. She'll be coming home at Christmas.'

'That'll be nice for you.'

'With a suitcase full of washing, I expect.'

'Just her?' Jack meant was she coming on her own or with her boyfriend, Ryan, who was studying in the same place.

'I think so. I didn't ask. She doesn't seem to talk about Ryan much these days. I assume they're still together. I hope he does come with her; I've a couple of things around the house that need doing.'

'I can do them, Maddie. You don't need to wait till then, just in case he comes with her. Cathy and I could come down for a few hours over the weekend. Have you spoken to Mum and Dad recently?'

'I did at the weekend. Mum still keeps saying I should sell up and move down to Eastbourne to be nearer to them. I always say yes, I'll think about it, but I'm afraid Eastbourne's not for me.'

'Same here; at least, not for another forty years. I must

take Cathy down to see them as well.' He paused. 'That's an idea. I'll have her at the weekend. I'll check that she doesn't have any other plans. Why don't we drive by yours first Saturday or Sunday, then the three of us can drive down.'

'I don't know. That's quite a drive for you.'

'It's not too bad. From yours, it's the A22 all the way. Can be there by twelve; don't need to stay too long.'

'All right. Let's do that.'

The call ended soon after, and Jack hung up. He was always weary after any conversation with his sister. He loved her very much, but she could be hard work.

In the just over two years since Graham had died, she had become very narcissistic, as if she was thriving on sympathy. She had made no effort to get back out into the world; rather, she expected everybody, her daughter, Jack, and their parents, to reach out to her. She and Graham never seemed to have many friends – Jack always put that down to Graham being weird – but those that they had seemed to have drifted away. Jack understood why they had gone, but was still concerned about her pottering around on her own in that four bedroomed house. There was a lot of logic in their parents' idea of her relocating. She didn't even have any pets to focus on. When he suggested she get a dog for company, she said no, as they were dirty. Maybe move to somewhere smaller? No, there were too many memories here. It was where Amanda grew up, and there were too many memories of Graham. Jack would have been less sceptical had Amanda not left home as soon as she could, and had Madeline not treated Graham like dirt when he was alive. It was true that Jack thought his late brother-in-law was an idiot, up to the day he died – it was his foolishness which led to his death – but Madeline did treat him badly.

So, that was the weekend sorted, potentially. He sent Cathy a text message – did she have any plans for the weekend, and what did she think about going down to Eastbourne to see Grandma and Grandad? And of taking

Aunt Maddie with them? He suspected that it would be a thumbs up to the first question; not so much the second.

CHAPTER FIVE

THE LOCAL AUTHORITY.

He had the number saved in his phone from previous stories, so just hit speed-dial. Eventually he was passed to somebody who was able to, and had the authority to, speak to him. Reluctance to give out information was always a frustration to people in Jack's position: a major piece of United Kingdom legislation was the Data Protection Act. Passed in 2018, and replacing an Act of Parliament of the same name dating back twenty years, this piece of legislation was frequently used by organisations as an excuse for not providing information which may be in the public domain, or had already been provided, or was already the subject of a Freedom of Information request.

'I'm sorry, I can't provide that information,' was a common reply.

'Why not?' Jack would ask.

'Because of data protection,' came the reply, which

was totally irrelevant to what he was asking.

Another beef Jack had was when he received an unsolicited, cold, call from a company which was normally trying to sell him something, he was expected to give his full name, address, date of birth, to prove his identity. Faced with that kind of request, Jack would just hang up. When he was in a good mood, that is; if he was in a bad mood, he would be more colourful in his response.

Today was midway between the two. After speaking to two people, he was passed to an apparently knowledgeable lady who was able to provide the information he was seeking. Some companies went into panic mode or pulled down the shutters as soon as they learned he was from the press: this lady knew what she was allowed to say, and gave him no personal details of the people involved, just details of the ongoing dispute, and what the council was doing about it. Nothing that was not already in the public domain, and that was all Jack was asking.

In fact, most of what she told him, he knew already. A resident, clearly unhappy about a pathway running alongside her house, had apparently unearthed a letter from the builder confirming that the path was not dedicated to the public and was for the private use of the residents. There was no discussion about the authenticity of the letter; no mention of anybody contacting the builder to validate this letter. However, whether the builder's letter was genuine, or correct was neither here nor there now: the fact that it had been used as a public right of way for so long - over twenty years - meant that it was now a legal, public right of way. A representative from the council had visited to request that she remove the fence; she had refused, and so the council had issued an order requiring her to do so. She had twenty-eight days to appeal, and after the twenty-eight days had passed and the fence was still extant, then the council would remove it. End of story.

Nothing Jack didn't know already – just confirmation

of what he already knew, and what he had been told. He took a last mouthful of sandwich, pulled the laptop closer. He wrote the article, checked it twice, made a few change, uploaded a sample of the pictures he had taken, checked the story once more, then filed it. Job done.

As he typed the quote from Susan Farmer, he paused. She volunteered a lot about her personal life, her single status, her son. Was she just being friendly, or was she letting him know she was single and available? Jack parked that thought.

Next, he turned to the two assignments in his inbox. It was now early afternoon. Enfield was the nearest: he could get over there in the car quite quickly and get this story done today. Wanstead was further, and could wait till tomorrow. He called the two contact numbers. The football team would be at a training session in the morning, and that would be an ideal time to get over there. The man in Enfield who called the paper about the shed thefts was retired so yes, he would be around this afternoon.

Soon, he was back in the car and began the drive to Enfield. There were road works on the A110, and as he waited in traffic his thoughts went back to Susan. Was she giving out signals? Immediately, he saw a problem. Subject to work, he was free all week, but not at weekends. She was free at weekends, but not during the week. But she told him she had a day off today. What about having lunch another day? His train of thought was interrupted as the light turned green and the traffic began moving again.

The neighbourhood where these break-ins had been taking place was in Enfield Wash, a district just outside the main town, and bordered by a motorway, two main highways, and a large reservoir.

The person he had arranged to see was called Isaac Baines. Jack found the address easily, and was greeted by Baines himself, standing by his gate, waving. Nothing like being discrete, Jack thought.

'I'll show you the shed,' Baines said after they had made their introductions. He was a short man, with a bald head, and was wearing a red and blue checked shirt. Jack put his age at late sixties, early seventies, but had to walk fast to keep up with Baines, who half ran, half trotted down to the shed.

Access to the shed was down a wide driveway, street end of which was a double gate.

'Here,' said Baines, pointing to the damaged door. 'That's how they got in.'

It was quite obvious what had happened. There had been a rudimentary padlock on the door, but had been forced open with a crowbar, or even a large screwdriver.

'Was anything stolen?' Jack asked.

'Some power tools. A saw, a drill, a hedge trimmer. The lawn mower was too big to take, I expect.'

Jack turned to the house. 'Did they try to break in? To the house, I mean. Using tools from here?'

A woman appeared out of the back door. White hair, same height as Baines. Mrs Baines, presumably.

'No,' she replied. She must have been in the doorway, listening. 'But our neighbour said she heard some kids round here. We'd been out shopping, and when we got back from the shops, the double gates were open - not wide, but not fastened shut, like we always do. He went to close the gate, then noticed the shed door open.'

'Bloody kids,' Baines said. Then, addressing Jack, 'Is this going to get in the paper?'

'Possibly,' Jack replied. 'It depends on my editor. Is it all right if I take a few pictures? Of the broken shed door, I mean?'

'Do you want one of us?' Baines asked, stepping over to stand next to his wife.

'Couldn't hurt,' Jack replied, and took one of the couple. It might help, from a human interest angle.

'Where are you going now?' Mrs Baines asked.

'It's er… Castle Street,' replied Jack. 'Is that far?'

She pointed up the street. 'It's just up there. First on

the right.'

'They've suffered the same as you. Can you claim on your house insurance?'

'Maybe,' Baines replied. 'But if we do, they'll put the premiums up next year.'

'If I were you,' Jack said, as he made his way to the gate, 'I'd put a fence up across here, with a gate if you need one.'

Mrs Baines said, 'That's what I keep telling him.'

Baines asked, 'What edition will this be in?'

Jack said, 'Probably by Friday, earlier online.'

Baines said, 'Good. I'll keep checking the internet.'

Jack had reached the street, so he thanked them again and said goodbye.

Jack drove round to the house in Castle Street. It was less than a minute's drive. The occupant was a Steven Bellingham. Jack rang the doorbell, and it was answered in seconds. Steven Bellingham was at least twenty-five years younger than Mr Baines, as tall as Jack. Thin, heavily tanned, and highlights in his blond hair. He had a short beard. Jack wondered if that was how he looked.

'Mr Bellingham? Jack Richardson. We spoke on the phone.'

'Yes,' said Bellingham. 'I'll take you round the side. Wait by that gate, would you?'

Jack did as instructed and after a minute, the side gate opened. Bellingham led him to the garden shed. 'Not much to show you,' he said, showing Jack the shed. 'That side gate we always kept shut. Now we keep it bolted too.'

Jack nodded and looked at the damaged shed. The damage was similar to that suffered by Mr Baines around the corner.

'Did they steal much?' Jack asked.

'Nothing in there worth stealing. Just junk. They did ransack it, though, looking for something valuable, I dare say.' He pointed over to the house. 'It looks as if they tried to prise open our patio doors, but Lemon stopped them.'

'Lemon?'

'Our Alsatian. We were both out. I normally work from home now but had a call to make in Central London. My partner, he was at work. Lemon must have heard the noise, ran to the door, and scared them off.'

'Did they drop whatever they use to jimmy the door? A crowbar, a screwdriver, something like that?'

'No. We wondered that. The police asked that too, but…'

'But?'

'To be honest with you, they weren't interested. We dialled that non-urgent number, 116 or something, and it was two days before a police officer called us back. Simon – my partner – said if we called and said there had been an intruder and we'd shot him, a car would've been round here in seconds.'

Jack nodded. 'Probably a lot more than a car. It was probably kids. A house round in Bell Lane, they had something similar happen, and a neighbour apparently heard kids in their garden.'

Bellingham sniffed with disdain. 'Little shits. I know what I'd do if I caught them. Is there anything else you need to know? I have a Zoom meeting in ten minutes.'

'If I could just take a picture of the damage to your shed, and to the patio door, then I'll be on my way.' Bellingham waited while Jack took the pictures, then led him out of the side gate. He heard Bellingham padlock the gate.

Back in the car, Jack trawled through the pictures. Bound to be just kids, he thought. Hardly a major crime story. Just a piece advising people to make sure their outbuildings are properly secured.

Time to drive back home, write up and file this non-story.

As he was negotiating the road works once more, his phone rang. The number showed on his car's LCD screen, but was not one he recognised. He answered and almost drove into the car in front when he learned it was Susan Farmer. Suddenly, his palms became sweaty.

'Oh, hello,' she said. 'Sorry to have bothered you, but I thought you'd like to know that somebody from the council has just been to the alleyway.'

'They've cleared it? Taken down the fence?'

'No, they've just put up a sign saying they're going to. Is that something you need to know?'

It wasn't really, but Jack told her, 'Yes, that's useful information. It means the council are on the case. Thanks for updating me.' Then he paused. *Go for it Jack*, he thought. 'Now that you've called, there is one more thing I'd like to ask you.'

'Yes?' she replied, quickly.

'You, um, said that you are off today, for working Saturday?'

'Yes, that's right.'

'Does that mean you're back at work for the rest of the week?'

'Yes, I go back tomorrow.'

'Okay. I was wondering if you'd let me take you to lunch. As a thank you, of course.'

'My mother is always happy to babysit if that's what you're asking. I can check if she's free tonight, if you like.'

Taken by surprise, Jack asked, 'So you'll let me know?'

'She's usually amenable. Why don't we assume it's a yes unless I call or text you otherwise?'

'That's good for me. Pick you up at seven?'

She agreed and they ended the call. Jack continued his journey home in a much lighter mood than he had been up till now.

There was life in the old dog yet, he thought. He still had it in him. Three shit assignments, and yet he still managed to pull.

CHAPTER SIX

AMANDA GLOVER, JACK'S niece, used her back to push the pub doors open. It was late Wednesday afternoon, and *The Penny Black* was busy. She had a plastic supermarket bag in each hand, and a full backpack strapped around her shoulders. She paused at the door, looking around: eventually she picked out her boyfriend, Ryan O'Connor, sitting the other side of the bar. She squeezed her way through the throng to where Ryan was sitting.

'Hey,' he said. 'What kept you?'

'Sorry I'm late. The shops were busy. It's like Christmas out there.'

'What? Lights and stuff?'

'No, idiot. So busy.'

'You want a drink? I've just got this.' He raised his half-drunk glass of lager.

'I'll have a dry white wine.'

As Ryan went to the bar, Amanda took off her coat and

settled down on the bench seat with the small circular table. Ryan returned after a few minutes. 'Here you go,' he said, sitting next to her. He looked down at her supermarket bags. 'What did you get?'

'Just pasta.'

'I'm sure everyone will like that. Even Sun.'

'I'm sure. That's assuming he comes back to eat. He's been away a while.'

'I think he's got a friend at Bowland. He spends a lot of time over there now.'

Amanda and Ryan were both in their third year at County, one of the nine colleges comprising Kendal University. Amanda was reading Business Management, Ryan Engineering. In their first year they resided on the Campus; since the previous September, they had been sharing a house in the City of Kendal with two other students, Anjita Banerjee, and Sun Lee. The house was a large Victorian place, with four bedrooms. Amanda and Ryan officially had a bedroom each, but each room only had a single bed, so whether they spent the night together depended on what kind of mood they were in. The other students knew they were together, and respected their privacy, but Amanda and Ryan tried not to make things obvious. The house also contained a shared kitchen, bathroom, and living room. At the beginning of term, they all agreed a rota for cleaning and cooking: this meant that each one had to cook for everybody every four days, and tonight, it was Amanda's turn.

'After dinner,' Amanda said, sipping her dry white wine, 'do you fancy going to the movies? It's cheaper midweek.'

'Sorry. I have an assignment to finish tonight, for tomorrow.'

'Really?'

'Yeah, my final assignment on Catalytic Engineering. I'll need to hit the laptop big time. And yes, I know I shouldn't have left it so late. Why don't you see if Anji wants to?'

'She won't want to.'

Laughing, Ryan said, 'Ask Sun then.'

'Yeah, right. As if he's going to say yes. It'd be different if you asked him.'

'I could ask him on your behalf. It's not like he'd make any moves on you.'

'Forget it. I'll catch something on Netflix. I have some stuff to finish off anyway.'

Ryan downed the last off his lager. 'It's Wednesday, anyways. You going to FaceTime your mum?

'Shit. I forgot. Yeah, I expect I'll have to.'

'Give her my love,' Ryan laughed.

'It's all right for you. Your parents are different.'

'She is widowed, remember.'

'She was like that when Dad was alive.'

'Mm.'

'What?'

'I was going to say, like mother, like…'

She elbowed him in the ribs. 'Don't you dare.'

Ryan laughed and stood up. 'Come on, let's go back.'

The house they all shared was in the Bowerham district, a ten minute bus ride away from College, and a seven minute bus ride from *The Penny Black*. On the bus back, Amanda rested her head against the window and stared out. It was dark now, raining, and the windows were beginning to steam up.

Ryan looked up from his phone. 'What's up?'

Amanda turned from the window. 'Nothing, really. I was just thinking about Mum. And Dad. I think she's lonely, really. Missing him. It's times like this I wish I wasn't an only child.'

'Why didn't they have another?'

She shrugged. 'I don't know. I did ask her once or twice, but she didn't really give me an answer; you know what she's like. She said something like it wasn't meant to happen. I never pushed it with either of them. I do know I was born C-section, so there might have been some kind of complication, if that had anything to do with it. But you know Mum: she'll never open up, even to me. She didn't much to Dad, either.'

'Think she'll ever remarry? She's only – what? Mid-forties?'

'I doubt it. I think she's very lonely, very unhappy. And not just because of Dad. It seems she's always been like that.'

'Do you ever feel guilty about not being there with her?'

'Now and again. But Uncle Jack said I should put my life first.'

'Did he? Well, he's right.'

Amanda nodded. 'He told me Mum made choices years ago about stuff, what she wanted. I need to put my life and future first, and if push comes to shove, he wasn't that far away. Plus, my grandparents are only on the South Coast.'

'Why doesn't she move down there, to be closer to them?' Ryan asked.

Amanda gave a wry smile. 'Grandad might have other ideas.'

Ryan asked, 'Do you miss not having a brother or sister? It must have been tough for you when you were a kid.'

'It was what it was. I didn't know anything different. I had lots of friends: from school, from Guides.'

Ryan laughed. 'You were in Girl Guides?'

'Yes. Brownies, then Guides. Were you?'

'In Guides?'

'No. In… Scouts?'

'No, I think I missed out there. Deprived childhood and all that.'

They stood up as the bus had arrived at their stop. It was raining harder now. They both pulled up their hoods, Ryan took one of the plastic bags, and they hurried, half walking, half running, around the corner and the last fifty yards or so to the house.

The house was in darkness, except for either a light on the landing or one of the back bedrooms. No downstairs lights on. It looked like they were the first to get back. Amanda and Ryan took off their wet coats, shook them and hung them up, and Amanda took both bags of shopping into the kitchen, which was at the end of a long hallway. Ryan followed her, but noticed that there was a small light on in the living room, too faint to be seen from the outside. He put his head round the door. He went in.

Amanda was crouching in front of the open fridge, putting away lettuce, when she heard Ryan call her. She tutted, stood up, closed the fridge door, and went to see what he wanted.

Ryan was in the living room. He was not alone: Anji was sitting in near darkness on one of the sofas. From the faint light from the lamp, Amanda could see she had been crying. Ryan stepped back a couple of paces to allow Amanda to get closer and sit on the sofa with Anji.

'What is it?' she asked. 'What's happened?'

'It's Sun,' Anji said, between sobs. Amanda looked up at Ryan at the mention of their fourth housemate. 'He's dead.'

CHAPTER SEVEN

RYAN LEFT THE girls in the living room while he made tea for them all. He took their mugs in, then returned with his own. Amanda had just asked Anji how she found out.

'His father called to tell us.'

'From China?' Ryan asked. He looked at his watch. 'It's just after six now; so it must be – what? Twelve, one in the morning there.'

Amanda looked up at him. 'I doubt they are getting much sleep.'

'It was Hong Kong,' Anji said quietly. 'He was calling from Hong Kong. He apologised if he was calling at a bad time, but there was so much to do, and the distance and time difference were making it difficult.'

'I'm sure.' Ryan perched himself on the arm of one of the chairs.

Amanda asked, 'Did Sun's father say anything else? How, where?'

Anji took a mouthful of tea and blew her nose before replying. 'He said Sun fell off Tower Bridge.'

'Tower Bridge?' Ryan gasped. 'In London?'

Anji nodded. 'Yes. He said Sun was walking along Tower Bridge, and fell in.'

'How could he have fallen off Tower Bridge?' Amanda asked, looking up at Ryan.

Ryan shrugged. 'Maybe he was doing something stupid. Maybe he was drunk. Was he alone?'

Anji said, 'I don't know. He didn't say how Sun fell, but he did say the police will be talking to us. He said he wanted to tell us personally before the police contacted us. So we didn't get any surprises, he said.'

'Surprises?' said Ryan. 'Jesus. And this isn't a surprise? And what was he doing in London?' And when did this happen?'

'Over the weekend,' said Anji.

'Then why didn't we notice he wasn't here?' Ryan asked. 'Why didn't we realise he was gone? We all live in the same house, for God's sake.'

'But he used to go away for days, weeks, sometimes,' said Amanda. 'To do stuff, he said. Even when he was here, he'd always keep himself to himself. He'd appear down here to eat with us, then he was back up to his room. I'd always assumed he was doing course work, or chatting to his family in China. Hong Kong, rather.'

Ryan agreed. 'Sometimes I think we used to see more of him at college than here. I thought he had a friend over in Bowland, and spent a lot of time over there with him. Sometimes I could tell he hadn't been here the night before, so I guessed he'd been staying over there.' He asked Anji, 'So that's all Sun's father told you?'

'He would have been upset,' said Amanda. 'It was just a courtesy call, just to warn us the police would be in touch. He didn't have to; it's not like we're family. Or friends.'

Anji nodded, blew her nose.

'So what about the college?' Amanda asked. 'Do we

have to report it?'

Ryan shook his head. 'Not down to us, babe. The authorities will deal with that. I expect the college will be in touch with us as well.'

'Yeah,' said Amanda, sitting back on the couch. 'I expect they will.'

That evening, Amanda, Ryan and Anji ate their pasta meal almost in silence, nobody wishing to speak. Any conversation was stilted small talk, not the normal animated banter. After they had eaten, and cleared up, again with very little conversation, Anji announced she was going to her room as she had to work on an assignment; Ryan said the same, leaving Amanda downstairs. This was nothing unusual, but tonight there was a sombre atmosphere in the house.

Amanda finished cleaning up, locked the doors, and went up to her own room. Most nights she and Ryan would do their course work in the same place, but clearly he had no appetite for company, and neither did she.

In her room, she sat crossed legged on her bed, leaning against the corner of the room. She had one of her textbooks, and began browsing through it. It was going to be a long night: none of them was going to get much sleep. Maybe after she had given Ryan a chance to finish working, she would see if they were going to sleep together tonight.

She had skimmed through a few pages when she heard a noise. She looked up. It sounded if it was the door to Sun's bedroom being opened. She laid the textbook on the bed and got up to see what was happening.

Sun's bedroom door was a few inches ajar. She padded over and peered around the opened door. Anji was sitting on the edge of Sun's bed.

Anji looked up, not registering any surprise at seeing Amanda. 'I couldn't concentrate on anything.'

Amanda stepped in, perching herself on the corner of the bed. 'Me neither.'

'I just can't believe it,' Anji said.

Amanda shook her head. 'No.' She looked around the bedroom. It was immaculate. The bed was neatly made, the closet doors were shut, two pairs of trainers were neatly lined up against the wall. On Sun's desk, textbooks were in a neat pile in one corner; above the desk were two bookshelves, both neatly stacked with books. It looked very much like a hotel room, awaiting its occupants. 'He always kept his room so neat and tidy,' she said.

Anji looked around. 'I wonder if that's because he's Chinese.' She paused a second, then added, 'That was a silly thing to say.'

'No, it might be a cultural thing. Aren't they very regimented out there?'

'Maybe,' said Anji. 'He always did keep it like this. Except one time, I needed to borrow something, I can't remember what it was, and I knocked to see if he could help. He was in, but he only opened the door a foot or so, and stuck his head around. I could see he didn't have a shirt or anything on. And as we talked, I noticed, behind him, the bed. There was another boy in the bed, and the sheets were all ruffled and untidy. He could see I noticed, so laughed as he shut the door.'

'Really? I didn't know that.'

'I think it was the boy from the other college. His face seemed familiar.'

'That was probably why he spent so much time over there,' said Amanda.

'Probably. He probably felt more secure over there. He was always very discreet.'

'He certainly was.'

They both laughed, a sad, humourless laugh.

The following morning, Amanda and Ryan decided to

walk to college. Both were awake early, neither having slept much that night. The rain had stopped, and the sky was bright blue. As they walked along, still not saying much, Amanda heard her phone ping. She ignored it as they were crossing a road. Momentarily, Ryan's also pinged. He stopped and checked it.

It was a text message from the Vice-Chancellor's office, asking if he would be so kind as to call in to see the Vice-Chancellor before the first lecture. Amanda checked her phone, and she had received the same message.

Momentarily Amanda's phone pinged again, this time with a message from Anji. She had received the same message.

When they arrived at the office, Anji was already sitting on the long couch outside the Vice-Chancellor's office. On seeing Amanda and Ryan arrive, the Vice-Chancellor's secretary picked up the phone. Moments later, the door opened, and the Vice-Chancellor stepped out.

Professor Louise Newbury was a tall, slim woman. Late fifties, grey hair neatly permed. She wore a blue business suit. She would not have looked out of place if the suit had been made from grey tweed and she had on green wellington boots rather than the expensive looking matching court shoes she was wearing.

'Thank you for coming,' she said, her voice showing a slight Scottish brogue. 'Please come in. Take a seat.' She pointed at the three chairs one side of her large dark mahogany desk. She walked round to the other side and sat down. She coughed as she began to speak. 'I'm afraid I have some very bad news for you.'

'If it's about Sun Lee, we already know,' said Ryan, earning himself a glare from Amanda.

Professor Newbury paused. It was not clear from the expression on her face whether she was surprised they knew already, or irritated that Ryan had interrupted her. She raised her eyebrows. 'Oh?'

'Yes,' explained Amanda. 'Anji took a call from Sun's

father yesterday afternoon. He wanted to tell us personally before we heard it from yourself.'

'Or the police,' Ryan added.

'Mm,' Professor Newbury said. 'First of all, on behalf of the University, I am sorry for your loss. I don't know if you were all friends, or just housemates, but it must have been a shock for you.'

Ryan, Amanda, and Anji said nothing, just nodded.

'I don't know yet what's going to happen with Sun's personal effects. That is something about which I am going to liaise with his family. If I could ask you, though, not to touch any of his property; just leave his room, and his effects untouched.'

They nodded again, all of them thinking how they would ignore this request.

'You will, however, I am afraid to say, need to speak with the police, who have said they will be contacting you independently of the University. This is partly down to the manner of Mr Lee's death.'

They sat up in their chairs.

'I don't know how much Mr Lee Senior told you, but it is my understanding that he was seen to jump from a bridge in London. When his body was recovered from the river, they carried out a routine post-mortem, and his body was found to contain a large amount of a drug known as MDMA.'

Amanda, Ryan and Anji looked at each other.

Professor Newbury added, with the air of imparting specialised knowledge, 'Also known as Ecstasy.'

CHAPTER EIGHT

JACK HAD ARRANGED to meet Susan at an Italian restaurant in Cricklewood High Street. Local for her; a short drive for Jack. He said he could pick her up, but she said no, she would meet him there. Jack's chivalrous, some might say old-fashioned, self felt like saying no, I'll pick you up, but it was obvious this was what she wanted, so he agreed and left it. He didn't want to screw things up this early by coming over too pushy or controlling. So they were to meet outside *Elementree* restaurant at seven.

On the way to the restaurant, Jack couldn't believe it – he actually had butterflies in his stomach! What to do, the first date protocol, kept running through his head. Should he greet her with a kiss? Should he try to hold her hand? Or should he let her initiate any physical contact? When they were done at the restaurant, should he suggest going on somewhere else? A bar, or a nightclub? He realised he didn't know any bars or clubs in the locale: he had found the restaurant on Google. Should he offer her a ride home? If she said she would get a cab, should he accept that? If he did take her home, and she asked him in for a coffee, should he accept? And would it be literally a coffee, or a euphemism for something else? So many questions. And another: was he expected to pay the bill? That would be his default position, but would she be expecting to split the bill?

'Get a grip, Jack,' he said aloud. 'You're a middle-aged divorcé, not a bloody teenager.'

He found a metered space on a side street off the High Street, and walked round to the restaurant. She was not waiting outside as they had arranged. There were three empty small circular tables on the pavement outside. It was cold, and he had no intention of having a meal with her out here. He peered inside: the restaurant was half full, and there was no sign of her waiting for him inside, out of the cold. He shivered and checked his watch. It was just after seven: four minutes after, to be precise. She was four minutes late. So what? He still had butterflies: 'God's sake,' he muttered under his breath. How long should he give her, he wondered. How long should he wait before calling or texting her?

Jack rubbed his chin. This hadn't occurred to him before: should he have shaved? It was still half beard, half stubble. Looking slightly neater than the other day. She had already seen him looking like this obviously, so was clearly happy with his appearance, otherwise wouldn't have accepted his invitation. Or did she consider the unshaven look his work normal, and expect him to have shaved for their date?

Much to his relief, Jack noticed a car pull up on the corner a few yards away. A figure got out and he saw it was Susan. Jack breathed a huge sigh of relief. She was wearing a long coat over a pair of trousers, and she was wearing her hair down, looking different, older, than previously, when she had it tied back. She looked around, saw Jack, smiled at him, and walked towards him. Jack gave her a little wave – the sort of wave his daughter would have done, he thought as he did it. He decided not to kiss her; neither did she, so it was obviously not expected. So far, so good.

'Sorry I'm late,' she said, a little out of breath and flustered.

'Don't worry; you're not late,' he lied.

'The cab came late,' she explained as they stepped into the restaurant. 'I was going to text you and let you know, but then it arrived.'

'It's fine. Hungry?'

'I'm starving,' she laughed as they stood in the doorway, waiting to be seated. After a few seconds they were shown to a table, one for two near the back of the restaurant. They were offered a drink while they consulted the menu. Both opted for a still water.

'I'm driving, so I'm going to save the wine for the meal,' Jack explained.

Taking a sip of her water, Susan looked around the restaurant. 'It's funny,' she said, 'but I don't live far from here, but I've never been in here.'

'Me neither.'

'Really? How did you…?'

'I found it online.'

'Really?' she laughed. 'It looks nice.'

'I checked out the photos on their website. It looked good. I hope the food is just as nice.'

'I'm sure it will be.' She picked up the menu and started to study it. Momentarily the waiter appeared and asked if they were ready to order.

Jack ordered the Smoked Norfolk Duck Breast with celeriac Remoulade to start, followed by a rib-eye steak with dauphinoise potatoes and peppercorn gravy; Susan started with deep fried calamari with tartare sauce, and for the mains seafood paella and vegetables. These dishes were accompanied by the *Vino Della Casa Trebbiano*, one glass for Jack, and two for Susan.

As they ate, Jack asked, 'You obviously got your

mother to babysit tonight.'

'Yes, I did. He's staying over at hers tonight. She's taking him to school in the morning. A little midweek treat for him.'

'If it's anything like my daughter staying at grandparents overnight, it's a treat for both of them. When Cathy was younger, it was more of a treat for my mother, I think, than for her.'

'My mother's on her own; they split up years ago. Are your parents local?'

'They were, when Cathy was younger. When my father retired, they moved down to Eastbourne. As you do when you retire, apparently.'

The conversation continued in this vein, Jack talking about his family, his job, Susan doing the same. When it was time for dessert, Jack chose the Belgian dark chocolate parfait with mixed berries, Susan the Apple Tarte Tatin.

Followed by coffee.

She was single, not divorced: she and her son Kyle's father never married. Two years after Kyle was born, he had an affair with somebody he worked with, and moved in with her. She was supposed to get child support from him, but he split up with his workmate eighteen months later, and disappeared off the radar. Susan did get some money from him around that time, but had no idea where he was now. What assistance she did get in raising Kyle, she did with her mother's help, both financially and in terms of childcare. Susan had a senior position at the estate agency, and was fortunately on a good salary, so she made do, in her words. As he listened, Jack was pleased to hear this: in his mind, a single mother making it so obvious she wanted to see him again; well, he could not be sure of her motives, but he recalled from a previous story that working in a supervisory position in an estate agency, she would be looking at a salary of around forty thousand, very comparable to a journalist, ironically. So he was hoping that she was going out with him for the right reasons.

She already knew Jack was divorced; he decided to leave it at that, and not tell her about his former girlfriend, Lucy Ryder, who had been killed in a car accident engineered by his ex-wife's ex-partner. Probably too confusing and messy for a conversation on their first date, especially if she was going to wonder if that happened to all his girlfriends.

It was eleven o'clock when they finished their coffee. When the waiter placed the bill on the table, Jack immediately slid it closer.

'Let me get my share,' she said.

Jack shook his head. 'No. This is on me.'

'You need to let me pay the next time.'

'Absolutely,' Jack said. He spoke jokingly, but was pleased that she offered. Pleased that she was talking about a next time.

She took out her phone.

'What are you doing?' he asked.

'I've got the number of that cab firm stored. I was just going to call them.'

'No way. I'll run you home.'

She put her phone down. 'Thanks. I'd like that.'

CHAPTER NINE

'YOU OKAY, BABY?' Amanda ran her hand over the side of Ryan's face. 'You look pale.'

Ryan said, 'I'm okay.'

'You a bit shook up about Sun?'

'I guess I am. It came out of the blue. I'll be okay.' He leaned down and kissed her.

After their meeting with Professor Newbury, Anji said goodbye and quietly made her way to the college library. She had no lectures till after lunch. She appeared to be in shock: as they listened to the Vice Chancellor talking about Sun, she sat there quietly, just slowly shaking her head. At least Amanda and Ryan had each other for support.

Folding her arms tightly around herself, Amanda said, 'See you after the first lecture? Around ten forty-five at the refectory?'

'Yeah,' said Ryan. 'Sure thing.' They said their

goodbyes and went their separate ways, their lectures being in different parts of the college.

Ryan arrived at his lecture hall and sat in the second row. He took his finished assignment out of his backpack and laid it on the desk. He checked his watch, then checked his phone.

'Hey, wake up! Can I get by?' said one of his fellow students, as he brushed past Ryan to take a seat.

'Sorry, mate,' Ryan said, adjusting his position. 'Miles away.'

He stared into space for a few seconds, then squeezed the assignment into his backpack, got up, and hurriedly left the lecture hall. Once outside, he looked around to make sure Amanda was not still around; satisfied she was not, he walked briskly out of the building. Ryan paused on the piazza outside, took a deep breath, and began walking to the main road, where he would find the bus stop.

Just before the perimeter road - South West Drive - he had to pass the college basketball court. A group of students was playing. Ryan recognised one of the players, and to make sure he was not seen himself, he hurried past.

He walked the few yards down the perimeter road to the bus stop. He looked around: there was no sign of any buses at all, so he decided to walk. It was a nice, bright morning, if not a little chilly; better than last night. He began to walk back to the house.

Amanda's first lecture had ended. Inequality Module One. She had not really been paying attention: her mind kept wandering back to Sun, trying to recall the last time she saw him. Maybe she and Ryan could speak to the boy in the other college Sun was friendly with, although she wasn't sure who he was. Perhaps they should go and see him, once they had found out who he was. But what sort of relationship was it? They were sleeping together, for sure, but was it just casual, or were they an item? The

Vice-Chancellor didn't mention anybody else, so maybe it was the former. That was always the problem with Sun: he was so private, and always kept himself to himself. Very enigmatic, Ryan would say. Maybe the boy knew what Sun was doing in London that night.

When they were both at college for lectures, or working in the college library, they tended to meet mid-morning at the refectory for a coffee. Maybe a snack, maybe a late breakfast. Her first period done, she gathered up her belongings, and walked round to meet her boyfriend. No sign of him inside, so she leaned on a wall, and checked her messages and social media. Strange: there was nothing about Sun on there: one would have thought the death of a student would have generated chatter, but there was nothing. Maybe word hadn't got round yet.

The place was filled with students milling around, but no sign of Ryan. She waited a few moments, then texted him. After two minutes there was no reply, so she called him.

He answered immediately. He seemed out of breath. 'I was going to call you.'

'Where are you?' Amanda asked.

'I'm headed back to the house. I feel like shit.'

'Oh, no. You okay?'

'Yeah, I just don't feel too good, that's all. Maybe you were right: maybe the news about Sun shook me up more than I thought.'

'You want me to come back?'

'No, no. It's okay. I just want a couple of hours downtime, get my head around what's happened. I'll come back to college this afternoon.'

'Are you still on the bus?'

'No, I walked.'

'Walked?'

'Yeah, it's a nice day, and it gives me a chance clear my head. I'll let you know when I'm back in college.'

'All right; fine. You sure you're okay?'

'Yes, I'm fine. I'll see you this afternoon.'

'Okay,' she said, slowly. 'Love you.'

'Love you too,' said Ryan, then hung up.

Amanda put the phone back in her bag and went to get coffee on her own. She took it to go. She thought about Ryan as she stepped out into the sun to drink her coffee. Sun's death must have shaken him up; Amanda didn't realise her boyfriend had such a sensitive side.

Ryan got back to the house. Thank God Anji was at college as well this morning. He ran upstairs to his bedroom. Went to his wardrobe, and crouched down to where he kept his shoes. Behind the trainers was where he kept it. It was in a clear resealable plastic bag, inside a manilla envelope.

Then he went into Sun's room. With much urgency, but without disturbing anything, he went through all of Sun's stuff: his clothes, carefully feeling between each items of underwear, inside each sock, all four of his dresser drawers. The same with the wardrobe. And the desk. Nothing. Ryan scratched his head, puzzled. It had to be here. He hit the floor and felt under Sun's bed, inside the bedframe. There it was: a similar envelope, white this time, filled with two clear resealable bags.

He took Sun's two bags and his one into the bathroom. Realizing the stupidity of furtively looking over his shoulder as he was alone in the house, he tipped the contents of the three little bags down the toilet, and flushed. Flushed three times. He turned the bags inside out, and rinsed them. Just to be sure, he would get rid of the empty bags on the way back to college.

Ryan leaned back against the bath and began taking deep breaths.

CHAPTER TEN

RAPTURE.

Meaning a feeling of intense pleasure or joy. Or at least, that was Jack's understanding of the word. Synonyms would be bliss, euphoria, elation, ecstasy.

Whichever words one chose, that was how Jack was feeling that morning. He was even smiling to himself as he waited in a long line of traffic to get onto London's North Circular Road at Edmonton.

The previous evening couldn't have gone better; well, he reflected, maybe slightly better. The meal was great, the conversation couldn't be faulted. Susan wasn't some vacuous blonde; there were no awkward silences; and as two single parents, they had plenty in common to talk about and even swap experiences about. She accepted his offer of a ride home. As they drove to her house, Jack wasn't sure if she was going to invite him in. If she did, would it be genuinely for coffee, or would it be for coffee and sex? If it was for coffee and sex, would she come straight out with it, or would it be coded, and would he be able to read the signs correctly?

Jack pulled up outside her house. As they arrived, he paused to let one of the people in the house at the end pull out onto the street. He set the handbrake, but decided on the spot it might be presumptuous to switch off the engine.

'Thanks for a lovely evening,' she said, gathering up her bag.

'Thank *you*. I had a great time.'

She seemed slightly ill at ease as she said, 'I would invite you in for a coffee, but I'm tired, I need to call my mother to check on Kyle, and I have some stuff to do for work tomorrow.' She paused a second, then added apologetically, 'I tend to leave things to the last minute.'

Jack shook his head. 'Don't worry; it's fine. I have an early start too: I need to be in Wanstead for ten.'

She nodded slightly, and leaned forward to kiss him. He gently responded, brushing one hand against her cheek. She smelt great still, and he could taste the sweetness of her Irish Coffee on her lips and tongue.

After a few seconds, their mouths parted.

'I'll call you,' they both said simultaneously, then laughed.

Jack got it in first. 'I'll call you. Message you.'

'Yes,' she said, smiling, and got out of the car.

Jack watched as she walked up to her front door. She paused in the doorway, waved, then had gone. He waited a second then drove away.

When he woke the next morning, there was a message waiting for him, sent at one fifteen that morning.

Tx again 4 last nite wish u had come in now, lol maybe next time x

He responded: *Don't worry. Next time then. Have a good day. Be in touch soon x*

That should keep things simmering for a few days, he thought. He needed to get round the challenge of her unavailability during the week and his at weekends.

However, he needed to focus on today's story: the football club in Wanstead. He was almost at the destination now. He was due to meet the owner and the team at the sports ground on the edge of Wanstead Park, where they were in training. He left the North Circular at the roundabout by Redbridge Station, and a couple of side streets later, he was there.

His appointment was with the club owner, Mo Khan.

Jack parked in front of the sports centre. He could hear the sound of a football match, so followed the sounds, and walked around the building to the pitches at the back. Only one pitch was in use, and he could see the team on the pitch, an older man in kit calling out instructions to the players. There was only one figure on the side-lines: a small man wearing a large black padded coat.

The man noticed Jack and turned round. He was Indian, so Jack guessed he was the owner.

'Daily News?' Khan asked.

'That's right.' Jack introduced himself and they shook hands.

'You're on your own?' Khan asked. 'Are you the reporter or the photographer?'

Jack held up his phone. 'Both.'

'A sign of the times.'

'It's been that way for a while,' said Jack. 'Especially with local newspapers. Technology has changed the job, as I supposed it's changed most jobs. During COVID we were doing interviews over the phone or Zoom and getting people to send in their own photographs.'

Khan nodded, his gaze darting back and forth from Jack to the pitch. 'There's the team, in training. They're almost done for this session.'

He was on the button. There was the sound of a whistle, and the team stopped and walked into the clubhouse. The coach picked up the ball. Khan and Jack followed.

For the next hour, Jack was introduced to and spoke to the players. He had no interest whatsoever in football, so a lot of the conversation went over his head. But he listened, nodded in the right places, took written notes, and recorded some of the conversation. He took photographs of Mo Khan on his own, of Mo Khan and the team, and a couple of the team on their own. He wondered whether he was here to write an article on the team, or on Mo Khan.

As he listened, the words local, and parochial, came to mind as his thoughts kept drifting to the previous evening and his longing for a bigger story.

CHAPTER ELEVEN

FOR MANY YEARS, *West Coast* has been a popular night spot in the City of Kendal. It is especially popular with people attending the University, as it offers a ten percent reduction in admission and at the bar on production of a National Union of Students identification card.

It is normally particularly busy on a Saturday night; tonight was no exception, as Amanda and Ryan had to wait in line outside for twenty minutes before they could gain admission. Amanda was reluctant to go tonight, but allowed herself to be persuaded by Ryan, who said after the events of the week, she needed to get out and have some fun. He had arranged to meet some other guys there too, he said, so it should be a good evening.

'Let's not make it too late,' Amanda had moaned. 'I'm supposed to be on FaceTime with Mum at one tomorrow.'

'That's no problem; you'll be ready in time.'

They arrived at the club around nine, and finally passed

the bouncers at nine twenty. As soon as they got inside, Ryan rubbed his hands together.

'I just need to take a piss first.' Amanda raised her eyes to the ceiling, but visited the ladies' while he was in the gents. When she came out, there was no sign of Ryan, which was unusual as he was always quicker than she was. Momentarily, she spotted him at the bar, talking to somebody. Ryan noticed her, said something to the man, who slipped off his stool and left the bar. Ryan walked over to Amanda.

'Who was that?' Amanda asked. 'I've seen him before. He's not from the uni?'

Ryan led her back to the bar. 'That's Will. He must come here regularly. That's where I know him from. We were just chatting. That's probably where you've seen him. Here.'

'Probably. Where'd he go?' She looked around.

Ryan shrugged. 'Don't know. He's around here somewhere. Perhaps he's gone for a piss too. Get a drink?'

They went to the bar, and Ryan got a bottle of Bud Light for himself and a half pint of lager and lime for Amanda. 'There's Samir and Paul,' he said, pointing to one of the tables, leading Amanda over there.

Once they had settled at the table, Samir said, 'That was bad shit about Sun Lee, wasn't it? You guys shared a house with him, didn't you?'

'We did,' said Ryan.

'What happened?' Paul asked.

Amanda replied, 'We don't really know. He wasn't here; he was down in London.'

'Really?' said Samir. 'I didn't know that. What was he doing there?'

'The breast stroke, by all accounts,' Paul sniggered. Nobody responded.

'Nobody knows,' said Ryan.

'Was he high?' Paul asked, keen to make a sensible contribution.

'Why do you ask that?' asked Ryan.

'His rep,' replied Paul.

Samir cut in. 'He had a bit of a reputation here and there. You know, he liked tasting Molly.'

Amanda said, 'You sure? I hadn't heard that.' She turned to Ryan. 'Had you?'

Ryan shook his head. 'No, I didn't. Not until the VC spoke to us.'

Amanda said, 'The police spoke to us as well. Came round to the house yesterday afternoon.'

'What did you tell them?' asked Paul.

'Exactly what we've told you,' said Ryan. 'We might have lived in the same house, but he kept himself to himself. We hardly saw him.'

'They searched his bedroom,' added Amanda. 'The police, I mean.'

'Did they find anything?' Samir asked.

'No,' said Ryan.

'Well,' corrected Amanda. 'We don't know that for sure. It depends on what they were looking for. But they never told us anything.'

'What do you think they were looking for?' Samir asked.

'According to Newbury and two cops who came round, when they found him, he was full of E.'

'I told you,' said Samir.

'So they found him… where?' Paul asked.

'In the river,' said Ryan. 'Or rather, he had got beached on a mud bank in Wapping.'

'That's kind of east, along from the bridge,' Amanda explained.

'Bridge?' Samir asked.

'Yeah,' said Ryan. 'Apparently he fell off Tower Bridge.'

Paul and Samir both laughed. Paul giggled, 'Trying to fly was he?'

Ryan and Amanda said nothing. She linked her arm into his, and he took a mouthful of beer.

Trying to change the subject, Paul said, 'There's not

much talent in here tonight.'

'I don't know,' Samir said. 'Look at those two over there.' Across the dance floor, on the edge, were two girls - the right age to be fellow students - dancing a slow dance together. One of them had both hands resting on the other's backside.

'I'll give the one on the left a seven,' said Paul.

'Please,' Amanda said. 'Must you?'

'Just a bit of fun,' said Paul. 'You'd do the same if you were here on a hen party.'

'No, I wouldn't,' said Amanda, taking a mouthful of lager and lime.

Ryan said, 'Calm down, everyone. Why don't you two go dance with them. You might end up giving them a higher score.' He could feel Amanda's angry gaze.

Paul stood up. 'Come on, then,' he said to Samir. 'Let's give these lovebirds the table to themselves.'

They left, much to Amanda's relief. She finished her drink. Ryan put an arm around her shoulder, and drew her close for a long kiss.

'Can't we go back?' she asked. 'It's so crowded here. And,' she added, putting a hand on Ryan's leg, 'Anji's out tonight.'

Ryan was about to say no, but the hand on the leg was beginning to sway him. 'Just a bit longer? One more drink?' She agreed.

Ryan kissed her again, and wandered over to the bar. While he was waiting to be served, he began fishing in his wallet for his Students Card. He didn't notice Will slip onto the next stool. Will was already holding a bottle of lager.

'Hey,' Will said.

Ryan looked up. 'Oh, hey, man.'

Will said, 'I hear you had a visit from the police.'

'We did, but everything's cool.'

'They didn't find anything?'

'I told you: everything's cool. I flushed it down the toilet. Chucked the empty bags in a bin in the street.'

Will pulled a pained expression and winced. 'Had to be done, I suppose.'

Ryan nodded. He ordered two more drinks for him and Amanda. 'Best to be safe.'

Will nodded, and slid his bottle in a circular motion on the bar. 'Well, now that's all out of the way, you'll be wanting to replenish?'

CHAPTER TWELVE

SUNDAY MORNING AND Jack should have seen this coming.

The weekend was starting so well. He was working from home on the Friday; he had filed all of his outstanding stories, leaving a few things to tidy up, but he could take care of these over the weekend, leaving the rest of the day to himself. First thing, he messaged Susan, to ask if she was free for lunch. She replied in seconds, much to Jack's delight, to say she was, but only had an hour, so maybe they could meet somewhere local to where she worked. Jack replied that was fine.

She worked out of an office in Finchley Road, West Hampstead, not too far from where she lived; not an area Jack knew that well.

We can pick up something at the O2 x, she messaged.

OK. Wheres that? x

On Finchley Rd, you cant miss it x

Is there parking? x

Loads, at the back. Go down the side rd. Meet u upstairs in the food hall x

Cool, cu 1? x

xx

So they met in the Food Hall, just after one PM, a quick lunch – a sandwich at the Soho Coffee Company. They chatted about the weekend. Susan was dropping her son off at her mother's Saturday morning, meeting a couple of girlfriends for lunch, then picking him up early evening for a movie and pizza. Sunday would be just stuff at home, probably vegging on the sofa while he played on his Wii, after housework and laundry.

Jack's was looking similar. He would be meeting Cathy after school that afternoon. Dinner would be fish and chips, after which he caught up with emails, and she chatted online in her room. Saturday, she wanted to go to Westfield, so he would take her there. Dinner would be somewhere out, or a Deliveroo. Sunday, they would be going to Eastbourne with his sister to visit their parents. When they got back he would drop Cathy off at his ex-wife Mel's.

'I try not to push the boat out too much with her,' Jack said. 'If I do, I get aggro from her mother about it. You know, "nice things with your father, routine stuff with me." She thinks it's a competition, sometimes.'

'But you have her two nights a week; your wife -'

'Ex-wife.'

'Ex-wife. She has her for five. You have to compensate for that, surely?'

'Yeah, I suppose so. Not sure if she sees it like that.'

Susan asked, 'Is she old enough to babysit?'

'I'd have to say no, not quite yet; maybe in a year or so.'

'Just a thought,' she said. Jack nodded: he had had the same thought.

After he had said his goodbyes to Susan, and an agreement to chat Sunday night, he drove back home and tidied his flat. Then picked up Cathy from school. As he had predicted, dinner was fish and chips, delivered, and then Cathy asked if they could watch a movie on Netflix: *Rabbit Proof Fence*. Jack had heard of it; apparently a girl in Cathy's class said it was 'brill'. As the movie progressed, though, she became more and more engrossed in chatting on her phone, and finally left Jack slumped on his sofa watching.

Sunday morning began with, 'Do we have to go there?'

'You haven't seen them in ages, Cathy, and they'd love to see you. Your Grandma keeps asking about you.'

She sighed and gave in, but he could see that today would be hard work, especially as they were going with her Aunt Maddie.

'We'll be back by seven,' Jack said as they set off, 'and I'll take you straight back to your mum's.' As if that would diffuse her lack of enthusiasm.

They had arranged to meet at Madeline's at eight thirty. Jack decided to shave that morning. He knew he would be interrogated about it by his mother and sister, and it just wasn't worth it. It wasn't yet a proper beard, just four to five days' stubble, and he could easily grow it again.

'I'll make breakfast,' Madeline told Jack on the phone the previous morning. Jack read into this that she would be giving them a cooked breakfast, and told Cathy as much; both found it hard to hide their disappointment to find that breakfast was two slices of toast and a cup of tea. They were both starving, and had to pull into a service area on the way down to Eastbourne to pick up coffee and something to eat. A sausage and egg panini for Jack and a chocolate croissant for Cathy.

'Wasn't the breakfast I gave you enough?' Madeline asked, huffily.

'It was at the time,' Jack lied, 'but we both had to get up extra early.'

Cathy rolled her eyes and returned to her phone.

They arrived at Jack and Madeline's parents at around eleven thirty. Some years ago, when their father retired, they sold the semi-detached four bedroom house in Purley in the county of Surrey, and relocated to a two-bedroom bungalow just outside Eastbourne. Their father was a keen gardener, and both front and back gardens were immaculately maintained. If the bungalow had a thatched roof, it would be the archetypal chocolate box dwelling.

Lunch was traditional roast beef, and while Jack was washing up, Cathy helped her aunt and grandmother set up the antiquated laptop for the booked FaceTime call to Amanda. He walked back into the living room while the call was in progress.

'Here's your Uncle Jack,' said his mother, moving aside so Amanda could see him.

'Hi, how's it going?' Jack asked, standing behind his mother.

'Everything's cool here. Still working hard.'

'Glad to hear it. Where's Ryan?'

'Oh, he had to pop out. He might be back in time.'

The next ten minutes were filled with chit chat and small talk. Cathy had a giggly chat with her older cousin, and the others left Madeline alone to speak with her daughter. Cathy went out into the garden with her grandfather and Jack's mother joined him in the kitchen.

'I'll make tea,' he said.

'She didn't seem her normal self,' his mother said. 'She's usually so bubbly.'

'It's Sunday lunchtime, Mum. She was probably hung over. She's a student, remember.'

His mother nodded, then took five cups and saucers out of the cupboard. 'She seemed tired.'

'Hungover. Or, just tired. It's not all fun and games being a student, you know. They have lectures, and studying, and exams to worry about.'

'Is she still with that boyfriend of hers? He wasn't there.'

'As far as I know. She said he had to pop out. Perhaps he was talking to his own family.'

Madeline joined them. 'Well. She seems fine.'

'I thought she looked tired,' said their mother. Jack groaned. 'What do you think, Jack?'

'Maybe. I thought she seemed a little, what's the word? Preoccupied.'

Madeline shrugged. 'Maybe.'

'Then you'd expect that, wouldn't you?' added Jack. 'I mean, she's away from home; she's working hard, she has exams soon. Students have a lot on their plate.'

Their mother finished the tea, and as it was a bright day, they agreed with her suggestion of going for a walk along the cliffs. This they did, Cathy walking with her grandfather, Jack with his sister and mother. As they strolled along, their mother said, 'I still don't know why you don't sell up and move down here, Madeline.'

Jack quickened his pace to avoid getting into this conversation. The wind was blowing hard, and he couldn't make out how the conversation went.

When they got back to the bungalow, it was almost time for Jack, Madeline, and Cathy to leave. As they gathered in the hall to say their goodbyes, Jack's mother said, 'I've just realised: I've seen both my granddaughters today. Not in the flesh, I know; but I've seen them in the same place.'

'Yes,' said their father. 'A rare event, having all the family together.'

'That's a most precious thing,' said their mother. 'Family, I mean. You can replace a car, or a house, or anything, really. But you can never replace family.'

A chill went down Jack's spine.

CHAPTER THIRTEEN

IT WAS A strange call that Jack took when he got home.

They left his parents at around four, dropped Madeline off at her house then headed back up to North London. The journey through London would take longer than the one from the South Coast. With Madeline no longer in the car, the atmosphere seemed more relaxed.

'Was it nice to see everybody?' Jack asked.

Cathy looked up from her phone. 'Everybody?'

'Grandma, Grandad, Aunt Maddie and Amanda.'

'Oh, yeah. That was good.'

'It's been a while since you saw them last.'

'I saw Grandma and Grandad in the holidays.'

'That's right; so you did. What about Maddie and Amanda?'

'Don't know. Ages.'

'You know, there's no reason why you can't talk to them yourself. On Skype, or FaceTime, or however you want to do it.'

Cathy looked up at her father with a look of incredulity. 'Aunt Maddie?'

Jack laughed. 'No, I mean Amanda. She is your cousin; you're the same generation. Your only cousin.'

'No, she's not. I've got -'

'From my side of the family, I mean.'

'Right.'

'I mean, she's what? Only ten years older than you. You've much more in common with her than with Aunt Maddie. And as you get older, the age difference becomes less and less relevant; you'll have much more in common.'

'Like what?'

'Same interest and attitudes. Same experiences. When you're eighteen, she'll be twenty-eight. If you end up going to uni, then the two of you can chat about her experience at Kendal.'

'Okay,' Cathy replied, plainly not meaning it.

'I'll send you her number, so you can reach out to her.'

Cathy said nothing; she was busy checking messages on her phone.

'You want to text your mum and tell her we'll be a little later back? Say by eight.'

'Okay.' Cathy typed in a brief message, then returned to TikTok. A reply came through in seconds.

'What did she say?'

'Just okay.'

Jack nodded.

It was six minutes before eight when they arrived back at the semi-detached house Cathy shared with her mother. She reached to the back seat and took out her backpack then she and Jack walked to the door. Mel, Jack's ex-wife answered the door seconds before they were about to knock. It was obvious she had been watching out for them.

'Sorry we're a bit late back,' Jack said. 'The traffic.'

'I saw Grandma and Grandad,' Cathy said. 'And Aunt Maddie and Amanda.'

'Oh?' said Mel, arms folded against the cold. 'Amanda's home?'

'No, it was on Skype. FaceTime, rather.'

Mel nodded, taking it all in. 'How are your parents?'

'They're fine, thanks.'

'And Amanda?'

'She seemed good, too. So's Maddie,' he added, mischievously. Through their marriage, Mel and Madeline never got on that well. Too similar, in Jack's opinion.

'Oh, good.'

'Everything okay with you?' Jack asked.

'Yes, everything's good.'

This was one of those meetings where the conversation was difficult and hard going. Jack was tired and tried to wind things up so he could get home. He wanted to relax and get in touch with Susan. 'Well, I'll let you two get on, then. School night, and all that.'

Cathy reappeared at the door. 'I forgot – there's no school tomorrow.'

Jack pulled an inquisitive face.

Mel explained, 'It's one of those teacher training days. She goes back Tuesday.'

'Okay. I didn't know that. Cathy didn't mention it. Anyway, it's still a school night for me.'

They said their goodbyes, and Jack walked back to his car, and drove home. He got indoors around eight thirty, and as he placed his phone on the table, he noticed a message from Amanda had come through about forty minutes ago.

uncle jack, r u free 2 chat?

He replied to the effect that he was free now.

A minute later, the phone rang, and he could see Amanda was calling him on FaceTime. He answered, slumping onto his sofa.

'Sorry, I didn't mean to FaceTime you; my phone's

still on it from this afternoon.'

'That's okay. I'm at home now. What's up?'

'Are you alone?'

'Of course I am. Who else -?'

'I just wondered if Cathy was with you.'

'No, I've just dropped her at her mother's. I'm on my own here. What's the matter?'

'Something's happened here at the house. I didn't want to tell Mum, but I have to tell someone, or I'll go nuts.'

'Sure, I get it. What's happened?'

Amanda took a deep breath. 'We share the house, Ryan and me, with two other students. There's Anji, she's cool, and there's Sun.'

'Sun?' asked Jack. 'As in… moon?'

'Yeah. He's Chinese. But he died the other day. Last weekend.'

Jack sat up. 'Shit. Died? How? What happened?'

'He was down in London, don't ask me why, but…' She paused to swallow. 'According to witnesses, he jumped off Tower Bridge.'

'What? Are you saying he killed himself? Suicide?'

'I don't know what I'm saying. But, Uncle Jack, according to the Vice Chancellor, when they found him, he was full of E. Ecstasy.'

'I know what E is. It has lots of names. So, he OD'd? Or was at least under the influence?'

She shrugged. 'Suppose so.'

'Did you know he was taking?'

'Both of us had no idea. He always kept himself to himself, very private, although we think he had a kind of boyfriend in one of the other colleges. But, Uncle Jack, the police came and spoke to us.'

'Don't worry about that. That's standard procedure. They have to do that. They need to find out where he got it from. I take it they searched his room.'

'They searched the whole house. Even our rooms. Without a warrant.'

'They don't need one. It's not your house. They just

need the permission of the owner if they don't have a warrant.' He paused. 'I'm assuming they didn't find anything?'

'No, nothing.'

Jack sighed with relief. 'That's good. What does Ryan think? Where is he, by the way? Didn't see him earlier.'

'He's in his room. He's working on assignment. That's why he wasn't on the call this afternoon. He's left it all until the last minute, as usual.'

Jack said, 'Look, I think you did the right thing by not telling your mum. She'd have been up there on the next train to bring you home.'

'That's why I didn't tell her. Uncle Jack, what should I do?'

'As they say, keep calm and carry on. Just keep your head down, get on with your studies. And be alert. It's possible, only possible, that whoever was supplying him with the E might approach you, any of you, to supply you. They've lost a customer, remember.'

'Oh my God! What should I do?'

Jack paused a second, then said, 'Call me and talk to me if anybody does approach you. Or Ryan. Day or night, yes? I'll tell you what to do. Just call me.'

'I will. Thanks, Uncle Jack.'

'And I've told you before, drop the Uncle bit. And thanks for letting me know. Now go and get some sleep.'

The call ended. Jack leaned back, looked up at the ceiling and shut his eyes.

Oh, shit.

Thank God she didn't tell Maddie.

He was planning on contacting Susan, like he said he would, but at the moment was not really motivated to do so. He'd get in touch in the morning.

Tower Bridge.

What the hell was a student from Kendal doing on

Tower Bridge? It wasn't if it was a holiday, just an ordinary weekend.

Jack rubbed his chin. The kid might have got the E he was taking from somebody in London. It might be worthwhile asking around about this. There might even be a story in it, somewhere.

Oh shit, he thought again.

A couple of hours ago, he was talking about Cathy going to university in five years. It had always seemed a good idea to him.

Now he wasn't so sure.

CHAPTER FOURTEEN

JACK COULDN'T RESIST it.

In fact there was no way he ever could.

When he logged on in the morning and checked his emails, he saw that, at 5:18 that morning, Mike Smith had emailed over a story for him to look into, and mail a five hundred word piece by Tuesday, five PM. The lead was about a row which had arisen in the Brent Cross area of North London, where visitors to the Shopping Centre had taken to parking on nearby residential streets, parking on the verges, to avoid using the Centre car parks, where the tariffs had just been raised.

'Give me a break,' he muttered, before checking the paper's database for any reports of his niece's housemate, Sun Lee. Nothing there, so he checked other local and the national papers. Finding nothing there either, he googled the name Sun Lee, and got a number of responses, notably a photographer in Melbourne and dozens of Chinese restaurants.

He was not really surprised: sadly, how newsworthy was the drowning of a twenty-three year old student from overseas?

So now, after making a couple of calls, he was on the Piccadilly Line, heading for Tower Bridge station. He also replied to Mike's email telling him about the story he was following up. He made no mention of his niece, only that he felt that a possible student drug ring was potentially more newsworthy than shoppers parking on grass verges.

It was not a long journey, changing onto the Circle Line at Kings Cross. In the short term, today's trip might well yield nothing. But it was something he always did, visit the scene, to get a feel for the events. He felt that made his writing better.

Arriving at his destination, he exited Tower Hill (the station), then walked along Tower Hill (the street), turning right onto Tower Bridge Road. Once at the actual bridge, he walked the length of it, crossed over, and walked back to the north side. As he walked along the pavement, sometimes having to squeeze past throngs of tourists, he ran a hand along the handrail. He found it hard to imagine how somebody could end up in the water below. It must have happened, though, on more than one occasion in the past, as every twenty yards or so, there was a sign stating there was an alternative to ending it all here, with a freephone number for the Samaritans. He looked over the railings down at the water. It was dark and flowing rapidly. It looked cold. Freezing cold. Jack shivered and hurried to the end of the bridge.

One of the calls he had made before he had left home was to the local police. He wanted to speak with one of the officers dealing with the Sun Lee case. He always found the Metropolitan Police cooperative with the news media, and had arranged an appointment with a Detective Sergeant Eve at the Marine Policing Unit. Based not far away in Wapping High Street, the Unit is responsible for policing the river and its environs, including the bridges.

He paused and looked back at the bridge. According to Amanda, witnesses saw him jump. He would need to get that claim validated, but couldn't see how he could have got to a place from which it was easy to jump. Did he climb onto those railings? Hardly – the top railing was semi-circular, and it was physically impossible to stand on there to jump.

Either way, he ended up in the river. Jack wondered where he was found. Depending on conditions, his body could have ended up anywhere from Wapping to Southend on Sea to… well, Rotterdam. Geography wasn't his strongest point.

Back on Tower Bridge Road, he hailed a cab which took him to the Police Station in Wapping. His appointment with DS Eve was at eleven forty-five. He arrived at eleven forty, and DS Eve appeared ten minutes later. She was short - the days of police officers having to be at least six feet tall had long gone – and had short red hair. She was in her forties and wore a crisp white blouse and black trousers with shiny black shoes.

'Mr Richardson?' she asked. 'You want to come through?' Jack followed her through a keypad-guarded door and into an interview room. 'Sit down, please.' When they were both seated, she asked, 'Which paper are you with?'

'The *London Daily News*,' Jack replied.

She nodded. 'I know that. When you phoned, you said you had specific information about the investigation.'

'No, I said I had a specific interest in the investigation. I know he was seen to fall off Tower Bridge, and I know his body was found to have a large quantity of Ecstasy present.'

She slowly nodded. 'Okay. And what is your interest exactly?'

'My interest is two-fold. First of all, there is a potential story, if I'm honest. Something along the lines of the dangers of recreational drugs, aiming for the younger reader. Secondly, he shared a house with my niece.'

Until now, Eve had that *I've heard all this before* look on her face; at the mention of Jack's niece, her expression changed.

'Up in Kendal?'

Jack nodded.

'Can she shed any light on what happened?'

'Not really. She called me about it last night. It seemed the boy was very solitary. There might have been a language barrier; I don't know, I didn't ask. But he kept himself to himself, so it wasn't unusual for him to be absent. She was surprised to hear he was in London, though. She has no idea why he jumped off Tower Bridge, none of them have.'

'The local police have spoken to her?'

Jack had the feeling DS Eve already knew the answer to this question. 'Yes, they have.'

'Okay.' DS Eve sat back in her chair. 'From the top, then. He died from drowning. No surprise there. But to be precise, he didn't jump off Tower Bridge. According to our two witnesses, a couple upstairs on a passing Night Bus, it looked as if he was trying to fly. Launching himself into the air. Of course, it was two in the morning, it all happened quickly, and they were on top of a passing bus.'

'And that was probably the last thing they expected to see.'

'Quite,' she agreed.

Jack paused and scratched his chin. 'Trying to fly. I know a little about recreational drugs. From a research point of view,' he added jokingly.

Her expression remained frozen. Jack wondered if being humourless was a prerequisite for joining the police. He continued, 'But trying to fly: isn't that consistent with having a large quantity of MDMA in your system?'

'I never mentioned drugs. Where did you hear about the Ecstasy?'

'From my niece, and she was told by the University Vice-Chancellor. And of course, by your colleagues in Kendal, who apparently searched the house for more. And found nothing.'

Eve nodded. 'Yes, that can be one of the side effects.'

'Where was he found?' Jack asked.

'Ironically, not far from here. The river flows west to east, as you might know, it was a low tide that night, and his body was beached on some mud banks by the Old Stairs.'

'Jesus, what if it hadn't been low tide?'

'Daytime he might have been spotted: this part of the river is quite busy. But at two AM; well, that's anybody's guess.'

'Any nobody has any idea why he was in London?'

'Not at this time, but we do know he was due to return to Kendal on the Tuesday morning.'

Jack gave her a puzzled look.

'He had a wallet in his back pocket. Bank card, Student ID card, Railcard, and a return ticket for Tuesday. He'd been in London since Saturday at least, as we discovered that he had made two large cash withdrawals over the weekend.'

'How large?'

She paused. 'Two hundred and three hundred.'

'That's five hundred.'

'Yes? And?'

'ATM withdrawals. There's a limit on ATM withdrawals, I think, Something like three hundred a day. So he must have needed a monkey for something specific. The supply of Ecstasy, maybe?'

She nodded. 'That's what we are thinking, although it is more likely that a student in possession of Ecstasy obtained it nearer to home.'

'The university?'

'Too early to say yet.'

'What about a mobile? He would have had a phone, surely?'

'He did, but it was waterlogged. We're hoping it'll dry out so we can check it out.'

'Try rice,' Jack said.

'Excuse me?'

'Leave the phone in a bowl of rice. Grains, dry. They'll help to soak up the moisture.'

'I didn't know that. I'll tell my DI. So, to recap: you, or your niece, rather, have no idea why he should have come to London?'

'No, but as I said, he apparently kept himself to himself. But she told me he had a friend, a boyfriend, maybe, from one of the other colleges. He might know why, or may have travelled with him.'

Eve nodded. 'I'll relay that to my colleagues. They can speak with the University. Anything else?'

Jack paused a second before replying. 'He could have travelled to London with this friend, yes? I suppose the university will know if any other students are missing.'

'They will, but -'

'I'm thinking aloud now. I'm thinking this was an impulse trip, not planned.'

'How do you figure that out?'

'He had a paper ticket, a card ticket, yes? You know, the same size as a bank card?'

'That's correct,' she replied, a little impatiently.

'He would have bought this ticket either from the Kendal ticket office, or from one of those ticket machines they have in the stations.'

'Of course,' she said, not knowing where this was going.

'Not bought in advance. Look, I'd say most students - or anybody under thirty for that matter - do everything on their phones. Right?'

DS Eve gave a slight nod.

Jack continued, 'Surely, if he'd booked this trip in advance, he'd have done it online, and just got himself an e-ticket.'

'I see. That's possible.'

'Then, if he bought his ticket online, there might be seat reservations. Then you could see if he travelled down here alone. But he didn't buy online. Was there anything on the ticket about seat reservations?'

'No.'

'They could probably tell you how the ticket was bought – card or cash.'

She looked at her watch. 'I'm sorry, Mr Richardson, I have another meeting now. I'll update my DI with what you've told me. Hopefully that can help us to move the investigation on quicker.'

'How much would a return Kendal to London cost?' asked Jack. 'Fifty, sixty quid? That's quite a sum for a student, even with a Railcard. So the journey must have been an important one.'

She stood up. 'As I said, I need to go now. But I appreciate you taking the time and trouble to come in and see us. All I can tell you is the investigation is still ongoing.' As she spoke, she opened the interview room door and indicated for Jack to leave.

A minute later, he was standing on the street outside the police station. He felt he had been given the brush off, but it was clear they knew very little either.

He turned and walked down Wapping High Street. He was headed for the Old Stairs. He paused and checked online the exact location.

Wapping Old Stairs is one of several steps leading down to the river, in past times used by fishermen landing their catches. This particular location saw the hanging on 23rd May 1701 of the infamous Captain William Kidd. After his execution, the steps were named Execution Dock; it is now the site of a pub called Town of Ramsgate, named after the Kent town where the fishermen would fish.

And, fifty yards away, he saw the pub. At the side of the building was a narrow alley. Jack walked down the alley, which took him to the back of the pub. At the end of the alley were the Old Stairs. It must have been midway between high and low tides, as around a dozen steps were above the surface of the water. The tide must have been going out, as these exposed steps were wet, and there were small puddles in the imperfections of the stone.

Looking down the steps at the dark water, he could just imagine what it was like here at the end of the nineteenth century: the cobbled streets, the gaslights, the fog. Jack the Ripper. Chestnuts roasting. He could almost hear a street woman saying, 'Gawd bless ya, guv.'

He shivered again. His imagination was getting the better of him. There was no fog, and it was the early part of the twenty-first century. He walked back along the alley. He noticed the pub was open. That would figure – it was lunchtime.

He walked in, ordered a beer and a sandwich, and sat down, working out where to go next.

CHAPTER FIFTEEN

JACK TOOK A bite from his chicken sandwich and texted Susan.

hi u free?

He waited a few seconds for a reply, but when none came, he returned to his pint of beer. He had had no feedback from Mike Smith after his email saying that this story, which was essentially what it was, was more newsworthy than people parking on grass verges, pissing off the residents. He read into this lack of response that Mike reluctantly agreed with him, or that he just hadn't read Jack's email. One way or the other, Jack would have to contact him, to get agreement for him to go to Kendal, which was what he would have to do. Even if Mike said no, he would not authorise the trip, Jack would go anyway. It would only be a matter of him having to pay the expenses himself, which wouldn't be excessive. A couple of nights in a Premier Inn or something and a three hundred or so mile round trip on the motorway.

His phone chirped. He put the beer down and picked up his phone.

sorry was with a client. good w/e?

There was no point in dressing things up. *soso, difficult convers with niece*

sorry 2 hear. where ru?

wapping

wapping! long way.

lol, on a story

am free 2nite if u want 2 chat

great, call u l8r?

anytime after 8, is ok?

great. later

xx

Satisfied, he put the phone down and finished his drink in one swallow. At least things were still good between them; he had had the nagging feeling that she might have been upset he didn't contact her last night, as he had said he would. He could explain everything to her that night. It would in fact be helpful to him to talk about what was going on with somebody not involved.

He set a reminder on his phone to call her eight fifteen. She had said any time after eight, presumably after she had put her son to bed. Even though she said any time, if he called too late, then she might think he didn't feel it important enough; if he rang too early, like on the dot of eight, she might think him too pushy and desperate. Eight fifteen, eight twenty seemed about right.

He bought another pint and sat considering what he should do next.

The first thing had to be to find out more about Sun Lee, and what happened to him in his last couple of days. He had booked a journey to London, arriving Saturday, returning Tuesday. He died in the early hours of Monday morning. In student-speak, that was late Sunday night. It was likely to have been arranged at short notice, as he explained to the police; otherwise he would have booked his ticket online. And where was he staying in London? Why had nobody in London reported him missing? And why withdraw all that cash? Was it to pay for his accommodation? And why were no drugs found on his person? And why Tower Bridge? Did this mean he had been staying or seeing somebody in that locality?

So many questions. It was a shame he had been such a loner, and that Amanda knew so little about his private life. He needed to find out who this friend at the university was: he might be able to shed some light on what had been happening. He might have been in London as well, travelling down with Sun. Maybe he should ask Amanda, or Ryan, to see if they could find out who this person was. It was unlikely a newspaper reporter would be able, or be allowed to, find out much first hand.

His thoughts turned back to his niece. His comment last night about whoever was supplying Sun Lee looking for replacement buyers was just off the cuff; however, it was a strong possibility if Lee's supplier was in Kendal. He might be supplying more students. He might see Amanda and Ryan as potential clients. It was most likely to be a he although there were no certainties.

Jack needed to get up there.

He finished his beer, visited the gents, then left the pub. He checked the time: he'd actually been in the pub just over an hour, so headed back down the alley at the side of the pub to the Old Stairs. A couple of twenty-somethings were standing at the top of the stairs; at first they were oblivious to Jack's presence, but when he put his foot on the top step and said, 'Shit!' at the slipperiness of the steps, the man pulled his mouth away from the girl's and led her back up the alley.

In the time Jack had been in the pub, the water had receded quite a bit, and now Jack could see that the steps led down not to the water, but to a mud bank. If it comprised sand and not mud, it could be called a beach. But here, it was soggy, mud. This must have been where Sun Lee's body had fetched up. For a moment, Jack stared down at the mud bank, visualising a young man's body, beached on the mud. He had no idea when the body was found: if he entered the water at two, it would probably still have been dark when the current brought him here; there was no reason for anybody to be down here that time of the morning, so it had to be the first person down here in daylight. Jack sighed: the thought of Sun Lee lying here in the mud, alone, for three or four hours at least was tragic; the reality was, though, that he had drowned long before.

He attempted to go further down the steps, but even holding onto the handrail, he could feel his shoes losing their grip. He climbed back up to dry land.

Before returning to the High Street, he perched on the low wall separating the pub's terrace from the alley, and began to text Amanda, letting her know he would be going to Kendal. He got four words typed when he gave up and called. It would be easier to leave a voice message.

Much to his surprise, she answered.

'Uncle Jack! Jack. This is a surprise.'

'I was going to leave a message. I assumed you'd be in a lesson.'

'Schoolchildren have lessons; we have lectures.'

'Okay, lectures. Pardon me.'

'Anyway, it's lunchtime now. Is everything okay?'

'Yes, everything's as okay as it was yesterday. Look, I wanted you to know, I'm coming up to Kendal for a couple of days.'

'Uncle Jack, you don't need to fuss. I'm a big girl now. I'll be all right.'

'That's not why I'm coming up. I'm looking into your friend Sun Lee.'

'For an article? Cool.'

'Maybe; I'll need to find some things out first. I spoke to the local police this morning, the ones who pulled him out of the river.'

'What did they say?'

'Not much. I'm not sure if they didn't want to tell me

much, or they just didn't know much.'

'What do you think?'

'I think the latter, and I also think – from my experience – that there might be some tug of war situation with the police where you are as to who's leading the case. Anyway, I didn't really get much from them, only that he travelled down here Saturday and was booked to go back north Tuesday. I think a good way forward is for me to speak with this friend he had.'

'You mean the person at the other college?'

'That's right. It was a he, wasn't it?'

'It was, yes, and they were more than friends. Anji caught them in bed together once.'

'Do you know who he is?'

'No. He always kept his private life… well, private?'

'Any chance you could ask around? You and Ryan? It might be easier for you, being his housemates. I've got no status up there.'

'I'll see what I can do. Are you coming today?'

'No, it'll be tomorrow. I have some things to finish off, and I want to drive up. I can't do that now as I've had a couple of beers here.'

'Where? In London?'

'To be honest, in the pub in Wapping where he was found.'

'Ugh, gross.'

'I'll let you know when I arrive tomorrow. I'll find a hotel in the town centre.'

'City centre.'

'I stand corrected. Maybe we could have dinner together or something.'

'Us two, or Ryan as well?'

'Entirely up to you. And by the way, if you happen to talk with your mother, don't tell her I'm going up there.'

'No way would I tell her.'

'Good. See you tomorrow then. And do your best.'

'Best at what?'

'Finding who Sun's boyfriend was.'

'Will do.'

The call ended, Jack walked back to the street. He considered going back to the pub and talking to anybody who was around when Sun's body was found, but decided he would leave that for now. If this panned out into a story, he could always return when he was at the finishing off stage.

It was getting darker already, and there was moisture in the air. He shivered, pulled his collar up and looked around for a cab. Rather than loiter around here on the off-chance a taxi should appear, he began a brisk walk back to Tower Hill. The drizzle was turning into light rain, and the sky was growing darker. He quickened his pace; he wanted to reach the tube station before the rain got harder.

He was looking forward to getting home, to planning his trip up north, and particularly to talking to Susan.

CHAPTER SIXTEEN

IT WAS MID-AFTERNOON when Jack pulled into the car park of the Holiday Inn hotel on the outskirts of Kendal. He parked, checked in, and went straight to his room.

The previous day, after leaving Wapping, he headed straight back home. The first call he made was to Mike Smith, to get his agreement for a work trip to the Lancashire city. Expecting an interrogation, or an argument about why he was going there, and not speaking to pissed off householders about motorists parking on their grass verges, to Jack's surprise, Mike was quite amenable.

Jack had to sell the idea to him, though.

'So, you're thinking this might be a drugs ring at the heart of the educational establishment?' Mike asked. Jack wasn't sure if he was being sarcastic, genuine, or a prat. Probably the latter, but Jack played along.

'Too early to say at this stage, Mike, but I think we need to establish why a student like him suddenly took a trip down to London.'

'How long will you be away for?'

'I reckon a couple of nights, three days, should be enough.'

'Two nights, that seems reasonable. But don't go booking yourself into the Hilton or somewhere. A hundred a night max. Okay?'

Jack said that was okay and that he would update Mike on his return to London.

The next call he made he made at six thirty, to his daughter. As usual Mel, his ex-wife, answered. Jack decided not to say anything to her about this, just he needed to ask Cathy something. When Cathy came to the phone, Jack told her that he had to go up north for work for a couple of days, and as he was near Kendal, he was going to see Amanda. Did she have any messages for her cousin?

'Like what?' Cathy asked.

'I don't know. Or shall I just tell her you said hi?'

'Yes. That's strange: we only talked to her the other day.'

'We did. Strange coincidence.'

Jack ended that call and waited till the appointed time of eight fifteen before he called Susan. In fact he waited a whole extra two minutes, just to appear extra cool.

There was no point dressing things up for her: he had already told her about Mel and Cathy, and about Madeline, her late husband Graham, and about Amanda. He heard her gasp as he told her about Sun being found in the river, and understood his reasons for going up there. Firstly, as it could be a potential story; secondly, she agreed that Sun's supplier might be looking for a replacement customer.

'How long do you think you'll be up there?' she asked.

'Couple of nights.'

'Well, if you're coming back Thursday, why don't I see if my mother can have Kyle, then I can cook you dinner. Here. You won't feel like cooking after a long drive.'

Jack was glad this was not a video call, as she would

have seen him punch the air. 'That would be great, if you're sure,' he said casually, and wondering if that offer included breakfast as her son was at his grandmother's. 'I'll message you while I'm up there, so we can square everything up.'

After some brief chit chat, he ended that call too. That sounded promising, and he couldn't help noticing he had got aroused at the thought of dinner with Susan. It was about time he had some action, he thought.

Once in his room, he dropped his bag on the floor, kicked off his shoes and lay down on the bed. Checked his phone. While he was driving, Amanda had messaged him to check he was still coming and if he didn't mind her cooking, he could come round to the house that evening.

He replied, yes he'd like that, he just needed the time and the address.

He arrived at the agreed time of seven thirty with a bottle of Chardonnay. Ryan answered the door as Amanda was in the kitchen. They shook hands and Ryan led him out to the kitchen.

'I hope you don't mind pasta?' Amanda asked.

'Pasta? I should have brought red,' he joked. 'No, pasta's good.'

'By the way, this is Anji,' Amanda said, introducing their other housemate. Anji was in the kitchen, perched on a stool, sipping a glass of red.

The food was soon ready, and they ate sitting around the table in the large kitchen. The conversation started with some small talk: Amanda asking about Cathy, and Jack telling the others a couple of stories about Amanda when she was a little girl. Cue much laughter, and Amanda's red face.

Eventually, Jack took a sip of wine and asked, 'Did you have any luck with Sun's friend?'

Amanda and Ryan looked at each other and shook their

heads. 'Anji didn't, either,' Amanda added. 'I told her why you were coming, was that all right?'

Jack shrugged to say yes.

'He was more than a friend,' said Anji sardonically. Jack looked over to her.

'Oh yes,' Amanda said. 'Anji caught them at it.'

'Is that so?' asked Jack.

Anji took some more wine. 'Not exactly *en flagrante*, no. I had to knock on his door to borrow something, and when he answered, I could see a figure in his bed.'

'A man?' Jack asked.

'Or a very sturdy woman with hairy legs.'

'Would you recognise him again?' asked Jack.

'I doubt it. As soon as Sun realised I could see, he began to close the door. He had dark hair, I do remember that.'

Ryan clicked his fingers. 'What about his accounts? Facebook? Insta? The guy's picture might be on there.'

Amanda said, 'But we don't have his phone. How can we…?'

'The police said his phone was waterlogged,' Jack explained. 'They're waiting for it to dry out.'

'We don't need his actual phone,' Ryan said. 'We can just look on his profile page.' He pulled his own phone out of his back pocket and typed in Sun's name. 'Jesus, there's hundreds.'

'Are you friends with him on there?' Amanda asked.

Ryan shook his head. 'No, I'm not.'

'I think I am!' Anji exclaimed. She took out her phone and after a few seconds, 'Yes, I am. Here he is.'

'Look at his friends first,' Jack said. 'We'll get a name then.'

Anji scrolled through his friends. Shook her head. 'Sorry. Nothing here. Nobody I recognise, anyway.'

'What about his photos?' Amanda asked. 'Does he have many on there?'

'Loads. Let's see.' She began trawling again. 'Sorry. Nothing.'

'What about Instagram?' Amanda asked.

'I think I followed him there too.' Anji began searching. 'Here he is. Let's have a look. Hundreds here as well.'

While she was doing that, Jack retrieved Sun's profile and did the same. 'I don't know why I'm doing this,' he said. 'I don't even know what he looked like. Hold on: who's this?' he showed Anji a picture he had reached.

She looked and shook her head. 'That's Sun; but I don't know who the other guy is.'

Jack showed the picture to Ryan and Amanda. It was taken in a club, or even a pub. It was a close-up, head shot of Sun and another man of similar age. He had dark, shaggy hair, and a beard. Amanda shook her head, but Ryan frowned.

'Well?' Jack asked.

'He seems familiar,' said Ryan. 'But I can't place him.'

'He never had any visitors here?' Jack asked.

'No, obviously apart from that time Anji…'

'I think,' added Anji, 'that day we were all due to be out, but I came home unexpectedly.'

'What are you going to do with the picture?' Amanda asked.

'Do any of you know what college this boy was in?'

'I seem to remember,' Anji said, 'that he mentioned he knew somebody in Bowland. Bowland rings a bell, that's all. It might be something else.'

'How many colleges are there here?' Jack asked.

'Nine,' Amanda replied.

'Great,' Jack said. 'He's not in yours, so if it's not Bowland, I've got seven more to check.'

'How can you check?'

Jack laughed. 'By standing outside as everyone goes in and out, seeing if I can spot this face, and asking the students if they know who he is. That's until I get kicked out.'

'Why would you get kicked out?' asked Ryan.

'I'm not a detective. Even the police would ask the

university's consent. I'm just a reporter; there's no way any authority is going to sanction this. I'll just have to keep at it till I get my collar felt. I had to do this once before, a few years back. And by coincidence, that guy was called Lee. Bruce Lee, would you believe?'

Ryan laughed. 'Bruce Lee? You're kidding.'

'No. Straight up. But this time I'm looking for a little guy with a beard and shaggy hair.'

'How do you know he's little?' asked Amanda.

'Look at this photo. He and Sun are around the same height.'

Amanda laughed. 'Sun wasn't little. He was tall.'

'Over six foot,' Ryan added.

'You just assumed,' said Amanda, 'that as he was Chinese, he was short. That's so racist, Uncle Jack,' she added, in a mock reprimand.

'Maybe a racial stereotype,' Jack admitted. 'My bad; I withdraw that. A guy with shaggy hair and a beard.'

As the others began to clear the table, Jack looked down at the photo of Sun Lee and the other boy.

Maybe he had made a little progress today.

CHAPTER SEVENTEEN

JACK ARRIVED AT the college at eight the next morning. He had decided to leave the car at the hotel and get a cab to the college. All on expenses, anyway.

His plan was something he had done many a few times before; namely, to stand outside the college, approaching as many students as he could and show them the photograph of Sun Lee and the bearded boy. Hopefully there would be some recognition. Unless he got lucky and saw the boy himself.

It was cold, damp, and had started to drizzle. He pulled his coat collar up around his neck. At breakfast he decided to forgo the second cup of coffee as he needed to be here until the last of the students had arrived: the last thing he wanted was to miss the right person due to an emergency bathroom visit.

As he waited for the students to arrive, he thought about prioritising who he should approach, as there was no way he was going to speak to everybody, and yet remain discreet. From what Amanda had told him, Sun and this other student were sleeping together, so should he just speak with the single, male ones, as they were more likely to be in the same circle of friends - solitary males? He decided that probably was not a good idea: what he really needed to do was get as much coverage as possible this morning. It was possible, maybe likely, that he would get nowhere this morning and would have to come back later. The disadvantage with that was that the longer he stood here, the greater chances of being spotted by the university authorities. Of course he could position himself at the main gate, on the public highway, but being actually at the college the boy attended was more likely to get a result quicker. He considered cropping Sun out of the picture, but decided against as having his face might help recognition.

At around ten past, the first began to arrive. Two girls. A boy. Two boys and a girl.

'Excuse me. Sorry to bother you, but do you recognise either of these?' was his standard question. Some glanced quickly at his phone before saying no they didn't recognise either; others stopped and looked more thoroughly. A couple of solitary male students were unable to hear his questions as they were wearing earphones.

Two approached, a boy and a girl, chatting to each other animatedly. Their body language suggested they were a couple, or at least close. They paused as Jack spoke with them.

The boy frowned as he looked closely at Jack's screen, then looked over at the girl. 'They look familiar. What do you think?'

The girl looked and then said, 'No, I've never seen them before. Sorry.'

The boy added, 'I might have seen the one on the right around here. The Asian.'

'But not the one with the beard?' Jack asked.

The boy looked again. 'Difficult to tell. Most guys

around here look like that.'

'I appreciate that,' Jack joked back at him. 'Thanks anyway.'

Nobody had asked him why he was asking: if anybody did, he was planning on giving them some bullshit story about being a relative or something. He would not say anything about what had happened to Sun: he was not sure whether it was public knowledge all over the campus, and to give out that kind of news might draw more attention to himself.

He thanked the couple for their time and turned to look down the road leading to the college steps. Students were arriving in greater numbers now: a group of five or six, couples, threes, and some walking in on their own. Jack paid particular attention to those on their own. Two were girls, laughing loudly; two others were male students, on their own. One had blond hair and was clean shaven. He took Jack's phone and looked carefully at the photograph.

'I might have seen them around here,' he said. 'Or maybe in town. Sorry.'

'No problem,' said Jack as he took the phone back. 'Thanks for your time, anyway.'

The second solitary male was dark-haired, and had a beard, but he was short, and the assumption was that Sun's friend was over six feet as well.

'The one with the beard,' he said, 'does seem familiar. He might be from around here. I don't know the Chinese one, thought. Why?'

'Oh, I'm just a friend of the family. Long story. Thanks anyway.'

Jack managed to stop two girls who studied the picture. As they did so, Jack spotted a figure walking along the road, around fifty yards away. Tall, around the same height as Jack, stocky, wearing a jacket with the hood up. Under the hood, though, Jack could see he was bearded. He took his phone back from the two girls, hurriedly thanking them for their time, then walked to the other side of the road to intercept the hooded figure.

He noticed Jack approaching, and made to walk around, but Jack stepped in front again and spoke.

'Excuse me. Sorry to bother you, but do you recognise either of these?'

The student stopped and looked at the photograph, and then at Jack's face.

'Yes, that's me.'

'You're a friend of Sun Lee?'

'I am, yes. What's all this about? Do you know him as well? Do you know what happened to him?' Jack thought he could detect an American accent.

'I'm a friend of the family, kind of. Can we talk?'

'I can't now; I have a lecture. I'm free this afternoon.' Definitely an American accent.

'Can we talk then?'

'Sure.' He looked around furtively as he spoke to Jack. 'Fenton House. Room 326. Any time after two o'clock.' With that, he hurried inside the college building.

Jack waited until he had gone inside and spoke to a few more students. As before, those he spoke to did not recognise either, or said the faces seemed vaguely familiar. Until the last student Jack spoke to.

He was short - around five feet - wore thick glasses, and had a bad complexion. His image conjured up the word geek. He studied the picture then said, 'Yes, I recognise them both. That's Sun, and that's Guillaume.'

'Guillaume?'

'Yes. French for William. I don't know why he calls himself that. Just being pretentious, if you ask me. Guillaume Wickham.'

'Are they students here?' Jack asked.

'Guillaume is. I think Sun is too, but at another college. I met them both at a night club in the city some months back. That's how I know them; we're not friends. I'm Josh, by the way.'

'I'm Jack. Thanks for your help.'

'Jack? A J as well.'

'What? Oh, yes. Small world. Thanks again.'

'Any time.' With that, Josh left Jack and walked into the college. Jack left the area in front of the college and found a bench a few yards down the road. He sat and studied the photograph again.

So, this mysterious boy in the picture with Sun Lee was called Guillaume. French name, American accent: quite the enigma.

It was eight forty-two. He had an appointment with Guillaume at two. There was no need for him to be cool this time: he would arrive at two.

As he started to formulate the conversation he wanted to have with Guillaume, the drizzle turned to light rain. He got off the bench and tugged on his coat collar. Then the light rain turned to heavy rain. 'Shit,' he muttered and hurried to the nearest place of shelter.

CHAPTER EIGHTEEN

UNTIL HE HAD spoken to Guillaume, there was very little Jack could do to move things forward. He considered getting a cab back to the hotel, but as all he had consumed that morning was a single cup of coffee, dodging the rain, he walked into the city centre and found a café where he had breakfast. It was a matter of killing time before his appointment.

He checked online for the exact location of Fenton House, and saw it was on the campus, a couple of hundred yards from the college. Then checked his emails, of which there was nothing of consequence. He texted Susan to tell her he was having breakfast in the pouring rain and that he hoped she was drier; she replied that it was raining in London too.

His next online enquiry was of things to do and see in Kendal. He had to kill time somehow, and napping in his hotel room was not the best use of his time.

So he spent the next few hours wandering around the Historic Charter Market, the City Museum, and a couple of pubs towards the end of the morning. Just after one thirty, he walked back up to the university. The rain had stopped now, and there were breaks in the cloud.

Once on the campus, he used the map he had downloaded to locate Fenton House. He was surprised he had already spent so much time on the campus without being challenged. Was there no security? There was a guy in a booth at the main entrance, but he seemed more interested in his phone than who was entering the campus.

Fenton House looked no different to any ordinary block of flats. There was a telephone style keypad by the door, with a speaker grille. Jack keyed in three, two, and six, and waited. After a few seconds, he heard the lock on the set of double doors click, and he was able to push his way in. He had the choice of the lift or stairs to the third floor: the lift was already on the ground floor, so he used that. A couple of seconds after he knocked on door 326, it opened.

Without the cover of a hooded raincoat, Guillaume was easily recognisable as the person in the picture with Sun Lee.

'Come in,' he said, ushering Jack into the flat, checking nobody else was in the corridor. Flat was probably an exaggeration: it was a medium sized room, a single, unmade bed in an alcove. There was a desk against a wall upon which a large A4 binder lay open, with a couple of text books and a laptop. A small closet, and in one corner a sink unit, and cupboards, and a small stove. There was one other door, presumably to a bathroom. There were two piles of books stacked against another wall, and clothes strewn over the floor. Guillaume was barefoot, and was wearing a black tee shirt and grey shorts.

'You've changed,' Jack commented.

'Yeah, I got drenched walking back here from the college,' Guillaume explained, pointing to the pair of jeans hanging over a radiator. 'So, you were asking about Sun?' he said.

'You're American?' Jack asked, casually peering out of the window.

'No, Canadian actually.'

'Sorry.'

'That's cool. Most people make that mistake.'

'I'm Jack, by the way.'

'I'm Guillaume.'

Jack decided not to divulge he knew that. 'Guillaume. That's French, isn't it? For William?'

'I told you, I'm Canadian. I was raised in a place called Drummondville.'

'Never heard of it.'

'It's a small town, not far from Montreal.'

'So why are you over here?'

'My folks split up when I was a kid. My mother's still out there; I have no idea where my old man is. I wanted to travel Europe, and as I have an uncle and aunt in the UK, I settled here.'

Jack nodded.

'You want to sit down?' Guillaume asked, pointing down to the bed.

Jack was unsure what that meant, so he pulled out the chair by the desk and sat down on that. 'Thanks.'

Leaning against the sink unit, Guillaume asked, 'So what's this about Sun? You know him?'

'Not exactly.' Jack paused. 'You don't know, do you?'

'What are you talking about? I don't know what?'

'I'm so sorry to have to tell you, but Sun died a few days ago.'

Guillaume pushed himself off the sink unit. 'You get the fuck out of here. You some kind of nut? You get your kicks by -'

Jack held out both hands to pacify him. 'No, I'm not a nut. Please… Hear me out.'

'Go on then.' Guillaume stood up straight, arms folded. 'Tell me then.'

'You want to sit down?'

'I'm good,' Guillaume snapped.

Jack slowly and calmly explained to Guillaume the whole story, from who he was, and how he had got involved; where Sun's body was found, and that he was seen on Tower Bridge. And that his body was full of Ecstasy. As he spoke, he could see Guillaume's face grow paler, and his body language was less defensive. It was clear he believed Jack.

By the time Jack had finished, Guillaume was perched on the edge of the bed. 'I don't believe it.'

'When did you see him last?' Jack asked. 'You want a glass of water or something?'

Guillaume shook his head. 'A week ago, maybe two. I didn't know he'd gone to London. But then he didn't tell me everything. He was very, kind of private, you know?'

'When you saw him last, where was it?'

'Here,' he said quietly, running a hand down the bed.

'So, the two of you were…' Jack tried to find the right phrase.

'We weren't together, if that's what you're asking.'

Jack shrugged. 'You were friends. With benefits, as they say.'

'Pretty much. And you're positive it was him?'

'I didn't see the body, if that's what you're asking. But the police in London said his ID was in his pocket.'

'His cell phone?'

'It was waterlogged. They're waiting to dry it out.'

'It'll be fucked then.' Guillaume reached over for his own phone and speed dialled.

'Who are you calling?' Jack asked.

After a few seconds, Guillaume shook his head and ended the call. 'I was calling Sun's number. It went to voicemail.'

'I'd expect that. And you had no idea? Nothing from the university?'

'Nothing. But then, our relationship wasn't common knowledge.'

'The Vice Chancellor told my niece and her… and Ryan and Anji, his housemates. You know them?'

Guillaume shook his head.

'I think they were told to keep it to themselves. They were told as they lived with him, but the university probably doesn't want it public yet, although it'll have to be, eventually.'

Guillaume nodded. 'Guess so.' He looked up at Jack. 'How did you find me?'

'That picture I showed you this morning? I assumed it was of someone he was sort of close to.'

'Can I see it again?'

'Sure.' Jack stepped over to the bed and handed Guillaume his phone.

'I remember when that was taken,' he said, passing Jack the phone. 'It was in the summer, at *West Coast*, a club in the city centre.'

'Happier times.' Jack returned to his seat. 'Did you know he was on drugs?'

Guillaume let out a big sigh. 'Yeah, Kind of. He used to when he was here sometimes. Called it tasting Molly. He said it made him last longer.'

'Did you take it?'

'Didn't need it to perform.'

'I see,' Jack nodded knowingly.

'No, dude: I'm passive, so he did all the work.'

'Oh, I see. Sorry.'

Guillaume shrugged dismissively. 'We both used to use poppers, though.'

'Did you know where he got the stuff from?'

'The E? No, I didn't ask. Maybe that was why he was in London.'

'Possibly. You don't know of anybody up here, trying to sell?'

'I told you, I don't use.'

'I get that, but have you ever heard anything on the grapevine? When you were in that club? *West Coast*? Any activity there that you were witness to?'

'No, nothing.'

'Where do you get your poppers from?'

'You mean do I get them from a dealer? They're not drugs. I get mine online.'

'Online?'

'Yeah.' He reached over to the chest of drawers next to the bed, and took out a small bottle with a bright orange label.

Jack read out the label. '*Iron Horse Leather Cleaner Poppers*. And that's what you use?'

'Yup. Thirty-five pounds for five bottles. Reduced from fifty-five. He unscrewed the cap and held it up. 'You just sniff, and…'

'I'm good, thanks.' Jack involuntarily took a step back. 'Look, you said you and Sun were friends with benefits. Would you know if he was seeing anybody else?'

'He might have been, I don't know. We weren't joined at the hip. Well,' he laughed, 'we were sometimes, I guess. I see a couple other guys now and again; I'm sure he was too. He was pretty hot.'

'But you don't know who?'

'Sorry, pal.'

Jack said, almost thinking aloud, 'So he could have been getting his supply from one of them.'

Guillaume pulled an apologetic expression.

'I guess so. Sorry I can't be any more help.'

CHAPTER NINETEEN

'SO HE WASN'T much use, this friend of Sun's?' Ryan asked.

After speaking with Guillaume, Jack returned to his hotel, where he got up to date online, and arranged to take Amanda, Ryan and Anji out to dinner that evening to update them and to reciprocate for the evening before. Anji was unavailable, so it was just Jack, his niece, and her boyfriend, which was really how Jack wanted it. Keep it in the family.

They ordered. Jack chose the rack of ribs with barbecue sauce, chips, slaw and buttered corn. Amanda thought that sounded good, so followed suit. Ryan ordered the rotisserie chicken, with seasoned fries, and corn.

'You didn't want the ribs?' Jack asked.

'No,' Ryan said quietly. 'Preferred the chicken.'

'No, you should have had them. Then we could have shared.'

'Uncle Jack,' Amanda said through gritted teeth, 'Ryan's Jewish.'

It took a moment for this to sink in. 'Oh, I see. Sorry. Well, I didn't know. How would I know?'

'Why would you?' Ryan asked.

'What's your surname?' Jack asked.

'O'Connor,' Ryan replied.

Jack nodded.

Amanda said, 'Jack, just because he's Jewish doesn't mean to say his name has to be Goldberg or something. You do need to take a look at your racial stereotyping: you assumed Sun was short just because he came from China.'

'Okay, okay. Point taken. I'm suitably admonished. Sorry to have embarrassed you, Ryan.'

'It's cool, honestly,' Ryan laughed, looking at Amanda. She briefly rested her temple on his shoulder.

'And in answer to your question,' Jack said, 'he was of limited use. But the visit wasn't a total waste of time.'

'Was he easy to find?' Amanda asked.

'It took a while. Some weren't interested in even looking; some looked, but there was no recognition; others said the faces looked familiar but couldn't place them. Then I saw the guy himself.'

'That was a bit of luck,' Amanda said.

'It was, and we arranged for me to see him at his digs this afternoon.'

'And what did he tell you?' Ryan asked, taking a mouthful of rotisserie chicken.

'Well, his name's Guillaume.'

'As in... William?'

'Yes. He's Canadian. French Canadian. He's studying - I don't know what, it never came up in conversation - at Bowland College, and his room is in Fenton House. You guys know it?'

Amanda and Ryan looked at each other. 'Sort of.'

'Okay. Well, he and your pal Sun weren't together, in that sense; more like...'

'Fuckbuddies?' suggested Ryan.

'Um, he said friends with benefits, but I suppose that's the same thing. He did say there were others.'

'What? He had others, or Sun did?'

'Both. He said he was sleeping with Sun, but said so were others.'

Amanda said, 'I never saw him bring anybody back. Did you?'

Ryan shook his head. 'I never knew about this guy – Guillaume?'

Jack asked, 'Didn't Anji say she saw him bring someone back once?'

'Yes, that's right,' Amanda replied. 'Once.'

'She didn't actually see the guy, though, did she?' Ryan said. 'She said he only opened the door slightly, and she just got a glimpse of a figure in the bed.'

'That could have been Guillaume,' Jack said, 'or that could be someone else. He told me he knew Sun used to use: he said he didn't, only poppers. Oh yes, when he told me that, he showed me a little bottle of what he used, said he got it online. But that was the extent of his drug taking. He didn't know where Sun got his from. You guys have no idea? You've not heard any talk, any whispers about drugs, any type? Even poppers? This is a university, after all.'

'Nothing,' Amanda said.

'Well, that's not one hundred percent true,' Ryan said. 'I know a lot of students use poppers, they talk about them. I don't know where they get them from; I've never felt the need to.' He looked over at Amanda. 'Have we?'

Amanda shook her head. 'No. Did you when you were our age? Take drugs, I mean.'

'In my day, it was mainly alcohol. I did smoke something two or three times. Marijuana, I think it was. But keep that to yourselves: don't tell your mother or grandmother.'

'I've seen people,' Amanda continued, 'and you think, you know, that they must be smoking or taking something. But that's the extent of it. That's right, isn't it?' She looked at Ryan, who nodded in agreement.

'Yes,' he said. And I'm sure Anji would say the same thing. Sun moved in different circles to the rest of us.'

Jack finished the last rib, dipped his fingers in the little bowl of water and wiped his hands and mouth with his napkin. 'You said the police searched his room?'

'Yes,' replied Ryan, 'and they found nothing.'

'You assume they found nothing. But what would they find?'

'Um, stuff like drugs. Whatever he was taking.'

'Is his stuff still in the room? His personal belongings, I mean. Did the police say anything about what was going to happen to it?'

'Only that somebody would be in touch about it.'

'Somebody?' Jack queried.

'One of the officers said the next of kin would be in touch.'

'But aren't they in China?' Amanda asked. 'I mean, when we found out, Sun's father called us from China. No, he said Hong Kong. It was Hong Kong.'

'So,' mused Jack, 'somebody could be on a plane now to get his stuff. If they don't, I would imagine your landlord will wait until the last rent payment has expired, then box everything up, store it for a while, then bin it. My point is, the police are unlikely to want to come back. I'd like to look through Sun's room. Is that okay?'

Amanda and Ryan nodded.

'The room isn't locked, or anything, is it?'

'No, it's just as they left it.'

'Great,' Jack said, as he asked for the bill.

'What are you looking for?' Ryan asked.

'Anything.'

'When do you want to come and do it?' asked Amanda.

'Why don't I give you two a lift back, and do it then? It'll save you a taxi fare, at least.'

*****

'So is your friend Anji out?' Jack asked, as he stood at the foot of the stairs.

'She's out on a date.' Amanda explained. 'Otherwise, she might have come with us.'

'Show me his room,' said Jack.

'Straight on at the top of the stairs. His room's at the end of the landing.'

'What about the bathroom?' Jack asked, as he went upstairs.

'Help yourself. It's to the left.'

'No, I don't mean that. Did he keep his toiletry stuff - shaver, shower gel and the like – in the bathroom?'

'Oh, yes,' Amanda called up the stairs. 'He had a black bag.'

'Okey dokey,' replied Jack. He went into the bathroom and found the bag. Unzipped it, and went through the items. A small battery operated shaver which Jack unscrewed and checked inside, a toothbrush which was bone dry, and a little tube of toothpaste. He reassembled the shaver and replaced it in the bag. He unzipped the side compartment inside the bag and took out a resealable plastic bag. He held the bag up to see the contents. It was a small, black douche bulb. He quickly folded the bag up again, and replaced it in the zipped compartment, and put the black bag back on the shelf. As he left the bathroom, he bumped into Ryan.

'I just need to use the...'

'Go ahead,' said Jack. 'I'll check his room now.'

He walked in and switched on the light. He was amazed how tidy the room was. Everything neatly in its place, the bed neatly made. It was hard to believe the police had been through this room, unless somebody had tidied it since.

He noticed Ryan standing in the doorway. 'Is this how he kept it?' he asked.

'Pretty much, although I think Anji put everything back in its place after the police had been through it. Mark of respect, she said.'

Jack nodded and walked over to the closet. The rail was full of clothes neatly hanging on a rail: shirts, jackets, a couple of coats, and a few pairs of trousers. He went through each item carefully, checking that each pocket was empty. Four pairs of shoes rested neatly at the bottom of the wardrobe.

A large black suitcase lay on top of the wardrobe. Jack pulled it down, and put it on the bed. He checked the outside, unzipped it and checked inside.

'Looking for secret compartments?' Ryan asked from the doorway.

'Something like that,' said Jack, not looking up.

'Can I help?'

'Thanks, but I need to do this alone. It helps me concentrate. Why don't you get some dessert? We didn't get that earlier.'

'Okay, if you're sure. I'll get Amanda to save you some.'

'Thanks.' Jack waited until he heard Ryan go downstairs, then he finished checking the suitcase, put it back, then turned to the chest of drawers. The top drawer was filled with underwear and socks, all neatly folded. He noticed the material of one pair of underpants looked different, and took it out, holding it up. It was made of a mesh type material and was open at the back. Sun had three pairs of these, black, red, blue. Under the items in the drawer were two packs of condoms and a bottle of sexual lubricant. Jack raised his eyebrows, and neatly and hurriedly replaced the items. Even with Sun being dead or maybe precisely because he was dead, Jack felt guilty and uncomfortable looking through what were very personal things. He wondered what Sun's next of kin would make of all this.

The next drawer was filled with tee shirts, neatly folded and in piles of matching colours, all white, all black, all red, all grey and a variety of brighter colours. Jack searched through here, and again found nothing.

It was the same story with the bottom drawer and its

trousers, jeans, and shorts. As he went through each drawer, he ran his hand along the underside of the drawer above, pulling the bottom draw off its runners to do the same, before replacing it. He checked behind all the furniture.

Jack sat on the bed and sighed. This was going to be fruitless. He went through the desk and the contents, even checking the books in case he had cut out a section of the pages, and unscrewed the pens. The little bedside cabinet revealed nothing, only tissues and more books. Jack wondered why Sun kept the condoms and lubricant over there in the chest of drawers, and not right next to the bed: maybe that was confirmation that he hardly ever brought anybody back here.

Next the bed itself. He went on all fours and checked under the bed, but found nothing there. He searched the bedclothes, inside the pillow case and quilt cover. He checked that the mattress was intact.

Then he lifted up the mattress and checked underneath. Now he could see through the slats holding the mattress onto the floor below. He looked all around under the bed then something caught his eye.

Downstairs in the kitchen, Amanda and Ryan heard him call them. They ran upstairs where they found him sitting on Sun's bed frame. He had peeled off a small piece of carpet, no more than three inches square. Lifting up the piece of carpet, he took out a small, sealable clear plastic bag.

Inside the plastic bag was a small amount of white powder.

CHAPTER TWENTY

'WHAT IS IT?' asked Amanda.

Jack held the plastic bag up to the light. 'In the movies, or on TV, they'd dip a finger, taste it, and say something like, "This is cocaine direct from Venezuela, seventy-six percent proof," but as a journalist, I can only guess. Your friend Sun was apparently full of Ecstasy, so it's probably that.'

'E?' said Ryan.

'Ecstasy, E, MDMA, Molly; it has lots of names. I'm guessing it comes in different forms.'

'Where was it?' Ryan asked.

Jack showed them. 'Under his bed. Under the carpet. I lifted up the bedding, looked through these – slats, I think they're called – and I noticed a short cut in the carpet. A deliberate cut, not just a tear. He showed them the flap. 'I lifted the carpet up, and hey presto! I found this.'

'No wonder,' Ryan said, then coughed. 'No

wonder the police never found it.'

'Yeah,' said Jack. 'Stroke of luck.'

'So what are you going to do?' Ryan asked. 'Go to the police?'

Jack straightened the bed and sat on it. 'I'm not sure. It's only a small amount.' As he spoke he held it up to the light again. 'Although it might depend on how refined it is.'

'Refined?' asked Amanda.

'Yeah, I think that's the technical term. Basically how strong, how concentrated the stuff in here is. It could be pure - depends how far along the distribution chain Sun was – or it might be mixed in with baby milk powder, or something similar.'

'What do you mean the chain?' Ryan asked.

'Well, we're assuming he was just a taker. He could be distributing himself. This could be pure: he'd mix it with something else, like powdered milk, and sell it on. Hard-up student, I don't know.'

'Jesus,' said Amanda, shivering and folding her arms.

'Do you think there's any more here?' Ryan asked.

Jack looked around the room. 'I think I've searched the place pretty thoroughly, as I'm sure the police did. I even looked inside his texts books; you know, to see if he had cut out a little compartment in one of them.'

'Had he?' asked Ryan.

'No.' Jack scanned the carpet. 'No, I think that's it.'

'So what *are* you going to do?' Ryan asked.

'I don't know. Strictly speaking, I ought to go to the police, but they might not take too kindly to me searching after them and finding something they missed. They might even accuse me of putting it there. They were obviously satisfied: they didn't declare this room as a crime scene; no locked door, no tape, or whatever they do.' He paused and clicked his fingers. 'I know what I'll do. I'm going to take it back to London tomorrow. We'll need to find out exactly what it is. I have a couple of contacts down there:

there's a good chance that they might have a friend of a friend, et cetera, who could identify it.' He paused and grinned. 'At least if I get stopped with this, I can say it's for my own recreational use, as it's such a small quantity.'

'Then what?' enquired Ryan.

'The whole point of my coming up here – well, there are two points, I suppose. The first was to make sure you guys are okay; remember I said that Sun's contact might get in touch with you and exert pressure on you to become replacement customers.'

'Oh, I can take care of that,' Ryan said, looking down at Amanda.

Jack looked up at him. 'I wouldn't bank on that.' He paused a second. 'And also, there might be a story here, a big one. You know the sort of thing, our reporter uncovers a major narcotics distribution ring based in one of England's prestigious universities.'

The others laughed.

Jack grinned. 'Something like that. We always dress things up to appeal to the readership. Sensation and scandal sell. But when I find out what this is,' he said, holding up the plastic bag, 'then I'll probably have to come back up here. Maybe use it as bait.'

'Bait?' Ryan asked.

'That's right. Use it to flush out whoever was supplying Sun.'

'How would you do that?' asked Amanda.

'Not sure yet. It depends on what I find out from my contact.'

'Is there anything we can do to help?' she asked.

'Thanks; there might be, though I don't know what yet. But whatever we do, you need to know… well, you need to be careful. It might be dangerous.'

CHAPTER TWENTY-ONE

'DANGEROUS? IN WHAT way?'

Jack looked over at his niece. 'In several ways. Firstly, we don't want the police involved right now. I know they're investigating Sun's death themselves, but I'm approaching this from a story point of view, and if the police crop up in the middle of things, I might miss out on something important. Plus, if we're using this shit as some kind of bait, then technically we're in possession. Well, I am. Now, I know that in the grand scheme of things, this is only a tiny amount, clearly for one person's use, but being picked up for it is only going to complicate matters.

'Secondly, and I've said this before, whoever's selling to Sun has lost a customer. He might think he needs to recruit a replacement customer. And we are assuming that Sun was just a user; that he wasn't part of a distribution network, selling on to other students. The tiny amount here suggests he wasn't, but he could have had more stashed away somewhere else - not in this house - or he could have just run out. That could well be why he was in London. He used as well as sold, although that's not likely, as somebody who is selling will know what the effects are, and won't take it themselves. Either way, we don't know how persuasive his sellers can be, especially if we're – sorry, I – am trying to draw them out. You guys understand all that?'

'Yes,' said Amanda.

Jack looked at Ryan.

'Yes,' said Ryan.

Jack nodded, not one hundred percent sure that they did.

The following morning, Jack was driving home, down the M6. He had just rejoined the motorway after a comfort stop at Knutsford. The further south he got, the heavier the traffic. He always hated driving on this road, and was hoping to get back while it was still light, and while he was relatively fresh. He had a date that night, and did not want to spend the whole evening suppressing yawns.

His journey took him around Birmingham on the M6 toll road, and eventually onto the M1, which would take him into London. One more stop, this time at Watford Gap, which is nowhere near the eponymous Hertfordshire town. Before re-joining the motorway, he paused in the services car park and sent a text to Amanda, checking if everything was okay; then a message to Susan, asking if everything was still on for that evening. He sat in the car for a few minutes, then to his satisfaction, replies came through, both saying yes. Now for the last leg of the journey, and for some heavy traffic as he approached the capital.

He finally arrived home around four. He texted Susan one more time, saying he forgot to ask earlier, but he would bring wine, and should he bring red or white. She replied in a couple of minutes, saying red she supposed, as she was cooking lasagne. She hoped he liked lasagne.

Jack didn't like lasagne. He replied, *luv it. cant wait. red it is.*

He showered, and, still wearing a towel, texted Cathy to tell her he was back home safely. He wondered if he ought to have brought her back a souvenir, but came to the conclusion that she was too old for that sort of thing by now.

She replied shortly, *cool, cu at weekend.*

Around six, he set off for Susan's, calling in at his local 7/11 for a bottle of Malbec. After choosing the bottle, he made a detour on his way to the checkout to pick up a toothbrush. Something to keep in the car as a just in case. He stopped again at the end of the aisle, paused a second, then turned back and walked down to the other end, where they stocked the condoms. Again, something to keep in the glove compartment with the toothbrush in case they were needed. He decided it would be tactful to keep these items back; the last thing he wanted was for her to think him presumptuous by arriving for dinner and expecting to have an overnight stay as well.

It was just after seven when he knocked on her door. As she held the door open for him, he took in what she was wearing. She had on a black dress, its hem two inches above the knee. Her hair was tied up in a bun, and she was wearing make-up, something she hadn't done when he first saw her here. When they met during her lunch break the other day, her make-up had been minimal.

She closed the door and he held out the bottle.

'Here you are. A bottle of red.'

She took the wine and stood it on the small table by the door. Reached up and put both arms around his neck, gently pulling him down to kiss her. He responded as their mouths met, putting one arm around her waist and the other around her shoulders. As they held each other, Jack felt himself harden immediately, and eased himself slightly away from her in case she could feel it too. He was too late; she pulled away and laughed.

'Let's eat first,' she said, picking up the wine and leading him into the kitchen. Slightly embarrassed and cross with himself for allowing that to happen, he followed her.

The kitchen was filled with the aroma of cooking. The dish of lasagne stood on the side, cooling. Despite the fact that he did not normally like lasagne, he had to admit it smelled good. The table was already laid: a tall white candle in the centre; two bowls of salad, and a stack of garlic bread next to the candle. Two empty wine glasses waiting for the Malbec.

'You okay to pour while I dish up?' she asked, handing him a corkscrew.

'Absolutely,' he replied.

They sat and ate, Jack actually enjoying his lasagne this time. The conversation began by being a continuation of the one they had had in the Cricklewood restaurant, segueing to their children, and their jobs. Jack had to admit, although did not say so, that he was glad he was the journalist and not the estate agent, as the job, from what she had told him, seemed boring compared to his.

Inevitably, the conversation drifted to his trip to Kendal. Jack kept what he told her to the bare facts that one of his niece's housemates had died of an overdose, and he was researching and preparing an article on the dangers faced by, to use a phrase he detested, but for which he could find no substitute, young people today.

She nodded thoughtfully as he spoke, and laughed with him at his tales of the less serious items he had had to cover over the course of his job. She admitted she didn't read the *Daily News,* so as well as his name, the stories he spoke of were unfamiliar to her. Unless she was just trying to be cool.

'I tend not to read actual newspapers,' she said at one point. 'Just get my news from one of the news channel apps.'

'We have an online presence too, as do all titles these

days. That gets updated first, then the paper edition. The news on the website tends to be a kind of interim piece, with the full story being done for the main editions.'

'It sounds far more interesting than what I do.'

Jack shrugged. 'Every job has its ups and downs. For every what you might call exciting story, I get fifteen, twenty, maybe more pieces that are mind-numbingly boring, lots and lots of waiting around, in the cold and wet. It's not as glamorous as you think.'

She stared at him a moment, then stood up. 'Give me those,' she said, picking up his plate, 'and I'll get dessert.'

'It's okay; let me help.' Jack stood and gathered the main course plates, while she busied herself on dessert, which was tiramisu, something Jack did like.

'I have to confess,' Susan said, as they ate, 'this is shop bought. I did put the lasagne together, but not this.'

'It's still delicious,' Jack said, this time honestly.

After the meal, she was about to clear up, but Jack insisted on helping her.

'Kyle's father used to let me do everything,' she said, rinsing the plates for the dishwasher.

'That's an outdate attitude,' Jack replied. 'In fact, truth be known, I rather enjoy clearing up after a meal. I don't even own a dishwasher. You want some more wine?' he asked, taking the bottle off the table.

'Won't it taste a bit bitter,' she asked, 'after the tiramisu?'

Jack pointed a few drops into a glass and tried it. Pulled a face. 'Yes, very.'

'I'll make us coffee,' she said, 'then I've got some brandy somewhere.'

'Wine, coffee and brandy. Not quite what I get at home.'

'What do you usually get at home?'

'Something delicious,' he said, pausing for the punchline, 'straight from the microwave. With maybe a beer, if it's a special occasion.'

'That's what I feel like sometimes, though I try to cook

something healthy most nights, for Kyle.'

'Cathy and I tend to get fish and chips on a Friday night. Really healthy.'

'Yes, but you only have her two nights a week. So they're special occasions. Let her mother give her healthy food.'

Jack couldn't argue with that.

CHAPTER TWENTY-TWO

JACK STIRRED.

For a moment he was not sure where he was. Then he realised.

There was a light. A white light. He blinked a few times to get his bearings.

He looked down at his bare chest. There were several small marks on the upper part of his chest, around the breast bone. Like scratch marks. They had bled a little, but the blood had dried. He brushed the flecks of dried blood off with his hand.

Now he had become orientated, and realised where he was. The white light was a street light. He had never noticed there was a street light outside Susan's house. In the past, not so long ago, streets were lit by sodium lamps, which would have bathed the room in a soft, yellow glow, almost atmospheric.

The light shining through the gap in the curtains was

not sodium-yellow, but white. Not bright, just a different colour. He looked down to his left, to Susan as she lay, face down. The top of the duvet was around her waist, exposing her naked back. Her hair lay over her right shoulder, revealing her left cheek, neck, and shoulder. She was fast asleep, breathing heavily.

He flopped back onto the pillow and took a deep breath. In the light from outside, he could make out the face of the clock on the wall, to the side of the wall-mounted TV. It was three-forty.

Six and a half hours earlier, they had finished their second brandy, and were standing together in Susan's walk-in shower, arms and tongues entwined. For the next half hour, they showered and soaped each other's bodies, leaving no part or crevice untouched. Still with arms around each other, they found their way into Susan's bedroom, and returned to those same spots, this time with lips and tongues.

It had been a long time since Jack had been with a woman, apart from a couple of quickies, and although he could never forget the mechanics, he hoped the technique which had served him so well over the years had not been lost. It had not, and it seemed she was as hungry as he was.

Susan locked her fingers around his neck as he entered her, and with a strength that belied her small stature, pulled them both over, so now Jack was lying prone. She remained sitting upright momentarily, as if to get used to the idea of having him inside her. Closing her eyes, and resting her hands on his chest she began to rock, the rocking increasing in pace and strength. Jack raised his knees to edge her closer, her movements and moans becoming greater. Eventually, as they climaxed together, she dug her nails into his skin, his cries of pain and passion becoming indistinguishable.

She could detect him moving, and began to stir. She

opened her eyes and looked across to him.

'Hey,' she whispered, resting a hand on his chest. 'You okay?'

Jack leaned over and kissed her gently on the lips. 'I'm okay. You?'

She gave him a sleepy smile of satisfaction and nodded. 'Mm.'

'You're quite the little tigress in bed, aren't you?' he said softly, running his fingertips through her hair.

'Oh Jack,' she sighed, 'it had been so long.'

'Same for me.'

'What's the time?' she asked.

'Almost four.'

'You're not going, are you?'

'Not unless you want me to.'

She shook her head. 'I don't.'

'I'll stay then.'

'Let me make you breakfast.'

'At four in the morning?'

'Whenever,' she murmured, still half asleep.

'Whenever?' he repeated, nibbling her ear lobe. She manoeuvred herself around so she was face up, put one hand on the back of his head, drawing him closer. While they kissed, Jack pulled the covers over them both and lifted himself onto her. She wrapped both arms around his back and raised her left knee to accommodate him.

After another shower, and a plate of scrambled eggs with two mugs of coffee, Jack drove home.

'I'm sorry to be so early, but I have to get ready for work.'

'Stop apologising. I understand, and I have to start work too.'

'Are you working from home today?'

'I'll start there, but I need to speak with one of my contacts, so I expect I'll go and see him.'

'Where is he, your contact?'

'Enfield, so not too far.'

'Not too far, no.'

So, at seven-thirty, after a long embrace and kiss at her front door and a promise to call her that evening, a euphoric Jack set off back home. The traffic was heavy and slow, but he didn't mind.

His eyes darted down to the glove compartment, where he had put the toothbrush and packet of condoms. He hadn't needed either, as he hadn't brushed his teeth, and she had produced the condoms. From her chest of drawers, not the bedside cabinet. He reflected that was just where Sun Lee had kept his. Surely that meant that she did not have a regular use for them. Even though it was none of his business and he was the last person to cast that particular stone, he was pleased at that thought. His bliss also arose from what she was like in bed. She had seemed so quiet, so innocent, almost: her ferocity in bed surprised him, and it was a surprise he liked. But he wondered, was that a one off, the result of ages of not having intimacy with a man, and all that pent-up passion and energy being released, or was it the norm? He hoped he would find out.

Privately, he was also relieved that he had been able to perform. He tried to recall the last time he had slept with a woman. He had a feeling it was early summer. May? June? It was a woman he had met at the gym. Just a one-night stand: her husband was away. He couldn't even remember her name. Marie? Mary? It didn't really matter. It was a quick frolic on her plush sofa, and he was on his way within half an hour. Hadn't seen her at the gym again, either.

But he did feel a sense of satisfaction. Here he was, in early middle age, and he could still manage it twice in the same night.

CHAPTER TWENTY-THREE

FOR THE THIRD time in twenty-four hours, Jack was in the shower. This time alone, this time reluctantly showering off the smell of Susan, the smell of her scent. Showering away immediate memories of a few hours ago. Showering away the odour of sex.

Once dried and in fresh clothes, it was time to reach out to one of his contacts. This particular source of information went by the name of P Parmar, and his meetings with Jack were normally in a pub in the centre of the North London suburb of Enfield. This time it was different: Parmar was due to tee off at Bush Hill Park Golf Course at twelve thirty, so could meet Jack at the clubhouse any time before twelve.

The golf course was not far from where they would normally meet, and so Jack left a little before he would normally have done, and pulled into a space at the golf course car park just before eleven thirty. Once he had done here, he would call to update Mike Smith; in fact, he had been expecting his supervisor to call any time to ask for an update on what was going on, and how much of his budget Jack had spent. He walked up to the clubhouse and found his friend sitting on a bench outside, smoking a large cigar. A trolley filled with golf clubs stood next to the bench.

'Jack, man,' Parmar said as Jack approached. 'How you doing?'

'I'm good, thanks.' Jack sat down next to Parmar.

'So what can I do for you, my friend?' Parmar asked.

'Well, you can get that bloody thing out of my face for a start,' said Jack, good-humouredly, and waving cigar smoke away.

'Sorry, guy.' Parmar carefully laid the cigar on the arm rest and moved towards Jack. 'So,' he said, 'let's do business.'

Jack spent the next ten minutes giving Parmar a rundown on the events of the last few days. Parmar nodded at intervals as he listened.

'So,' he said thoughtfully, picking up his cigar, taking a long drag, and replacing it, 'you need to find out where you can buy Ecstasy here in London?'

Jack pulled a face. 'That's part of it. Why? Is it an easy thing to find out?' he said, aware that in all his dealings with Parmar, not easy meant not cheap.

'I don't know personally; I might know someone who knows someone, you know. And if I can find all this out, do you just want names or contact details? Or do you want to meet them? You want to buy some?' he laughed, leaning over in Jack's direction.

'No, no,' said Jack.

'Ah. I was wondering if you wanted some for yourself, and the story angle was just cover.'

'Give me a break.'

Parmar patted Jack's arm. 'I jest, my friend.'

'In any case,' said Jack, reaching into his pocket, 'I have this.' He showed Parmar the bag he found under

Sun's bed.

'What's this?'

'My guess is that it is Ecstasy, but I don't know.'

'You tasted it?'

'Not touched it. Do you know of anybody who could identify it?'

Parmar nodded and held out the palm of his hand. 'Just by taste though. Not a chemical analysis. It'll be a best guess.'

'That's all I'm interested in.'

'Okay,' said Parmar. He closed his hand as Jack rested the bag on his palm. 'I think I know someone who could do that. Recognise the taste, I mean.'

'Great. How long will all this take?'

'I can get back to you by tonight about what this stuff is. As far as your other enquiries are concerned, that might be tomorrow. Now, to talk about money…'

'I've not finished yet; I've one more thing.'

'Jack, this is my lucky day.'

'I'm not sure if you will be able to help on this one. This kid Sun Lee died here in London. The local Bill told me he travelled down on the Saturday before, the eighteenth. It was a traditional paper ticket, a walk-on, not one booked in advance online, like most people of his age would do. I'm guessing that as he bought it just before travel, it was a sudden, last minute decision.'

Parmar nodded in agreement. 'Makes sense.'

'Ideally, I'd like to know where he went in London, where he stayed.'

'Before he jumped off the bridge?'

'Before he jumped off the bridge, although I'm not sure how I'm going to get that, if at all. But I'd be interested to know if he went into London alone.'

'Why would you want to know that?'

'I'm thinking if he travelled with someone else, then they might know where he went once he arrived at Euston.'

'Euston?'

'Yes, that's where the trains from Kendal arrive.'

'Way ahead of you, Jack. If I was to tell you one of my nephews is an absolute genius on his laptop, and that cyberspace was his oyster?'

'And?'

'There aren't many sites Sagar can't hack into.'

'So he could find out about that ticket? He'd hack into… is it Virgin?'

'I expect he could.'

'So if he could identify when Sun bought the ticket, could he get hold of the CCTV for the next train?'

'I'll ask him, yes. I can't see any reason why not. Assuming he can get into their site.'

'And he'd be willing to do this? I mean, would it be traceable back to him? It's probably illegal.'

'He'll say if he's not willing to do it. It's not like he's transferring funds to his Swiss bank account, or anything. Just retrieving information that any employee could probably retrieve. Anything else? I'm due to tee off soon.'

'No, nothing else; that's all. Apart from how much all this is going to cost?'

Parmar stood up, took a last drag and tossed the cigar butt into a flower bed. 'A hundred for the last two questions. As to sources: that might be another.'

'Two hundred?'

'I reckon so.'

'Can I give you a hundred now, then; well, you know I'm good for it.'

'There's a cash machine in the clubhouse,' laughed Parmar.

'You're kidding! Come on then; show me where it is. By the way, this is what the dead kid looked like.' Jack sent Parmar the photograph of Sun and Guillaume. 'He's the Asian; the other one's just another student.'

Parmar checked his phone. 'I got it.'

They both walked into the clubhouse, Parmar showed Jack where the ATM was. Once Jack had drawn out the cash and slipped it to Parmar, he walked back to his car.

'I'll expect your call tonight,' he said as he left.

'About what this is,' said Parmar, patting his back pocket, 'and maybe about the train ticket.'

'And the other tomorrow?'

'You got it, Jack.'

'Enjoy your game,' said Jack and walked back to his car.

CHAPTER TWENTY-FOUR

ONCE HE GOT back home, Jack thought he had better bite the bullet and update Mike Smith. Mike answered after a couple of rings and Jack told him the story so far.

'Is this one of your fishing expeditions, Jack?'

'No, absolutely not.'

'Yes, it is.'

Jack sighed. 'Well, sort of; but there's always a need to "fish", as you put it, to get the details of the story.'

'So what angle are you going to approach it from?'

'I'm minded to take it from the angle of somebody selling drugs - a drug ring, if you like. I don't know yet the size of what's going on - to students. Just there, or in other places, I don't know yet.'

'Aren't students supposed to be hard up?'

'Mostly, yes.'

'So how are they able to pay for all this stuff? A student discount?'

'I doubt that very much. And that leads to another question: how are they getting the money to pay for it?'

'Are you talking sex and drugs?'

'I don't know that yet. Anyway, the sample I got from the dead kid's room -'

'The what? The sample?'

Jack explained about the plastic bag of powder he found under Sun's carpet. 'When I got home, I weighed it – three point seven five grams. I googled the cost of MDMA, assuming the stuff is Ecstasy, and it's roughly a hundred and twenty pounds per gram. So, what I brought back: we're talking four hundred and fifty pounds, depending on its purity.'

'You still got it?'

Jack explained about passing the bag to Parmar for analysis.

'You what?' said Mike. 'Are you telling me you passed almost five hundred quid's worth of stuff to your informant?'

'I need to see what it is. It might not actually be Molly.'

'Who's Molly?'

'Molly. MDMA. Ecstasy. E. It's got lots of names. I need to see what it is. It might be that; it might be something else. If it's cocaine, for example, it changes the dynamic, as he was found in the Thames full of Ecstasy.'

'What are you going to do with it? If you're found with it in your possession…'

'Parmar's going to return it. Then I'm going to get rid of it. Flush it down the toilet.'

Mike sighed loudly and theatrically. 'All right. You've got till Monday to submit something, anything. Even if it's just an introductory piece. If not, you'll just have to take an assigned story.'

Jack agreed.

After ending the call to Mike, he noticed a text from Susan, saying how much she enjoyed the previous evening. And that morning, with a wink emoji. He replied he enjoyed it too and must reciprocate very soon, if she can stand his cooking.

For the rest of the afternoon, Jack pottered around his flat, tidying up, catching up with washing-up, laundry and the vacuum cleaner, so the place was presentable for when he picked up his daughter from school. Friday always came round quickly. He was just about to get in the car when Parmar called.

'That was quick,' Jack said.

'I've heard back from my friend. What you gave me was definitely MDMA. Only confirmed by taste, but he reckoned it was pretty pure. He said you are talking about a street value of five hundred pounds there.'

Jack whistled. 'Okay. Has he returned it to you?'

'I'm seeing him tomorrow. I can get it from him then. Unless you want him to get rid of it.'

'What do you mean, get rid?'

'Throw it away. Down the toilet, Jack.'

'And he'll do that? He won't sell it on?'

'He promises he won't, and I trust him, Jack.'

'Okay. Get him to flush it down the toilet. At least I won't have it here.'

'That's what I was thinking, Jack. Now, I have heard back from my nephew.'

'The hacker?'

'Yes. He got into the system easily. It's not Virgin anymore, but Avanti, but still easy to break into. He checked for tickets bought that day in question, Kendal to London Euston. There were sixty-five, but only two with student railcard.'

'That has to be him, and he didn't travel alone, then. Any joy with the CCTV?'

'That will take longer, and he had to go to work. But he tells me that these two tickets were returns and were paid for with a credit card in the name of G Wickham. Does that name mean anything to you?'

'G Wickham?' Jack thought for a second. 'No, it doesn't.'

'That's too bad. Well, I'll get back to you with the

other question you had and what my nephew finds out from the CCTV on the trains. The first train after the tickets were bought, I think.'

'Or if there's CCTV of the ticket machines at the time the tickers were bought.'

'Yes, that would be better. I'll call you tomorrow, my friend.'

Jack ended the call and whistled. Five hundred quid's worth just in a tiny plastic bag. Less than four grams.

He leaned back in his chair. G Wickham. G Wickham. He was sure he had heard the name Wickham somewhere, but where?

Then he recalled the conversation he had had with the geeky student. Josh.

'Yes, I recognise them both. That's Sun, and that's Guillaume.'

'Guillaume?'

'Yes. French for William. I don't know why he calls himself that. Just being pretentious, if you ask me. Guillaume Wickham.'

Jack let out a large breath. So that's who Sun Lee went to London with. His friend with benefits.

Guillaume.

CHAPTER TWENTY-FIVE

THE LYING LITTLE bastard.

Jack got angrier and angrier as he drove to his daughter's school. Had it not been a Friday, he would have driven straight back to Kendal to confront Guillaume. He was the person with whom Sun travelled into London, and he could well hold the key to the last few hours of the boy's life. Now it would have to wait until Monday, although he would have to spend the weekend putting together some kind of article to keep Mike Smith off his back.

His mood was obviously showing when Cathy got into the car.

'What's up, Dad?'

'Nothing. Just stuff from work, that's all. So, how's school?'

Normally, getting any information from his daughter about school was like getting blood from a stone, and today was no exception. Her mother had agreed to keep him up to date with what was going on, if there were any concerns and he was confident she was doing that; in any case, the school had an app he and Mel could both use: the teachers updated the app daily with the quality of her school work, what other activities in which she was taking part, and any positive or negative events. All Jack had to do was log in any time of day or night and check on her progress. Still, it would have been nice to get some verbal updates from Cathy herself.

They got back to Jack's around four thirty, and that evening followed their normal Friday evening routine: fish and chips, this time delivered for an extra pound, and Cathy in her room chatting with her school friends. The ones she was with two or three hours ago.

While she was chatting, Jack sat at his table and booted up his laptop. The first part of preparing an article was the research: Jack felt he didn't know enough about the drug concerned at the moment.

For the next hour, he sat at his laptop, scrolling down and taking notes.

Ecstasy is a common name for Methylenedioxymethamphetamine, MDMA for short. Molly and Mandy are also common names. A psychoactive, which means with the ability to change a person's mental state by affecting the way the brain and nervous system work, drug used primarily for recreational purposes. Effects include enhanced sensations, and increased energy, empath, and pleasure. Taken orally, effects begin within forty-five minutes and last between three and six hours.

In the seventies, it was used in psychotherapy and became a popular street drug in the eighties, being associated with raves, dance parties, and electronic dance music. It is sometimes mixed with other drugs, particularly LSD, a process known as candy-flipping.

Short term side-effects include grinding the teeth, blurred vision, perspiration, and a rapid heartbeat. Long term side-effects include addiction, memory problems, paranoia, and insomnia. Following use, once the euphoria has gone, people often feel depressed and tired.

No surprise here: it is illegal in most countries, and has no approved medical uses.

Another article gave more information about the effects: the euphoria, the increased empathy and feeling of closeness to others, relaxation, hallucinations, enhanced sensations or sexuality. The experience will depend on the user, the setting, and the dose.

It is often considered the drug of choice within the rave culture, and is found at clubs, house parties and festivals. In the environment of a rave, the sensory effects of the music and the lighting are synergistic with the drug. Some users say they enjoy the feeling of mass communion as a result of the inhibition-reducing effects.

Small doses are used by religious practitioners to enhance prayer or meditation.

The street name Ecstasy usually refers to the drug in its tablet form, possibly including diluents. The UK colloquial terms 'Mandy', and the US equivalent 'Molly' tend to refer to the drug in it, free of crystalline powder form, normally free from adulterants. When in tablet form, the tablets are sometimes produced in shapes that depict characters from popular culture, sometimes referred to as 'fun tablets'.

MDMA is normally consumed by mouth, and is sometime snorted. Powdered MDMA can vary in purity from one hundred percent pure to thirty percent pure, due to the addition of amphetamines, caffeine, opiates or painkillers. Some samples have been found to contain little or no MDMA. It had to be the case, Jack reflected, that the sample Sun Lee had was of very high purity. Was he going to make an addition, then sell it on?

Jack sat back, took a deep breath and pinched the corner of his nose. This was hard going. He needed coffee. He stood, stretched and wandered to Cathy's room, knocked on the door and put his head around the door.

'Hey, you okay?'

She looked up from her phone. 'I'm good.'

'Still chatting?'

'Yeah. With Kylie. She was off sick today.'

Jack nodded. 'I'm getting myself a coffee. You want one?'

'I'm good, thanks,' his daughter replied.

'Okay.' Jack left her to her conversation, made himself a coffee, and returned to his laptop. The next article he read was all about the side-effects, although this piece was filled with medical and scientific terms that went way over his head.

The next piece focussed on overdoses. He sat up, as this was more appropriate, he thought. Minor overdoses seemed limited to the central nervous system, and included agitation, paranoia, and mental confusion. When he got to severe overdoses, these could affect the whole body: haemorrhage, rapid muscle breakdown, acute kidney injury were just a few of the many outcomes.

Severe overdoses resulting in life-threatening conditions and even death occurred when the MDMA was mixed with certain other drugs.

He stopped reading and rubbed his eyes. This was enough for tonight. Apart from the depressing subject matter he was getting too tired. He would return to this over the weekend; there should be enough to base an introductory article on.

Over breakfast the next morning, Jack asked Cathy what she wanted to do. The reply was as he expected, and they spent the morning and part of the afternoon at the Westfield Shopping Centre, Stratford, East London. For three hours, Cathy browsed through various stores, while Jack sat outside, reading the morning paper.

They bought lunch in the Food Hall, and mid-afternoon, arrived back at Jack's flat. For the rest of the day, at Cathy's request, they sat and binge-watched a show on Netflix called *Shadow and Bone*, which Jack had never heard of, but quite enjoyed. Dinner was prepared in the microwave.

He had planned this evening to continue his research, even got his laptop out ready, but felt he had enough to work with. He would put together the piece the next day, once Cathy had gone back home.

He also planned to return to Kendal Monday morning, and confront Guillaume, who had obviously lied to him, and knew far more than he admitted. He pulled the laptop over, and went online to book his hotel accommodation for Monday night, extendable if necessary.

They finished the box set around midnight, and as they were going to bed, Cathy asked, 'We're not going to Grandma and Grandad's again tomorrow, are we?'

'No. What do you want to do?'

'Don't know,' she shrugged.

'What about a drive in the country? Have a pub lunch?'

She thought that was a good idea, and, after both sleeping in, and after their pub lunch, Jack drove her straight home to her mother's. They arrived there around five. School day tomorrow. It was only on her way home that she asked Jack about his trip to Kendal. He just told her that it was for work, and that he had had dinner one evening with Amanda and Ryan.

Once back home, he fired up the laptop again, and in a couple of hours had put together a two thousand word piece, leading on from the tragic discovery of the body of a student in the Thames to how concerned should we be about our children and recreational drugs. No conclusion; just a series of questions. Other articles to follow. He transmitted the piece before packing: that should pacify Mike for a few days, or until he read Jack's email which said he was returning to Kendal.

Early start tomorrow. A long drive, and another encounter with Guillaume Wickham.

CHAPTER TWENTY-SIX

JACK ARRIVED IN Kendal a few minutes after midday. It was too early to check into his hotel, so he headed directly into the city and found a car park as close as he could to the campus. Unlike the previous week, the sky was blue and cloudless. He could feel warmth from the sun, although there was a bitingly cold wind, each gust taking a pile of brown leaves and swirling them around the street.

He was working on the assumption that Guillaume would be following the same schedule as he had been the previous week; that is, lectures in the morning, and back to his room in the afternoon for studying, or whatever students did in the privacy of their own rooms. So he decided to hold fire until around two, and then head to the student building.

He found a pub in a side street off the main road, and bought himself a beer and some lunch. As he sat eating his cheese roll, he sent a text to his niece to say he was back up here for one night and if she didn't have plans tonight, he was free; otherwise, maybe coffee the next morning.

Just before two, he left the pub, and made his way back to the campus. He would leave the car in the long-stay parking until he was done here. He arrived at Fenton House at about the same time as he did the other day: with a bit of luck, Guillaume would be in.

Unfortunately, it was not as easy as him pressing the buzzer, Guillaume letting him in and saying, 'Sorry I lied to you, Jack.' But once Jack was inside the building, he was halfway there.

He knew what to do. He waited across the stretch of grass between Fenton House and one of the faculty buildings. Not standing suspiciously staring up at the place, but pacing up and down the path, with his phone to his ear. Now and again somebody walked past and then he took part in a fictitious conversation. People rarely interrupted a mobile phone conversation, real or imaginary, and this took away all suspicion.

This went on for ten minutes or so – a long conversation – before Jack spotted a group of three students heading for Fenton House. Guillaume was not one of them. Still on the phone, he approached the doors so he arrived a few seconds ahead of them then pretended to press one of the buttons. The leading students produced a plastic key card and swiped it in the reader adjacent to the doors, which unlocked with a click. Still on the phone, Jack smiled and held the door open for the other two and followed them inside. They proceeded down the corridor, still chatting and laughing, and Jack took the stairs up to Guillaume's floor. As soon as the other students were out of sight, he put the phone away. It always worked: people never interrupt a mobile phone call.

The corridor in which Room 326 was located was deserted. All the better, but he hoped the boy was in. He looked up and down the corridor and knocked three times.

No response. No sounds from inside. If he was inside and had gone to the door and looked through the spy hole,

Jack would have heard something. He was out.

Jack tutted.

A gamble that didn't pay off.

He walked back to the stairs and lift, and sat on the stairs leading up to the next floor, his phone at the ready, in case he needed it again. He was taking a gamble that Guillaume, being a student, would take the lift when he returned and would not notice Jack on the stairs.

After a few moments the lift pinged and Jack sat up. A female student got out of the lift and walked the other way down the corridor. He relaxed again.

Then he could hear voices on the floor above. The sound of the voices and the accompanying footsteps told Jack they were coming downstairs, so, still sitting on the lower steps but pushing himself to the sides to allow them to pass, he began another call. The group, three girls and a boy, brushed past him and continued their journey to the ground floor. Once they were out of earshot, Jack put his phone down again.

After a few more minutes, the lift pinged again, and the doors slid open. Jack sat up again, phone to his ear in preparation. No need: this was Guillaume.

He looked up at Jack: there was a brief flicker of recognition, then as Jack stood up, the student realised who he was.

'I've been waiting for you,' Jack said, as he walked down to the landing.

Guillaume looked around, almost in panic, uncertain of what to do.

'I think we need to finish our conversation,' Jack said.

'I'll call campus security,' Guillaume blurted out.

'And I could go to the police. Do you really want that?'

His eyes lowered, Guillaume shook his head.

'Shall we?' Jack asked, holding an arm out in the direction of Guillaume's room.

Guillaume led Jack to his room, unlocked and held the door open.

'You first,' Jack said.

Inside, Jack closed the door behind them. Guillaume took a few steps away from him. 'Don't hurt me; please don't hurt me.'

'I'm not here to hurt you. So why don't you relax? And I think you already know why I've come back.'

Guillaume said nothing; he shuffled around for a moment, then looked up at Jack. He had his hands in his pockets. The phrase *naughty schoolboy* sprung into Jack's head. Jack spoke first.

'I know you paid for Sun's ticket to London. Two return tickets, in fact. And I'm guessing that you went with him.'

Guillaume pushed his hands deeper into his pockets. 'How do you know?'

'Am I right?' Jack asked.

'Are you the police or something?'

'No. You know who I am, and why I'm asking. But I could go to the police, couldn't I? Then you'll be well and truly screwed.'

Guillaume nodded, silently.

'So,' Jack asked, 'why did you and Sun go into London?'

Deflated, Guillaume flopped onto the unmade bed. 'He wanted to meet his supplier.'

'Okay,' Jack said slowly. 'Supplier of MDMA?'

'His Mandy?' Guillaume asked.

'That's the stuff. So… where, how?'

'He's arranged to meet this guy somewhere near the bridge, Tower Bridge. Bermondsey? You know the place?'

'Yes, I do. Bermondsey, Rotherhithe. I know the area. It's not far from where he was found.' Ironically, not far either from his paper's offices across the river. 'So, give it to me from the top. How did it all come about, this trip to London?'

Guillaume sank on the bed. 'Can I get some water?'

'Go ahead. Your flat.'

Guillaume got up, walked over to the fridge, and took

out a bottle of water. He offered one to Jack, who declined.

'We were here,' Guillaume said. 'No, we were at his. His room.'

'But his housemates said he never brought you back there.'

'Sometimes. He was careful. He knew when their lectures were, when he knew they'd be out. Usually in the mornings. It might mean we'd miss a lecture, but nobody gave a shit. Anyway, that day, he must have realised he'd almost run out. He'd mainly get it for his own use - I didn't touch it, I told you that – but sometimes he sold some on.'

'He dealt?'

'Not really. All kind of unofficial. Just to some guys he was friends with. He always said if the guy he was buying from found out, he'd kill him.'

'Really?' That was interesting, and an angle that Jack hadn't considered. 'I found some in his room, not much; just a few grams in a little plastic bag. A contact of mine said it was pretty pure.'

'That's likely. He used to get it that way, he said. Then mix it in with formula; you know, babies' powdered milk.'

'I know that.'

'Sometimes with other milk powder, CoffeeMate, you know that?'

'I know the stuff,' said Jack. 'So, he was dealing as well.'

'Like I said, kind of.'

'If he was, he was,' Jack said. He paused to think. 'You said he realised he had run out.'

'Yeah. He said he was almost dry. Started to go crazy. Not crazy loud, or rough, but kind of "what am I gonna do?" crazy. You get me? Mainly because he said he didn't have enough to get down to London. That ain't cheap.'

'Which is why you bought the tickets?'

'Yeah.'

'So he never got any up here?'

'That's a no. Nothing here. All London.'

'Okay,' said Jack. 'Go on.'

Guillaume took a swig of water. 'I told you, he was going crazy. He knew what he needed to do to get some more, but didn't want to go down there to get it on his own. He was afraid of getting mugged. I don't mean mugged mugged, but of him handing over the cash, getting the stuff, then his guy sends some other guys after him to snatch it back.'

'Did that ever happen to him?'

'I don't think so, but he was just paranoid about that. Both with carrying all that cash, and the stuff.' He stopped and chuckled. 'Kind of like his bodyguard. His security detail.'

'So, you both decided to go to London. Was it a sudden decision?'

'It was. How did you know?'

'Because you bought paper tickets and left immediately. Most students would have bought in advance, online. How much were the tickets, just out of interest? You both have railcards, I imagine?'

'We do, yes. It was sixty something each.'

Jack whistled. 'So,' he said, 'you both got on the train to London. What happened then?'

CHAPTER TWENTY-SEVEN

Guillaume took a mouthful of water, swallowing hard.

'The train got us into London around five. We needed somewhere to stay that night, and the next couple of nights, so we went to some desk at the station that had names of places to stay. Sun told the guy behind the desk we needed to have a place near Rother…?'

'Rotherhithe,' said Jack. 'South East London.'

'Rotherhithe. That's it. There were a few there: the one they sent us to was a bit of a shithole, but Sun said it was just in the right place.'

'Where exactly was it? Do you remember?'

'Not far from the Underground station. Across the road from some park.'

Jack frowned. 'A park? Southwark Park? Did it have a big lake?'

Guillaume shrugged. 'I don't know. I didn't notice.'

'A big park?'

'I guess.'

'I think I know where you mean. So, this agency found you this shithole in Southwark. What did you do when you got there? You see this contact of Sun's?'

'No. Sun said he'd arranged to meet him later the next day. Middle of the day. So we went out and got a kebab somewhere. He knew where to go.'

'So, the next day then. When and where did you see this guy?'

'Sun said he was supposed to meet this guy at twelve thirty. In the park across the street. But he had to see him alone.'

'Alone? But you told me he wanted you to go with him in case he got mugged.'

'No, I don't mean alone exactly. He'd arranged to meet him in that park. He said he had been told to wait and sit on a bench in the park. Yes, I remember now: there was a lake in the park. He was supposed to meet him there. You know, sit on the bench and the guy would sidle up to him, kind of discreet.'

'While you stayed in the shithole?'

'No, no, no. He got me to hang about by the park gates, so I could see him, and make sure he was okay.'

'Did you see the guy? In the distance, I mean?'

'Yeah. Sun said he was supposed to be there twelve thirty, but said to get there twelve twenty. That was in case his guy had somebody else watching, and saw that I was there also.'

'I see. Very cloak and dagger. So, from where you were by the park gates, what could you see?'

'He sat there for ten minutes. He did call me on my cell phone to ask if I could see anybody around or watching him, and I said no, because I didn't. He was very nervous and jumpy. I kind of got the impression he was scared of this guy.'

'Then the guy showed up? You get a look at him?'

'He showed up on the dot of twelve thirty. Just sat down on the bench next to Sun. From where I was watching, they were just two guys sitting on a park bench together. I didn't see any movement, they were too discreet, but Sun passed him the cash, and he passed Sun the stuff. Oh, I forgot to say: when we got into London, Sun took some cash out of the ATM at the station, then some more that morning when we went out to get some breakfast.'

Jack nodded. 'That's because the ATMs have a daily cash limit – two fifty, three hundred pounds, something like that. He had to make two withdrawals over two separate days. How much did he have to pay for the drugs?'

'I think it was five hundred.'

'So he had to make two withdrawals of two fifty, or one of three hundred, one of two. Plus any incidentals, like your kebabs or breakfast.'

'Oh, I paid for those.'

'Okay. So what happened next?'

'I saw the guy get up and walk off. Sun stayed there for another five minutes - he said the guy told him to do that - then he walked over to where I was.'

'That was so he could be sure Sun wasn't following him. What did he look like?'

'I couldn't see very clearly. He was average height. Sun was tall for an Asian, six feet two, he told me once; I don't think the guy was as tall as that. Young; I could see he had dark hair slicked back. And he was wearing a black overcoat, all done up.'

'Trousers? Shoes? Could you see?'

Guillaume scratched his head. 'I think he was wearing black pants; I *think* he was wearing shoes, not sneakers.'

'I don't suppose you noticed if he was wearing a collar and tie under his overcoat?'

'I couldn't see,' said Guillaume, shaking his head. 'Why?'

'Because it all fits. Well, in theory, anyway. Smart, slicked back hair? Black overcoat, black trousers and shoes? Insisting on meeting your friend at half past twelve? This guy works in an office, and was meeting Sun in his lunch hour.'

'Oh? I hadn't figured any of that. That kind of makes sense.'

'What we need now is a name. And an address.' Jack smiled grimly. 'How did Sun contact this guy?'

'On his cell.'

'I guessed that. But did they speak, or text, or WhatsApp, or Messenger? Did he tell you what his name was?'

'No. It'll be on his phone, surely? Do you have it?'

'No, the police have it.'

'Oh, shit.'

'Yes and no. I spoke to the local police, from where he was found. His phone was in his pocket, but it was waterlogged. Useless.'

'Right.'

'I think they're going to wait for it to dry out, then see if it's operational. What they can get out of it is another matter.'

'Don't they have IT guys who can hack into phones or something?'

'The police do; but how much they can get out of a phone that's had half the River Thames inside it is another question. And another thing is: when I spoke to them, as far as they were concerned, it was either a suicide, or an accidental death caused by the taking of MDMA. A witness is said to have seen him try to fly off Tower Bridge. They're not going to spend thousands of pounds on IT to solve this.'

'So what do you think happened to him?'

'That's what I'm trying to find out. You said once the guy had left the bench, Sun waited a few minutes. Then what?'

'Then he came over to where I was.'

'And?'

'He was in a really good mood; happy that the meeting was over, I guess. We went back to the B&B for a session.

Sun took some poppers before we started, then when we were done, he took some of the stuff he'd just bought. Just a little: you know, he wetted his finger, stuck it in the bag and sucked his finger.'

'Then what? It doesn't take effect immediately.'

'I know. We just lay there some: no, I went and made a myself a coffee. Then, when I'd finished in the bathroom, he was getting dressed. I said, "What's up? Where are you going?" He gave me a big hug and a... well, you'd call it a snog. He said something like, "I won't be long. I'm just going out to get us something. Keep everything warm for me," then left. And that was the last I saw him.'

'You didn't hear anything from him?'

'No. It had been about an hour, and still no sign. I texted him a couple times, got no reply. I called two or three times, but he didn't pick up. I went to look around, see if he'd gone back to that park, but there was no sign. It was getting dark by that time, so I stopped off at the McDonalds by the station and went back to the room. I kind of expected him to come back next morning after he'd hooked up with someone, but nothing. Next morning, I tried calling, but it went straight to voicemail.'

'By then he was in the Thames. Did you think of going to the police?'

'I didn't think anything was wrong. Why would I? Plus, the fact we were down here to buy drugs. I packed up my gear, tried to call him again, he didn't pick up, so I left a message. Something like, "Fuck you, Sun." I went back to the train station, got my ticket changed for that day, and went back up to Kendal.'

He took a mouthful of water and tossed the empty bottle into the waste bin. 'That was the last time I saw him.'

CHAPTER TWENTY-EIGHT

'So that's it?' said Jack. 'You came back up here as if nothing had happened?'

'What was I supposed to do?' Guillaume asked. 'How would I know anything had happened? I thought he was just being an ass. I kind of expected to see him here or have him reach out to me here. I had no idea about what did happen to him until you told me.'

Jack nodded resignedly. The kid was probably right. 'And there's nothing else you can tell me? All you know is that Sun met a guy who was possibly wearing a suit, under a smart black overcoat. Probably works in an office, and told Sun to meet him in his lunch break in Southwark Park. He must work somewhere nearby.' Jack paused. 'Not much to go on, is it?'

'Guess not.'

'What about his stuff? You just leave it there?'

'Well, yeah. He only had a backpack with some clothes

and toothbrush and stuff. I checked there was nothing valuable in it. He'd taken his wallet and cell phone.'

'What about the package he'd just bought?'

'He took that with him. I just left everything else there, assumed he'd come back for it.'

Jack sat down on Guillaume's desk chair and leaned back, folding his arms. 'Is that the only time he met with this guy when you were around? You didn't go with him on any other trips to London before?'

'No. I didn't see that much of him really. Just when we met here.'

Jack scratched the back of his head. 'So you don't know if that was the normal way of Sun keeping in touch with this guy?'

'As far as I know.'

'And that's all you can tell me?'

Guillaume said nothing, just continued staring into space.

'Yes?' Jack pressed.

Guillaume looked up. 'Mm?'

'I asked if that was all you can tell me.'

'I've just remembered something,' Guillaume said. 'Ages ago, he needed to borrow my cell phone to make a call. We were here; he'd left his behind at his place, so I let him use mine. I didn't hear what he was saying, as he went out into the corridor to make the call. I mean, I could hear him talking, but I couldn't make out what he was saying. Then he came back inside.'

'Did he say who he was talking to?'

'No, he just came back in here. I didn't ask; it was none of my business.'

'No,' Jack agreed. 'But,' he added, leaning forward for emphasis, 'the call he made, the number – that could still be on your phone, yes? Can you check?'

'Okay, I'll try.' Guillaume picked up his phone and began trawling through his call log. 'It was in the summer,' he said, as he thumbed his way through the list. 'I remember it was in the evening, but it was still light.'

Jack watched as Guillaume checked, crossing his fingers metaphorically, if not physically.

Guillaume paused. 'Here. I think this is it. 20:42, June twenty-nine.'

'It would still be light. Right, can you save the number?'

'Sure. Under what?'

'Anything. Sun's Friend, Dealer, Fred, whatever you like. Just so it's saved.'

'I've done it under *Dealer*.'

'You got WhatsApp on there?'

'Yeah, I do.'

'Go to it, and retrieve that contact. As if you were going to send a message. Only don't send anything.'

Guillaume did as Jack said, then gasped.

'What?' Jack asked.

'I have a face.'

'Show me.' Jack leaned forward and took Guillaume's phone. In the little circle by the name *Dealer* was a face. A man, late twenties, early thirties. Dark hair slicked back. Wearing Ray-Bans. A confident smile, showing gleaming, unnaturally white teeth. He was topless and the background was sunny: Jack guessed it was taken while he was on holiday. It was difficult to tell if he was heavily tanned or of mixed race. 'Is this the guy Sun met?' he asked, returning the phone.

'I reckon so.'

'Can you send me his details?' Jack gave Guillaume his number, and held his phone out waiting for the contact details to come through. It pinged a few seconds later, and Jack took another look at the thumbnail, maximising it to get a better look. 'So this could be our guy.' Jack saved the contact on his phone. 'Oiled back hair, shades, stupid grin. Posey. Works in an office. Late twenties to mid-thirties. Piece of shit.' He looked Guillaume in the eye. 'Anything else?'

'No.' Guillaume shook his head. 'No. What are you going to do?'

'I don't quite know yet. I'll think about it on the way home.'

'Do you think the guy... do you think he killed Sun? By forcing him to OD on the stuff he sold him?'

'I've no idea. Maybe, maybe not. We'll probably never know for sure; unless he or anybody else confesses to it. You've got my number: get in touch anytime if you remember anything else.'

'Are you going to contact him?'

'I told you, I don't know what I'm going to do yet.' Jack paused, then stood up. 'I'll be off now, then.' He walked over to the door, paused again, turning round still holding the door handle. 'Thanks for your help. Although it would've been easier if you'd told me all this last week.' He looked Guillaume clearly in the eye. 'You're not going to fuck with me, are you?'

Guillaume got off the bed, and adjusted his shirt, pulling the bottom down over his waist. 'What do you mean?'

'You've been reminded of the guy Sun saw. Don't do anything silly like contacting him yourself. In fact, why don't you delete his contact details?'

Guillaume nodded.

'Now,' said Jack.

'Okay, okay.' Guillaume fingered the screen to get contacts, found *Dealer*, and deleted it.

'Now from your call log.'

'Shit,' Guillaume muttered under his breath. He did what Jack had said, and held the phone out. 'See?'

'All right,' Jack nodded. 'I'll let myself out.'

Jack spent the evening at Amanda and Ryan's. He ordered a delivery of Chinese food for the three of them and Anji, who was in that evening.

'Why didn't he tell you all this last week?' Amanda asked.

'I don't know. I didn't even bother to ask. The main thing is, I now know why Sun was in London. I now know he went out that night, with a bagful of Ecstasy in his pocket. Where he went, or who he saw, we don't know.'

'What are you going to do now, Uncle Jack?'

'Not sure yet.'

'Are you going to go to the police?' Ryan asked. 'That guy in London does seem to be a drug dealer.'

Jack nodded, and tossed a bare pork rib onto his plate. 'I know. But if I did that immediately, that closes off one source of a story, which is what this is all about, anyway.'

Ryan nodded. 'Yes, I agree. It would.'

'Are you going to contact him?' asked Amanda. 'The dealer, I mean.'

'I have his number. I expect I will get in touch with him, somehow. I need to work out how to do it, to draw him out into the open.'

'Sounds all very cloak and dagger,' said Anji.

'It is, although I have to make sure I don't break the law myself. I'll just have to move quickly when I get back to London.'

'From what Guillaume told you,' said Ryan, 'there aren't any dealers based up here.'

'From what he told me. Assuming he was telling me the truth, it means that Sun got his stuff from London, and was maybe selling some of it on. I'm talking about MDMA, Ecstasy, E, Mandy, whatever you like to call it. It doesn't mean there aren't any other drugs around, so you guys still need to be vigilant. Careful.'

'You still going back tomorrow?' Amanda asked.

Jack nodded. 'First thing. I'll keep in touch though, and you guys do the same. What I said before still stands: be careful, and have your wits about you.'

'You too, Uncle Jack,' said Amanda, resting her hand on Jack's arm. 'I've read enough to know what drug dealers are like. It could be dangerous.'

CHAPTER TWENTY-NINE

JACK DROVE HOME after an early breakfast the next morning. As he took the motorway south, his mind kept going back to one of the last things his niece had said to him last night.

'You too, Uncle Jack,' said Amanda, resting her hand on Jack's arm. 'I've read enough to know what drug dealers are like. It could be dangerous.'

Possibly she was right, but he could take care of himself. He was bigger than most guys and had enough nouse and experience to get himself out of most situations. After all, once he had found himself trapped in darkness in an abandoned tube station, but still got himself out.

'You too, Uncle Jack. I've read enough to know what drug dealers are like. It could be dangerous.'

He was reassured, though, that Sun Lee seemed to be getting his supply from London, and not from the environment of the university. So, he hoped, Amanda would not be contacted by anybody up there looking for replacement customers.

'It could be dangerous.'

He shook himself and tried to focus on something else. What he would do now he had the dealer's number, to start with. After thinking through his options, he decided once he got back to London, he would pick up a burner, a cheap mobile phone without an account, and contact the dealer that way, saying he was a friend of Sun's or something like that, and wanted some stuff as he couldn't reach Sun. Hopefully he would be able to draw the dealer out that way. What he would do when he had drawn him out into the open was another matter.

He stopped off for a comfort break at the Norton Canes Services, and before he got back on the carriage way, he decided to give Susan a call. Expecting to get her voicemail as she was at work, he was pleasantly surprised when she answered.

'It's my day off,' she explained. 'I'm working this Saturday. Where are you?'

'I'm on the M6 at the moment.' He explained briefly why he had to go back up to Kendal. Ironic, he thought, the very day she was off work and home alone, he was God knows how many miles away.

'What time do you expect to get back?' she asked.

'Oh, depending on the traffic, about half two, three o'clock. Why?'

'Kyle's going to an after-school club today,' she explained, 'and I don't need to pick him up until just before four. If you get back in time, why don't you come straight here for a coffee?'

'That sounds a good idea,' Jack replied. 'I'll see you when I see you, but if I'm going to be later than three fifteen, say, I'll let you know.'

His average speed was greater for the rest of the journey than it had been up until then; fortunately the traffic, though heavy, was moving quite freely. It would be different an hour or two later once the rush hour had begun.

It was actually ten past three when he rang Susan's doorbell.

'That's good timing,' she said, standing on her toes to kiss him.

'What time do you need to go to the school?' he asked, following her into the kitchen.

'About a quarter to four. I would say why don't you stay here while I go pick him up, but I've not told him about you yet, and…'

'No, that's fine. I agree. I've not told Cathy about you yet, either. Plenty of time for that.'

'There you go.' She poured him a coffee from her cafetiere.

'Thanks. Just what I needed. What are you doing?' She was leaning on her stove, pulling off her jeans. Then her panties.

'Shh.' She rested an index finger on his lips, then climbed on his lap. As she put her mouth on his, she rotated her hips, and reached down for him, deftly undoing his belt. As she pushed herself down on him, clinging on tight to his shoulders, Jack could hear her breathing heavily with each movement.

They were both done in a couple of minutes and she remained in that position for a while, only climbing off after a long sigh.

'My coffee's still warm,' Jack joked, as she got back into her clothes.

'So what next with your story?' she asked, pouring herself a coffee.

He told her again the reason for his return visit to Kendal, and what his plan for tomorrow was.

'Sounds exciting.'

'Maybe not quite the word I'd use.'

'Maybe not. Are you going to talk to this guy? I mean, what happens?'

'The chances are he's just another cog in the wheel, another link in the chain. The further I can go in this chain, the more stuff I'll have for my piece. But while all this is going on, my editor is jumping up and down for me to submit something.'

She nodded, thoughtfully. 'Do you get to go to the police?'

'Most likely. What normally happens is that we get enough detail to be able to publish an article, or series of articles, then pass the papers to the police. We try not to involve them too soon as once they get involved, in this type of case, for example, a lot of avenues close, people go off the radar.'

'Get arrested, you mean?'

'No, it's too early for that. They'll make their own enquiries to validate what we've given them. They won't proceed to an arrest without proper evidence. Which is how it should be, of course.' He checked his phone screen. 'Oops. Time's up.'

On their way to the door, he turned to Susan. 'What do you think about this? When I have Cathy at the weekend, I'll tell her about you. I expect she'll be okay about it. Then maybe the weekend after, when your son's at his Granny's, she could meet you.'

'Yes, I'd like that. She won't have any problem with me, will she? You know, thinking I'm replacing her mother.'

Jack laughed. 'That ship sailed long ago. No, I don't think she'll have any problem at all. What about Kyle?'

'I don't think so. He's not seen his father in ages. It would be good to have a man around. Be a role model, or something.'

'Me? A role model?' Jack laughed. He paused. 'Back then, earlier: it was all in the heat of the moment. We didn't use anything. I assume…?'

'Don't worry; that's taken care of. And you told me it's been a while for you so…'

Jack nodded, smiled, and after they had shared a long and gentle kiss, walked back to his car, with a promise to call her in a day or so.

On the way home from Susan's, he called in to a supermarket to get some provisions and a meal for that night, plus a small, cheap mobile phone. Once home, he checked the phone over and plugged it in to charge.

It was fully charged after he had eaten. He sent the number for Dealer to this phone, and sent a message.

Hello, my name is Joe. I am a friend of Sun Lee. I haven't seen him for a while and need some more stuff.

Once he had sent the message, he put the phone down, booted up his laptop and checked his own emails, personal and work. A few moments later, the burner made a sound. Jack picked it up; so that's the sound it makes when a text comes through. The dealer had replied.

How did u get this number?

Jack thought for a moment, then typed back, *I got ur number from suns phone when he wasnt looking, hoping I could deal with u direct so I don't have 2 pay suns cut, think he was ripping me off.*

A reply came back quite swiftly.

lol, fairs. U want 2 meet?

That would be great, replied Jack.

wen?

ASAP, Jack typed back.

2moro?.

Jack replied that tomorrow was good for him and at what time and where.

u know southwark park?

Bingo! Jack replied, *think so*

can u b there 1230?

Jack sent a thumbs up.

bench by lake 1230

Another thumbs up.

bring 50 4 small sample?

Jack replied that he would. Another thumbs up emoji might seem flippant and arouse suspicion. Jack then asked what the dealer's name was.

why?

Jack winced. Shouldn't have asked. *No reason, u know*

mine.

Rupert.

Hi Rupert.

1230 2moro then?

Jack replied in the affirmative. There was no further response from Rupert.

So, job done. He would be meeting Rupert tomorrow. With a name like Rupert he had to be some yuppie bastard in a flash suit dealing in his lunch time.

Still, he thought as he tossed the burner down, the meeting was arranged. He thought it would have been more difficult than that.

He paused and picked up the phone again. Tapped it on his chin.

It had been easier than he expected.

Jack hoped it hadn't been too easy.

CHAPTER THIRTY

NEXT MORNING, AND Jack was headed down to Bermondsey. It was not an area of London he knew that well, despite being so close to his newspaper's offices, although the other side of the river. He decided to make the journey by tube – around an hour, with one change at Green Park. There were two reasons for this: one, he needed to be there at a particular time, and there were no guarantees of this if he drove; and two, as always, there were uncertainties about parking, and he didn't want to waste time driving around looking for parking spaces, only to find the nearest was miles away. There was a small car park on one edge of Southwark Park, but no space guaranteed, or there would be plenty half a mile way at the shopping centre or leisure park. The tube seemed easier: once he was done there, he could just go through those gates and would disappear into the multitudes.

As he sat on the tube, he spent time trying to work out who Rupert was. Slicked back dark hair. Caucasian. Tanned. Ray-bans. Smartly dressed, probably with a nice suit underneath that expensive overcoat. Nice shoes, too; although how Guillaume could have worked that out from a distance, he would never know.

From the picture, the man in question - Rupert - was in his late twenties, maybe early thirties. If he was wearing a suit, he had to be working in an office, or certainly a customer-facing job. He met Sun Lee at twelve thirty, he told Jack to meet him at twelve thirty: that had to be during his lunch break. Also, Jack figured, he had to be not especially senior in wherever he worked, despite appearances. Otherwise, surely he would have been able to get out whenever he liked?

Of course, Jack could be totally off base with all of these guesses.

His plan was to arrive at around eleven thirty, a full hour before his appointment, to get a feel of the locale, what was at the end of the several paths that ran through the park. He was keeping his fingers crossed that Rupert was going there on foot, as if he did use that little car park, Jack would have to call in some very big favours to get a name and address from a number plate.

He arrived at just after eleven thirty-five, and got off at Bermondsey station. The station is situated on the A200 Jamaica Road.

This road came into existence in the late seventeen hundreds, when it was called Bermondsey New Road. It was renamed some years later, the new name deriving from the trade that was carried on with Jamaica at the nearby docks, stocking 'London's larder' with provisions. A handful of terraced houses survive on Jamaica Road from the early nineteenth century but the majority of the area was redeveloped with blocks of flats in the nineteen fifties and sixties. In Bram Stoker's novel *Dracula*, the Count has six boxes of soil from his native Transylvania delivered to an address in Jamaica Lane, Bermondsey, by which Stoker presumably meant Jamaica Road or one of its side streets.

Southwark Park is situated two blocks away from the station; when he reached the park, Jack took the southbound path, which led to a dogleg to the left just past the lake. Almost circular, the path led to the car park. He casually walked through the little car park, checking if any of the five cars were occupied. Occupied by Rupert doing the same thing Jack was doing. All of the cars were empty.

He turned back and made his way to a spot near the entrance in Southwark Park Road, from where he could watch the bench by the lake where he was supposed to meet Rupert. Maybe this was where Guillaume had stood.

It was five minutes past twelve. He waited. Several people passed by: people walking, people jogging, people dog walking. Concerned that one of these passers-by might be Rupert, he began to use his old trick of being on his phone, casually pacing up and down. This might be a long call. Pacing up and down on a fictitious call would make him less conspicuous than just standing there, under a tree.

It was now twelve fifteen. He wished he had asked Guillaume from which direction Rupert had come from and gone back.

Why not? He took the phone away from his ear and speed dialled Guillaume. To his surprise, Guillaume answered.

'Hey,' said Jack. 'I'm at the park now. Tell me again where you waited, and from which direction did he come from?'

'I was by the gate.'

'Opposite a school?'

'Didn't notice a school. But there was a kind of little statue in the middle of the path.'

'I got it. That's where I am. And when he arrived, where did he come from? Which direction?'

There was a pause.

'From the left,' said Guillaume. 'Crossed over the road, carried on down the path to the bench.'

'And he went back in that direction?'

'He did.'

'Okay. Anything else you can tell me?'

'No; I told you the other day.'

'I know. I meant, have you remembered anything else?'

'No, man.'

'All right, then. Remember to let me know if you do.'

'I will.'

'I have to go,' said Jack. 'I think he's here.'

Jack hung up, and discretely took a picture of the overcoated figure walking in the direction of the bench. He walked past the empty bench, pausing after a few yards. He stopped, and Jack could see him take something out of a pocket. Jack took another couple of pictures, sent them to Guillaume with the message, *is this him?* As he did so, he felt the burner vibrate and ping. He ignored it. Rupert waited a couple of minutes, looked around. Jack hoped he didn't have 20/20 vision. He then swung round on his heels and walked back the way he came, in the direction of Jamaica Road. Jack began to emerge from the cover of the trees.

Rupert was walking briskly, but stopped a hundred yards further on. Took something out of his pocket: obviously his phone as Jack felt the burner again.

This time Jack took the burner out and quickly checked the screen whilst keeping an eye on where Rupert was going. There were two messages.

Im here, where ru?

Fuck u, u timewasting cunt

'Nice,' Jack said aloud, and set off in pursuit.

CHAPTER THIRTY-ONE

JACK FOLLOWED HIM through the park, keeping sufficient distance between them so that he did not lose sight of him, and so that he would not realise Jack was following if he turned round.

He did not turn round, but headed straight to Jamaica Road, turning left as if he was heading towards the tube station. Jack quickened his pace, not wanting to lose his quarry amongst the other pedestrians.

Rupert was walking swiftly and Jack had to quicken his pace again to avoid losing him. Across the street from the tube station was a line of shops, continuing right along the bend in the road.

The third shop was a *Pret a Manger* outlet, and Rupert stepped inside. Jack came to a halt and waited in the doorway of the charity shop next door. Either he was popping in to pick up some lunch, or he worked there. The latter was unlikely.

After three or four minutes, he exited *Pret a Manger* and carried on walking, Jack once again in pursuit. He followed him over two side roads, then went inside one of the premises. Jack slowed his pace as he passed where Rupert had gone in.

That all figured. It was an insurance broker's office. Five or six desks on the premises, each desk having a large free standing PC screen. Two desks were occupied: at one desk a woman sat talking to a man the other side of the desk; at the desk behind sat a man who was chatting to Rupert who was standing, still with his coat on and holding his brown sandwich bag. So this was where he worked. Jack was right: the trips to Southwark Park to deal in drugs were made in his lunch break.

He sat on a vacant bench a few yards further down the street and made a few calculations in his head. It was a ten, twelve minute walk from the seat in the park to here. Call it fifteen. The meeting was scheduled for twelve thirty, so he would have had to leave work twelve fifteen. That would mean having to get back to work one fifteen. It was twelve fifty-five now; twenty minutes to wait. He was probably in a room out the back, eating his *Pret a Manger* sandwich.

He crossed over the road, and stood outside the tube station, with a clear view of the insurance offices, just in case Rupert left the premises, which was unlikely.

Jack waited until one twenty, then crossed back over. Walking slowly past the broker's office, he could see Rupert at a desk, the one behind the colleague he was chatting to earlier. He was talking on the landline phone, looking at his computer screen.

He took a deep breath and went inside. A woman sitting at one of the front desk looked up. 'Can I help you?'

'I'd like to see...' He looked over at Rupert and saw the name plate on his desk. 'Rupert Daggert. I've seen him before.'

The woman indicated that it was okay to go over to

Rupert's desk. Rupert looked up at him and indicated for him to sit down, as he was nearly done on this call. Jack sat in front of the desk and waited.

'How can I help you?' Rupert asked, after he ended his call. 'You said you've seen me before?'

'Briefly,' Jack replied.

'I'm sorry, I don't recall. What type of insurance did we talk about?' Jack could detect the sickly aroma of Rupert's aftershave.

Jack paused. 'Motor.'

'Okay. I'll get up your details. What name is it?'

'Richardson. Jack Richardson.'

'Address?'

Jack gave the address of the paper's offices. Best to use a real address in case it got validated online.

'Date of birth?'

Jack gave him his.

'And occupation?'

Jack leaned forward and spoke quietly. 'Timewasting cunt.'

All colour drained from Rupert's face. He swallowed hard. He spoke through gritted teeth. 'Who are you? What do you want? I can't talk to you here.'

Jack laughed a humourless laugh. 'No, I don't suppose you can.'

'What do you want?' Rupert asked again.

'I want to talk to you.'

'I told you, I can't here.'

'Where then?'

'My car's parked out back. A red BMW. We can talk there. For a few minutes, though. Give me five.'

'All right.' Jack stood up. 'See you there in five. No funny business, right?' He left the office and walked around the side street to the back of the parade. A small street ran parallel with Jamaica Road: Jack took this, counting the number of premises he passed. He came to the back of the broker's offices, and sure enough, there was a red BMW i4, crammed in a small space with three other vehicles. As he stepped over to the car, its hazard lights flashed and it beeped. He swung round to see Rupert behind him, holding out the keys. Jack climbed in the front passenger seat and Rupert got in the driver's seat. They were blocked in, so there was no way they would be going anywhere.

Rupert slammed his door shut and asked, 'So who the fuck are you? Obviously not the police.'

'Lucky for you, pal. I'm a reporter.'

'Newspaper?'

'U-huh.'

'Oh, shit.'

'That's right: oh, shit.'

'So, what do you want, then? How did you find me? You doing a piece on me? Am I going to be in your newspaper?'

'Not necessarily.'

'Not necessarily? What does that mean?'

'Sun Lee.'

'Who?'

'Give me a break.'

'Okay. You're talking about the Chinese kid. What about him?'

'You were supplying him, yes?'

'Supplying him?'

'Stop bullshitting me. You know what I'm talking about.'

'Okay, okay. I wasn't supplying him regularly. Just every few months or so.'

'Where? Southwark Park? Where you were going to meet me?'

'Yeah. He used to come down from Liverpool or wherever the fuck it was.'

'Kendal.'

'Wherever. We'd meet up, I'd give him the merchandise, he'd pay me, and that was it. He'd get back to me when he needed more.'

'The merchandise? You mean Ecstasy?'

'That's right. We called it Mandy. He's partial to that. He give you my number?'

'In a manner of speaking.'

'So what are we doing here? You want information? I can't tell you anything. Go talk to the Chinese kid.'

'I can't.'

'Why not?'

'He's dead.'

Rupert's face went as white as it had done a few minutes before. Sun's death was clearly news to him. 'What? When? How?'

'They found his body in Wapping, washed up on the river bank. He was last seen on Tower Bridge, trying to fly.'

'Fuck me. He was high?'

'As a kite. The post mortem revealed he was full of it. Full of Mandy, as you'd say.'

'Had he been drinking? You shouldn't mix Mandy with booze.'

'You people,' Jack spat. 'You sell that shit to vulnerable kids - he was only a student, for Christ's sake – then say he shouldn't mix with alcohol? What's that supposed to be? A Government health warning?'

'Just saying, that's all.'

'Who were you getting it from?'

'I can't tell you that.'

'Or would you rather tell the police?'

'You'd go to the police? Then you'd never get your story.'

'I'd get something.'

Rupert paused a second, thinking. 'If I told you anything, you'd keep my name out when you wrote your story?'

Jack nodded. 'I'd use an alias.'

Rupert leaned back on the headrest. Took three or four deep breaths. Still looking up, he said, 'All right, then.'

CHAPTER THIRTY-TWO

'I'M GUESSING,' said Jack, 'that you're just part of a chain. A tiny cog in a bigger wheel.'

Rupert nodded. 'Yeah. I just buy and sell on.'

'I guessed as much. You don't look like Mr Big material.' Rupert sniffed, and said nothing. 'So,' Jack asked, 'where do you get the shit from?'

'A guy.'

'Yeah? This guy got a name?'

Rupert paused and took a deep breath. 'His name's Kwento Usman.'

'Where's he from?'

Rupert shrugged. 'Somewhere in Africa, I suppose.'

'Don't try and be clever with me. Where in London? Where do you meet him?'

'I don't know where in London. West, I think. I meet him in the West End. In a pub.'

'Which pub?'

'It's called *The Three Dukes*. It's in a little side street, off Frith Street.'

'I think I know where you mean. Near Soho Square.'

'Yeah, that's it.'

'So what happens?'

'We meet in the pub. I tell him how much I need. We meet up later in the gents or at the back of the pub outside, where he hands it over.'

'And that's when you give him the cash.'

'Sure. Cash on delivery.'

'So, you contact him first? Like Sun Lee did with you?'

'No, I don't need to. He's always in the pub, every evening. I just make contact when I get there. It's always busy in there, so nobody notices what's going on.'

'What's he like, this Kwento Usman?'

'Black guy, big – about the same size as you, but bulkier. Head shaved, black beard.'

'Is he alone?'

'He's with a couple of similar fellas, but they sit at a table near the bar. He sits alone at the bar.'

'They're his minders, I guess.'

'Guess so. I just sidle up to the bar, stand next to him as if I'm getting a drink, and I say something like, "I need some biscuits".'

'Biscuits? Is that another name for it?'

'It goes by lots of names – didn't you know? Biscuit, E, Eve, Molly, Mandy, Beans, Disco Biscuit. Lots of names.'

Despite himself, Jack laughed. 'Disco Biscuit. I like that. So you tell him you want some biscuits?'

'That's right. How much I need, and how I want it. He'd say how much it would cost, and to meet him in an hour or so in the gents, or outside, round the back of the pub. Then I just wait; depending on the price, a couple of times I've had to go down to Leicester Square, to an ATM.'

'You said he asked how you wanted it.'

'Pill or powder. I normally have it in pill form.'

'I see. Hold on – we found some powder in Sun's

room.'

'Really? He always used to take pills. Then he must have got that powder from someone else, or ground the pills down. Especially if he was selling some on. He'd mix the powder with milk powder or something, make it look more than it was.'

Jack nodded slowly. That all made sense. 'So an hour later, you'd meet him in the gents, or outside the pub. What then?'

'We'd meet there. If it's in the gents, and someone's in there, we'd make out we were taking a piss or something. If the pub's really busy, we'd use the alley outside. But only if it's dark. If it's the summer, and it's not quite dark, we might use the gents then. I'd give him the cash, and he'd hand over the package.'

Jack shook his head sadly. '"The package." You people are unbelievable Then you just leave?'

'Yes, I just go.'

'Where does he get it from?'

'I don't know. I don't care, either.'

'Is he there all night? At the pub, I mean?'

'Seems to be. I tend to get there around eight thirty, nine. I see other guys talk to him too, then he goes to the gents with them later.'

'Hm. His place of business, obviously. Or one of them. So, if I go there tonight, around nine, he'll be there?'

'I don't see why not. I told you, I don't check with him first. I just show up, and he's always been there. Why? You going to go there?'

'I've not decided yet,' Jack said. Then he paused. 'Okay, you can get back to work now; I'm sure they're missing you.' He climbed out of the BMW, then, hand on the roof, leaned back in. 'Two things, though: I'm guessing there's no point me saying to you to stop selling that shit to vulnerable people. Or stop dealing, period.' Rupert shook his head. 'I thought not,' said Jack. 'Secondly, I don't want you contacting your pal Usman and warning him. If I get the slightest vibe he's expecting me, remember I know where you work. And remember as well, I'm sure he won't be too happy to learn what you've told me; that you've spoken to the press about your little trade. You get the picture?'

Rupert nodded. 'I get the picture. What about your paper? Will I be in it? You said you wouldn't use any real names. But, if he reads it, he might work out who -'

'Calm down. Nothing'll get published until I've finished this research. And, as a thank you for your help, I'll let you know when, assuming you've been straight with me. I might need to talk to you some more, anyway.'

'You're not going to go to the police?'

'Not right now, but that's going to be up to my editor. Knowing him, he'll probably want to. I'll try to warn you in advance, as a measure of my appreciation, once I've done with you. You might want to cut your losses and get out of this first. Put some distance between you and him.' He looked over at the rear of the office. 'You must be pretty well paid here. Commission?'

'I've got a lot of expenses,' Rupert said.

'Still paying for this?' Jack tapped the roof of the BMW. 'Wait a minute, I've just realised. You're using yourself, aren't you? Like Sun was. You're buying, then selling on, but keeping some back for yourself. You're dealing to finance your own habit.'

Rupert said nothing.

Jack shook his head and straightened up. 'I'll be off now. Remember what I told you: don't do anything clever. Or stupid.'

He slammed the car door and walked back to Jamaica Road. As he turned the corner, he heard the driver door shut and bleep locked. He paused a second and looked back. 'Little prat,' he muttered.

CHAPTER THIRTY-THREE

After meeting Rupert, Jack decided he would go to his office. The Daily News offices were on the A1020 Silvertown Way, the other side of the river, but not far as the crow flies.

Jack and most of his colleagues spent more time working remotely than at a desk in the office, especially so in the last two or three years, but there was still an expectation that there was a visit to the office at least once a week. From here it was only a short ten-minute hop on the Jubilee Line to Canning Town, then a ten-minute walk down to the office.

The place was deserted. Well, almost deserted. Just a couple of lonely figures in the middle of a desert of empty desks. As he walked into the empty office, Jack could hear the voice of his editor, Mike Smith, talking loudly on his phone. *Great*, Jack thought, *he would have to be in.*

As he walked down to his desk, Cliff Hughes, the

Entertainment Correspondent, called out, 'Jack! It is Jack, isn't it?' Jack smiled weakly and sat down at his desk. Then Eddie Hutchinson, who covered politics, appeared at his side.

'Jack Richardson, isn't it,' he said, offering a handshake. 'Eddie Hutchinson, Politics. Nice to meet you.'

'Piss off, you two,' Jack said, booting up his PC. 'Very funny. Where is everybody? I expected more than two of you. Where's little Sharon?' *Little* Sharon was the receptionist.

'They had to let her go,' Eddie explained. 'Most people are working from home now. There was nothing for her to do; she was just sitting there, painting her nails.'

'Aw, that's a shame. Poor Sharon,' Jack sighed, feeling a little guilty, as he was one of those who worked from home.

'Yeah,' Eddie said. 'Apparently, when we need a receptionist again, she's first in line.'

'Like that's going to happen,' Jack muttered cynically. 'Oh, shit.'

His editor, Mike Smith approached. 'Glad you came in, Jack. Saves me a phone call. You want to come and give me an update?'

Jack followed Mike into his office, and sat down and updated him on events so far. Mike sat and listened, nodding occasionally. He must have been interested as he made no attempt to check his phone while Jack was talking.

'Shit, Jack – what are you getting into?'

'Nothing I can't handle.'

'But realistically, you haven't got much at the moment. Perhaps a few hundred words, nothing more.'

'Early days yet.'

'That stuff you say you found in the Chinese boy's room. You only have the word of your contact's friend that it is what you say it is.'

'There's no reason for him to lie. No money had

changed hands. If it was real and he said it wasn't, just to get out of paying me, I can understand, but he's actually said it's the real stuff. And pure stuff.'

'And he's thrown it away? Right, sure he has.'

'I don't care what he does with it. In the grand scheme of things, it was only a small quantity, and I didn't want it on me.'

'This dealer, you spoke about. Us…'

'Kwento Usman.'

'What do you know about him? I'm guessing from the name he's Nigerian or something.'

'Big guy, apparently. Same height as me, but bulkier. Goes around with two similar fellas, minders I suppose.'

'And you're planning on going to this pub in Soho. When?'

'I plan to go tonight.'

'And do what? You're not going to pose as a user, are you?'

'No, no. Not at this stage, anyway. I thought I'd watch who he meets – I know his method of doing business – I could follow who he sees and try to speak to them.'

Mike sat back and tapped his fingers on the desk. 'You could make an anonymous call to the police. You know, so the Drug Squad raids the place. They might even know about the place already, about him.'

'True, but say they do raid the place. Take him in for questioning. He obviously doesn't carry the stuff around with him. There's no van outside. He'll get released without charge, move his operations to another location, there'll be no evidence for the police or for us. And that will be the end. No story. Or at least, we'll have to go back to square one.'

'All right,' Mike acquiesced, 'but for Christ's sake be careful. And keep me up to date all the time. Then we can agree when there's something to publish, a one-off or a series, then we can pass what we have to the police.'

Jack stood. 'No problem. I'll keep you in the loop.'

He returned to his desk, checked and actioned work

emails, all stuff he could have done at home on his laptop. When he had finished that, he checked the time. It was not worth going back home now; he would head directly to the West End for his visit to *The Three Dukes*. As he left the office, he glanced at the empty reception desk. The management were right: these days having a receptionist was an anachronism, even a luxury, although he would miss the banter he had, the numerous call-back messages. That was progress, was it? Maybe things would return to the way they were; most likely not.

It was almost five. He walked back up to the tube station on his journey to Leicester Square. As he waited for his train, he realised he had not eaten in hours and was starving. He would hold on until he got to the West End: he knew a place he could go.

As he had plenty of time, he stayed on the Jubilee Line as far as Green Park. He always enjoyed the walk along Piccadilly from the Ritz and the park to Piccadilly Circus, so took his time, in spite of his hunger. He stopped off at the ATM next to Fortnum & Mason, just in case.

The place he was headed for was a Chinese Restaurant – he had been there several times, but had forgotten the name – along Windmill Street, just off the Circus. He quickened his pace as he walked up Windmill Street, as he was getting hungrier by the minute. Much to his disappointment, though, the place was boarded up. It had been closed for a while, as the windows were dirty, and were filled with remnants of bills posted, probably the sort one found in phone boxes, advertising all kind of personal services.

That was a shame: he was in the mood for some Chinese food. But he was in Soho, where it was impossible to go more than two blocks without coming across a Chinese restaurant. Sure enough, he soon found another: it was on Lexington Street, itself a continuation of Windmill Street, on the corner with Brewer Street.

It was empty as you would expect at this time of the evening. He ordered Fried Crabmeat and Straw

Mushrooms with Rice, washed down with a bottle of Chinese beer. After he had finished, he settled the bill and walked back down to Leicester Square. He found an empty bench on the square and called Susan, as he had arranged. She was having a normal evening, just about to put her son to bed. Jack told her where he was, and that he was due to meet an informant here later. He thought it best not to give her too much detail.

Soon it was time to go to the pub. He found it easily, on the corner of Frith and Bateman Streets, as Rupert had said. And as Rupert had also said, it was quite busy, people at the bar, and standing around. He got himself a beer – a proper beer, he told himself, not that Chinese piss he'd just drunk – and picked up the copy of the *Standard* somebody had left on the bar, and found himself a table.

He took a mouthful of his drink and opened the paper. Over the top edge he saw him. Twelve feet away. Sitting on a bar stool, chatting with one of his minders.

Jack guessed he was at least six six, a muscular frame. Black open shirt, black trousers and pointed shoes. Purple jacket. Shaven head, black beard from the top of his ears. From his right ear lobe hung a ring on a little chain. Its gold colour matched the medallion hanging down his chest.

Kwento Usman.

CHAPTER THIRTY-FOUR

JACK HAD THE feeling this was going to be a long night. He had already read the discarded *Standard* twice, and now he was wishing he had a pen or pencil so he could attempt the crossword. It looked very much as if business was slow tonight for Kwento Usman. For the last hour, he had been sitting at the bar, chatting occasionally with the girl behind the bar, maybe the odd aside or joke with her or one of his minders, who remained at their table, just like any other two men enjoying a drink together. There definitely hadn't been anybody perching next to Usman, asking about Disco Biscuits, or the like. Maybe it wasn't going to happen tonight; maybe a meet had already happened, although if that was the case, he would be disappearing for a while for the transaction.

At that moment Jack noticed another figure. Also standing at the bar, two stools down, but surreptitiously moving closer to Usman. The figure had his back to Jack, but was wearing a white padded hooded coat. Over the top of the hood, Jack could see close cropped dark hair.

The white puffed coat leaned forward, elbows on the bar, almost mirroring Usman's body language. Jack could make out slight movements of their head, suggesting to him they were having some kind of conversation.

Then, white puffed coat leaned back, and just as furtively as he had joined Usman, returned to his original place. Usman leaned back and glanced at his two companions, one of whom gave an imperceptible nod, picked up his phone and left the pub.

This is interesting, Jack thought; maybe something's about to go down. He felt he had enough time to get another drink, so stepped over to the bar to get another beer. He returned to his seat and began to read the *Standard* for the fourth time.

It must have been forty minutes later when Usman's companion returned. As he walked past Usman, Jack noticed the tips of his fingers brush across Usman's back. Usman moved imperceptivity in response. He carried on walking to the gents door, pushed it open, and disappeared from view. A moment later, Usman stood up, stretched casually, and sauntered in the same direction. To the uninformed observer, there was no link here. Momentarily, the white puffed jacket got up and followed. From this angle, Jack could see he was a man of around thirty, maybe a couple of years under, maybe a couple over. He appeared to be South Asian, had a small black goatee, and a small gold chain hanging from his right ear lobe. Jack took one more mouthful of his beer, and readied himself for what he planned to do.

A couple of minutes later, Usman and the companion emerged and resumed their places at the bar and table respectively. A few seconds later the white coat emerged. Jack could hear the sound of the hand drier from inside the toilets. The white coat walked along the bar straight to the door and out into the night. Jack quickly stood up and followed, not even looking back in case that delayed him even a second.

It was fortunate that he was wearing a white coat, as otherwise Jack would have probably missed him in the darkened Soho streets. He was not walking particularly fast either, which helped.

Jack kept twelve feet behind as he followed the white coat up Frith Street, anticlockwise around Soho Square, along Sutton Row, into Charing Cross Road. Then he made a left, Jack quickening his pace as if he was going to lose his quarry, it would be now.

They continued up Charing Cross Road as far as the tube station, making the one eighty as they took the escalator down to platform level, Jack now keeping six feet behind. Within a minute they were on the Northern Line platform, heading south. The platform was not too busy; at least it was not two hours later, when the theatres would be emptying.

The first train to arrive was for Kennington. Jack readied himself to jump on, but to his surprise, the white coat did not board, but stepped back to the platform wall. Okay, thought Jack, what's going on? Why didn't he get on?

The next train was for Morden, due in three minutes. As he waited, Jack found himself staring into the blackness of the tunnel. He began to recollect the day, a few years back, when he found himself inside one of those tunnels in the long-since closed and abandoned York Way station, where he had to crawl in total darkness to the safety of a platform. He shivered at the memory, which ended with the draught and the sound of the Morden train arriving. The white coat boarded, as did Jack, using the next set of double doors. Jack stood in the vestibule of these doors, discretely watching his quarry, who had sat down and was leaning forward looking at his phone.

Eventually they arrived at Kennington, where the previous train had terminated: White Coat looked up, saw the station sign, and returned to his phone. I'm back south of the river, Jack reflected.

The next stop was Oval, the location of the famous cricket ground. White Coat looked up as the train came to a stop, then leapt out of his seat and onto the platform. Jack did the same, through the other doors.

Here, the station was quieter than Tottenham Court Road where they had boarded, so Jack felt it safe to put a bit more space between them as they ascended the escalator.

Out on the street, they crossed Clapham Road, and walked down Camberwell Road; only a couple of hundred yards, though, as White Coat took the first left, a side street at a forty-five degree angle from the main road. This road comprised a short row of shops: a newsagent, a vaping store, a mini-market, and a café, which was closed. After the café, White Coat took a left.

'Where the hell's he going?' Jack muttered, mentally preparing himself for a confrontation – if he knew he was being followed, he might be luring Jack to somewhere out of the way. However, Jack was at least a foot taller than White Coat, so did not feel particularly threatened.

Another right, and White Coat was going down a flight of metal steps. Jack walked past, taking in where White Coat was going. On this side of the street was a medium sized apartment building, and it seemed that White Coat was going down the iron steps to a basement flat. He paused, and heard the metal grille close first, then the door.

Jack turned and walked back to the top of the stairs. A light had gone on in one of the basement windows. Jack wondered if he had just followed White Coat home. And did he live alone?

Jack looked around, took a deep breath, and walked down the steps.

CHAPTER THIRTY-FIVE

HE WAS MAKING a lot of assumptions. He was assuming White Coat was a similar cog in the wheel as that odious little creep Rupert. He was assuming this was where White Coat lived. And he was assuming he lived alone, not with three others.

There was no door bell, so he reached through the bars of the grille, and knocked on the door, three times. There was no spyhole in the door; but if there was a metal grille in front, there was hardly a need for a spyhole.

The door opened. He had taken his white coat off, and was wearing a white tee shirt, and grey tracksuit bottoms. Jack guess he was Indian.

'Yes?' he asked, with a very slight accent.

'Hi,' said Jack, breezily. 'I want to talk about Kwento Usman.'

'Oh, yeah? I've just -' He stopped himself.

'Can we talk inside?' Jack asked.

White Coat said nothing; Jack could envisage him thinking this situation through.

'Don't worry; it's cool,' Jack said, disarmingly. 'If you feel safer with me outside, then that's okay.'

'I'm all right.' He unlocked the gate, and let Jack in, down a long hallway, past a bedroom, into a large lounge with kitchen space. The door to the bathroom was the other side of the room.

Jack looked around to make sure they were alone. 'Kwento Usman,' he said.

'Yeah,' White Coat said. 'Who are you, man? What about Kwento? I've just seen him. Did he send you after me? What's going on?'

'Okay,' said Jack. 'From the top.' He handed over a business card.

White Coat read the card. 'So you're from the press? Why are you asking about Kwento? I don't get it.'

'Drugs. Ecstasy. Mandy, Molly, Milly, whatever you guys call it.'

'Why are you asking me this? How'd you find out about me?' There was an edge of panic in his voice.

'I followed you from the pub.'

'From the *Dukes*? What do you want?'

Jack reached into his pocket and took out the five twenty pound notes he had withdrawn earlier that evening. 'Information. I need it for something I'm writing.'

White Coat stared at the notes, then said, 'What sort of information?'

'You buy your stuff from Usman, I know that. What do you do with it? Do you use it yourself, or sell it on?'

White Coat shrugged. 'I use some, I sell some.'

'Mixed with milk powder or something?'

'Yeah, maybe.'

'And is it Ecstasy?'

'Mostly. He calls it Disco Biscuits.'

'Pills?'

'Normally.'

'Then you grind them down?'

'To sell on, yeah.'

'How did you get to meet him? First, I mean.'

'It was in a club. He offered me some when I was in the toilet.'

'You were already using?'

'A bit, yeah.'

'So don't tell me – you bought a small amount, then went back again and again. He gets you to buy more and more. And now you need to sell more to feed your own habit.'

White Coat nodded, shuffling his feet.

'Bizarre economics,' Jack said. 'And who do you sell to?'

'Just people.'

'Regulars?'

'Yeah, you could say that.'

'Kids?'

'Not children, but older.'

'Like students?'

'Some are. Hey, you're not going to go to the police with this. Are you?'

'No,' Jack lied. 'This is just for my paper. Don't worry, it's all anonymous. I'll use a different name. What is your name, by the way?'

'It's Taheen.'

'Taheen. So we won't use that name.'

'Anything else? I have stuff to do tonight.'

'No, I don't think so. I'll leave you now. My number's on that card, if you think of anything else. And I know where you live now, if I need anything.' He handed Taheen the cash. 'Thanks for the information. Spend it on something other than Disco Biscuits. I'll let myself out.'

Jack left the flat, and as he got to the top of the steps, he heard Taheen lock the grille and the door. Then he began a brisk walk to the station; he had a long ride home.

Inside the flat, Taheen ran into the bedroom and looked up out of the window. The bedroom light was off, so he could see outside. He saw Jack's foot step off the top stair and onto the pavement. He took a deep breath, and rechecked the cash. Whistled. Then his phone rang. He walked into the lounge and answered.

'Yeah, this is Taheen.'

'………'

'Yeah, he just left. He followed me here from the pub. I didn't know he was -'

'………'

'No, I didn't tell him anything. Honest.'

'………'

'He's a reporter, from the *Daily News*. He gave me his card.'

'………'

'He said to call him if I could remember anything. He knows -'

'………'

'His number's on the card. You want it?'

'………'

'Sure. It's…'

CHAPTER THIRTY-SIX

JACK'S ALARM WOKE him at three minutes to eight.

He had got home from his trip to Oval just after midnight. He was tired, but felt he had achieved something that day. Now it was Thursday morning, and there was a lot he wanted to do before the weekend.

It would not be long before he was chased for his so many thousand words for the next edition, so today would be spent at home putting that together; not the finished article, but an introductory piece. Just something to keep Mike off his back a bit longer.

But first of all, he needed to carry out some research. He had already done some, but that was mainly related specifically to MDMA; now he needed a more general overview, something to put in his first piece.

His first potential source was his own paper's archives, looking at any articles about drug use in general, and any relating to drug-related crime. He searched the archives for the last three years, found a few pieces, then extended his research to other newspapers, both local and national. Some of these articles contained links to various official websites, which Jack also checked.

Two hours and three mugs of black coffee into the research, Jack decided he had almost enough material. He would spend till one doing this, take a breather, and spend the afternoon writing the piece, with a view to emailing to Mike by five.

The facts he had gleaned so far were random and needed ordering, but he was getting the picture.

In the most recent full year where records were available, it was estimated that there had been a hundred and seventy-five thousand drug-related crimes committed, a thirteen percent increase over the previous year. There had been four and a half thousand drug related deaths in that period. These statistics only related to England and Wales, but a bit of extrapolation would give him the complete picture for the entire United Kingdom.

Drug-related crimes tended to be using or supplying; driving and other offences committed while under the influence of drugs, with or without alcohol; and crimes of violence, mainly by dealers with users who owed them money, or with other dealers. As he read this, the face of Kwento Usman appeared in his head.

Jack whistled as he learned that to fund a habit can cost between fifteen and thirty thousand pounds a year. Shit, he thought; small wonder those two kids sold stuff on, as well as using. Most users stole to fund their habit. On average, the resale value of stolen goods is a third of the actual market value, so if somebody has a habit costing say twenty-five thousand, they would have to steal seventy-five thousand pounds' worth of goods a year to fund their habit. One of the official websites Jack was referred to estimated that there were three hundred thousand users in England and Wales alone. Even before extrapolation to get the whole United Kingdom figure, that was a hell of a lot of theft, burglary, fraud, and shoplifting. Fifty percent of acquisitive crime was thought to be drug-related, with the total amount of stolen goods having a market value of over two billion pounds.

Some of the links led him to information about MDMA itself. He knew a lot of this already, through his previous research. The nickname *Molly* comes from the word *molecular*. In the United Kingdom, it is a Class A drug. After cannabis, it is the most popular drug, especially in the sixteen to twenty-four age range. In powder form, thirty to fifty pounds per gram. A single pill will sell for five pounds, double that if it is higher strength.

In recent years, there had been evidence that doses were getting stronger: from 50 to 80mg per tablet to 125. *Super pills* would contain 125mg per tablet.

Jack came to dangerous interactions, something that he had wondered about in the case of Sun Lee: was it just the MDMA which had caused him to dive into the Thames? Was it a combination of Ecstasy and another substance, or just a *super pill*?

A mix with NBOMe, or n-bomb, could cause increased heart rate, and possible heart failure. Mixing with alcohol would exaggerate the effects of either, with the obvious results. Mixing with cocaine could lead to heart strain, possibly leading to death.

For those who try to kick the habit, some of the withdrawal symptoms were terrifying: electric shock sensations, chest pains and heart palpitations or attack, high blood pressure, seizures and muscle spasms, stroke, kidney failure, breathing difficulties were just some of the possible symptoms, the last being death.

A chill ran down Jack's spine: surely this distribution network had not stretched from Usman to Rupert, to Sun, then to who else? He had been living in the same house as Amanda.

Jack leaned back and rubbed his face. Usman was the start of this chain, but where did he get the stuff from? Sure, it was possible that he was just another cog in the wheel, another link in the chain as were Rupert, Taheen, and Sun; but Jack had the vibe that he was more than that, that he was a main source. So where did he get it from? Jack had a feeling he knew the answer.

The likelihood was that Usman was buying the stuff on the dark net, using a cryptocurrency.

The dark net, or dark web, is a network within the internet which can only be accessed with specific software or configurations.

In a previous assignment, Jack had come up against the deep web. The terms deep web and dark web are commonly used interchangeably, but whilst that is the case in terms of the technology, there is a difference. The deep web refers to webpages which are not indexed, as pages on the internet are. The dark web refers to parts of the deep web in which one can engage in illegal activities. The dark web comprises about five percent of the deep web.

When somebody makes use of the regular internet, the search engines scour the web for content and websites. For this it uses automated bots known as crawlers, which begin in sites already known to the search engine, and then visit every link on those sites. This is generally how sites like Google add web pages to their index. This allows users to find sites through its search engine. The next stage is indexing, which is the storing and categorising of the sites, in order to find the relevant results. Finally, there is serving, where the most relevant result in the index is served back to the user.

The deep web is different, in that the sites are invisible to the crawler bots and indexes, and are effectively hidden. Therefore, to find a site on the deep web, one must have the specific web address or a specific deep web search engine.

The dark web is a subsection of the deep web which provides illegal services. Whilst not fundamentally dangerous, its scope takes in personal and financial information, sale of arms, child pornography, and allegedly assassination contracts. It also includes the trade in illegal substances.

Assuming Jack's theory was correct, Usman was to all intents and purposes the original source of the drugs, as Jack would not be able to trace any dark web transactions. He was not sure the police would, either.

He took a sheet of A4 and drew a kind of flow chart, tracking the path the MDMA was taking. Starting off with the dark web, and Kwento Usman obtaining his supplies, Jack drew three lines from Usman's name, leading to Rupert, to Taheen, and to a third, marked 'Others'. How many others there were, was anybody's guess. From Rupert's name, Jack drew a line to Sun Lee, and also to another marked 'Others', repeating this for the other two strands. It was beginning to look like some grotesque family tree, a spider's web reaching out and multiplying again and again, more and more people being supplied. Like the spread of a virus, multiplying exponentially.

It was quite possible that that particular tentacle did not end with Sun Lee himself; why would it? Jack had already been told by the student Guillaume that he suspected Sun was selling some of the stuff on. Jack had the feeling he would be making another trip to Kendal soon.

Anyway, it was time to start writing. It was now two o'clock: if he produced a couple of thousand words by say three forty-five, he had another hour for checking, then he could send it over. Then there was the next day. He decided to see how today ended before thinking about Friday, apart from picking his daughter up from school. Their first father-daughter activity might be a trip to the supermarket.

Just as he was about to start, his phone chirped. He picked it up and checked the screen. It was a text from a number he did not recognise.

Is that jack rickardson?

He replied that it was, not bothering to correct the person's spelling of his name, and asked who he was talking to.

Its taheen, from last night.

I remember, Jack replied.

Can I cu? I have info 4u
Sure. When? I'm free this pm
Can we meet ur place?
No, not here, Jack typed back. *Yours?*

There was a pause. Then the reply came back, *cant, flatmate in.*

'Flatmate?' Jack wondered aloud. There was only one bedroom, surely. 'Oh, well.' *Where then?*

can meet by the 3 dukes pub

Where I saw you last night? Jack asked.

yeah, I work near there.

Jack replied that was okay, and he could be there by six. Was that all right? The piece for Mike Smith would have to keep till tomorrow. This was too good an opportunity to pass up.

ok, cu 6 text me when u there

Jack typed a thumbs up emoji and ended the conversation. Four hours, just a couple of things to finish off here.

Kwento Usman was sitting in an armchair in a flat. He also ended the conversation. He grinned and tossed the phone back to one of his companions.

CHAPTER THIRTY-SEVEN

UP IN KENDAL, Ryan was standing on the landing of the shared house. He was alone upstairs; Anji was out, and Amanda was downstairs busy at something.

He opened the door to Sun's room, and cast his eyes over the empty space. Not totally empty, but empty of Sun's personal effects, his stuff. The wardrobe stood where it had always been: one door swung open revealing an empty interior. The desk and shelves were devoid of any contents. A mattress lay on the bedframe, a solitary pillow laid in the corner. It was the sight of that which reinforced the idea that Sun had gone: no sheets, no duvet, no pillowcase.

The landlord had called at the beginning of the week to say that a representative of Sun's family would be calling round to collect his personal effects. Two days later, they came. Anji was in at the time, and said it was two young men from a solicitor's office who called round, taking all of Sun's stuff in two large cardboard boxes.

The landlord could not be certain when the room would be occupied again; he guessed it would be in the new year, at the start of the new term.

Ryan sat down on the empty mattress. He ran a hand over it, recalling the numerous chats he had had with Sun while he was lying on and in the bed. He smiled, sadly.

A voice came from outside, from downstairs.

'Ryan? Where are you?'

'I'm up here,' he called out. 'In Sun's room.'

In a moment, Amanda's head came around the door. 'What you doing, baby?'

'Just looking around here. Thinking about Sun.'

Amanda came and sat next to him, resting her head on his shoulder, and putting her hand on his. 'It'll seem weird without him around.'

'Yes,' Ryan sighed, 'I guess it will.'

'Even when somebody else is in here. I'll still keep thinking of it as Sun's room.'

'At least he didn't die in here.'

Amanda lifted her head off his shoulder and shook it. 'That would be so gross. I'm not sure if I could handle that.'

'I wonder what they'll be like,' Ryan mused.

'In what way?'

'A guy, a girl, you know what I mean. Will they be friendly, or keep themselves to themselves, like he used to?

'We might have to wait a while. Anji said that it could be after the holidays before they move in.'

'I know. She told me.'

She stood up. 'I'm going to get some coffee then start work on my assignment. You coming down for a cup?'

'In a moment. I just want to stay here on my own for a few more minutes.'

'Sure.' She leaned over and kissed him on the top of his head. 'See you downstairs.'

After she had left, Ryan sat quietly on the bed,

listening. He waited until he heard her footsteps reach the bottom of the stairs, then pushed himself off. He walked over to the other side of the room, where the empty wardrobe stood. He paused a second, ears cocked, then grabbed both corners of the wardrobe, and eased it away from the wall. It was much easier now it was empty. He paused again to listen, then knelt down. He reached for his back pocket, and pulled out the teaspoon he had brought up with him earlier. He reached to where the wardrobe had stood, and, using the spoon, he began to prise a small piece of carpet away from the floorboards.

Down in London, Jack had finished his piece. He had checked it. He had sent it for Mike to look over. In his covering email, he told Mike it was only two thousand words, an introductory piece. He would be able to submit the next instalment once he had finished this piece of research. With any luck, Mike would not look at it until the next morning. Today was Thursday: if it had been a day later, there was no chance Mike would be looking at it at this time of the afternoon.

He was due to meet Taheen at *The Three Dukes* at six o'clock. He just had a couple of things to do by way of preparation, then he would leave.

A short while later, he was making his way up Frith Street. There was the pub, on the corner with Bateman Street. He made a right turn, walking past, his head facing forwards, but his eyes glancing to his left. There was nobody hanging around. Taheen did not say *in* the pub, so Jack was expecting their conversation to take place outside somewhere. He made a right at the next corner and walked down Greek Street. As he passed the theatre stage door, he paused and checked the time. It was ten minutes to six. When he reached Shaftesbury Avenue, he paused in a bus shelter and texted Taheen that he was here.

A few moments later, the reply came.

where ru?

Cambridge Circus he replied.

ok, go to the pub, 2 doors away theres an alley, next 2 kebab house

Jack typed the okay and headed back up Greek Street. It was getting cold, and he pulled his collar up, against the biting wind. Back up Greek Street, back along Bateman Street to the pub. He looked around for the kebab house, and, as Taheen had said, *Soho Kebabs & Burgers* was two doors from the pub. There was an alley the other side of the kebab house: wider than a normal alleyway, and too narrow for a motor vehicle; wide enough, though, for a large wheelie bin, of which there were at least two against the wall.

Where are you? I'm here.

end of the alley, don't want 2b seen, on cig break

Jack sent another okay, put the phone in his pocket and stepped down the alley, stepping sideways to pass the two wheelie bins. He could smell burnt oil and rotting food.

The alley shortly opened up into a wider space, which was probably where the fire exits from the kebab house and neighbouring places led.

Jack blinked a couple of times to get his eyes used to the light. Before his brain registered that Taheen was not here, two figures leapt out of the darkness. He had no time to react, when one of the figures delivered a powerful punch to Jack's stomach, winding him, and causing him to bend double. The second figure was behind him, and roughly grabbed him by the arms, holding him tightly. Jack attempted to straighten up and steeled himself for a second blow. That never came; instead, he saw the first figure take something from a pocket and, under the pale light from the kebab house windows, Jack saw the knife, its blade pointing at his stomach.

CHAPTER THIRTY-EIGHT

JACK FROZE, HIS eyes fixed on the knife. It took him a split second to work out the size: six inches, he reckoned, with a smooth blade, not serrated. At least that was something.

Suddenly, the guy holding the knife cried out in pain, dropped the knife, and fell to the ground, clutching the back of his head.

'You okay, Jack?' asked Samir, one of his contact Parmar's nephews. He stood, grinning, holding a three foot length of timber, probably four inches by two.

Jack felt his arms being released, and his captor made an attempt to run, but was caught by Samir's brother, Deepak, who was also carrying a three foot length of timber.

'You're not going anywhere, pal,' Deepak said, pushing him against a wall.

Jack looked over. 'You people will need to get up

earlier in the morning to ambush me,' he said. Deepak prodded the guy in the chest with his length of wood, causing him to stagger back a couple of steps. He said nothing.

Jack had fully recovered now. Rubbing his stomach, he looked down at the prone figure of the one who had punched him. 'You've killed him!'

Samir shook his head. 'No, I haven't. Look: he's still moving.' He was right; Jack could see the guy was still breathing. He kicked the knife away, causing it to slide under one of the large wheelie bins. The sound of the knife clattering away must have woken the guy, as he made a sound and began to move. Samir lifted the wood as if to deliver another blow.

'No,' Jack said. The guy collapsed back onto the ground. 'He's out cold.' He reached down and found a pulse. 'Out cold,' he repeated.

Deepak brandished his wood and grinned at the guy against the wall. 'That just leaves you, pal,' he said.

The guy glared at him. 'Fuck you.'

'No. Fuck *you*.' The guy recoiled at another poke from Deepak's wood.

Jack walked over. 'I need some information from you.'

'Go fuck yourself.'

'A hundred quid?'

The guy look up at Jack. 'What?'

Jack reached into his pocket and pulled out five twenties.

The guy glanced down at his unconscious colleague, then back to Jack. 'What do you want to know?'

Jack turned to Samir. 'Can you keep an eye on him?'

'No worries, Jack.'

Jack turned back. 'Kwento Usman.'

'What about him?'

'What do you do for him?'

'Stuff.'

'What stuff? His minder, his bodyguard, his gofer?'

'All of that, yeah.'

'And you get the drugs?'

'No, he does that himself.'

'No, I mean, he tells you what to get, and to bring it to the pub. One of you disappears, and comes back with what he's going to sell.'

The guy nodded to his unconscious partner. 'He normally does that.'

'Where does he go?'

He hesitated a second, until he got another prod from Deepak's wood. 'Kwento's got a flat. He keeps the stuff there, in a safe. He tells us how much to get and take over to the *Dukes*, and we go get it. Just so he doesn't carry any himself.'

'In case the police raid the pub?'

'Yeah, something like that.'

'Where is the flat?'

'Not far. Near Covent Garden.'

'And that's where he keeps his stock?'

The guy seemed to become more defiant. 'Who the fuck are you anyway? You can't be the cops.'

'I'm the Press,' Jack told him.

'What? The papers?'

'You got it. I'm writing about the drugs trade; about your little supply chain. Whoever sells to your pal Usman, who he supplies, who they supply, who they supply, and so on. First question: where does Usman get his supply from?'

'Hey, if I tell you anything, you going to put my name in the papers?'

'I don't know your name, but anyway, I'll use a cover name, a false name. Now: quickly, before your boyfriend wakes up. Where does he get his supply from?'

'He gets it online. I don't know where online, but he did say once that it can't be traced back to him. And he doesn't use pounds, or euros, or dollars. He said he used special money that can't be traced.'

'He means he used cryptocurrency,' Jack said.

'He goes on the dark web,' Samir said.

'Is that right?' Jack asked.

'If you say so. I just knows he goes online.'

'Yeah, fucking eBay,' Deepak chuckled.

Jack grinned and turned back to Usman's guy. 'Tell me how he gets the stuff. Once he's bought it online, how does he take delivery? How does it get to his flat?'

'Guy on a bike.' As he replied, he glanced down at his partner, who was still prone.

'Best keep an eye on him,' Jack said to Samir. 'In case he's shamming.' He turned back. 'So, it arrives by courier. How does that all happen?'

'Kwento knows when it's due to arrive. He waits at the flat, checks it when it's delivered, then puts it in the safe.'

Jack nodded. 'And what else do you do for him?'

'That's it. We just drive him around, travel with him if he uses the Tube, stay there in the pub with him, do stuff for him.'

'Errands?'

The guy nodded.

'You're not very loyal,' Jack remarked.

'How'd you make that out?'

'Telling me all this just for a hundred quid.'

'He don't pay much.'

'This flat in Covent Garden; where is it?'

'I didn't say *in* Covent Garden. *Near* it. Neal Street. Above *Seven Dials*.'

'So the flat's in Seven Dials?'

'No, above a shop called *Seven Dials*. They sell watches.'

'And that's where he lives?'

'No way. He's got some fancy apartment out East. Shoreditch.'

'Very nice, very expensive,' said Deepak.

'Yeah,' Jack agreed. 'Very gentrified out there these days. Are you telling me he keeps his supply of drugs in an empty flat?'

'They're in a safe, and there's loads of security there. Sometimes he or one of us stays over there. He's got it in a different name.'

'So he can't be connected to it if the shit hits the fan,' Jack said. 'Look,' he said, glancing down at the prone body, 'you said he doesn't pay much.' As he spoke, Jack handed over the five twenties. 'There's more where this came from. You up for making this a regular thing?'

'You mean being some kind of informant?'

'Pretty much.'

'It'll take more than a hundred. What do you want?'

'I don't really know yet. Just somebody on the inside I can contact if I need to; or who can contact me if something is about to go down.'

'If the money's right. Two hundred at least.'

Samir and Deepak looked at each other, laughing.

Jack agreed. 'Where's your mobile?'

He reached into his pocket. Deepak grabbed his arm. 'Careful. Just the phone.'

'Unlock it,' Jack said, and send me your number.' He recited his own number, and checked his burner phone after it pinged. 'What's your name?'

'My name is Kasim.'

'Need anything else, Jack?' Samir asked. 'I think he's beginning to come round. Unless you want me to -'

'No, no. I think we're done here.' Kasim's partner was beginning to move about. 'Let's go.'

'Wait,' said Kasim. 'You need to hit me. When Idi comes round, he and Kwento will ask why I wasn't touched. They will get suspicious.'

'If you insist,' said Deepak, lifting up his wood.

'No,' said Jack. 'Not that.' Deepak backed off as Jack stepped towards Kasim. He took a deep breath and swung his right fist, impacting on Kasim's jaw. Kasim flew back, crash-landing on a pile of crates and tied up bin bags. 'I hope nothing's broken. You know what to do.' He turned to Samir and Deepak. 'C'mon guys, let's get out of here.'

Samir kicked the still prone Idi in the ribs for good measure, and he and Deepak threw their pieces of wood at Kasim and Idi's bodies, and followed Jack, who was already hurrying out of the alley, back onto Frith Street. From there, they slowed to a brisk walk back to Shaftesbury Avenue, then Gerrard Place, and the underground parking garage, where Jack had left his car.

CHAPTER THIRTY-NINE

'THANKS FOR YOUR help, fellas. Where do you want dropping?' Jack asked, as he unlocked his car.

'Tottenham Court Road tube, if that's not too much trouble,' Samir replied, opening the rear door.

'Okay, if you're sure.' The station was half a mile away.

'Drop us there, and we'll be back in Tooting in half an hour.'

'Whatever you say.' Once out of the car park, Jack turned off Shaftesbury Avenue into Charing Cross Road; soon he was pulling up behind a bus almost before the junction with Oxford Street. 'Thanks again, guys,' he said one more time as they got out.

He gave them a wave, pulled out into the other lane so he could overtake the bus, headed over the junction up Tottenham Court Road, and made his way back through the North London streets. He arrived home just after eleven, thinking how good a move it was not going there alone.

Earlier that evening, before he left home for the West End, he called Parmar, to ask a favour. He said he had a meeting planned for later, and things might get a bit rough.

'That's no problem, Jack; would you like to borrow two of my nephews?'

'That would be appreciated. How big are they?'

Parmar laughed. 'Around the same size as you, I think. Deepak might be a bit taller. Big buggers, both of them. Why? You expecting trouble?'

'Possibly. Remember that sample of Ecstasy you had checked out for me?'

'It's to do with that?'

'It is. I've been trying to identify the sale chain, and I think I've traced where the source is. I spoke to one of the people the guy is selling to. I didn't get much out of him – I'm not sure whether he genuinely didn't know much or was just bullshitting me – but he called me later, saying he wanted to meet with me to tell me more.'

'Isn't that good, then?'

'He asked if he could meet me at my place. I said no, of course; but I've never been asked that. It was a strange request. I suggested meeting at his, but he said no, as his flatmate was in. Now, I was at his place the night before, and no way did he have a flatmate. My suspicion is, it wasn't him. It wasn't a voice call; just texting. After talking to him the night before, it all seemed too easy, and things just don't add up. I need to go, but I think I need some back-up. Some muscle, maybe.'

The next morning, and Jack was working on his article. The piece he had previously submitted was an introductory article; now he was working on the main bit. He had been expecting some kind of communication from Mike Smith about what he had sent, and was a bit puzzled that he had heard nothing. It was Friday, so maybe Mike just had the day off. It was odd not to have heard anything, though.

He made himself more coffee and sat down to type. He referred to the introductory piece, and said that here there would be more specific detail. He planned on talking about the deep web and its place in the drugs trade, about Kwento Usman, and the people he was selling to, and so on. He never used people's real names, although there was a possibility he might use Usman's real name if the police were involved at the time of publication. Most times, he would use, and say he had used, an alias to protect the person's identity. In the narrative, he used the third person: *this reporter*.

He had managed to get the first few hundred words down when an email came through. It was from Mike Smith. Jack saved what he had typed so far, and read the email.

It was a reply to Jack's email sending the first article. Mike had attached the article to this email, highlighting certain words or phrases. In the comments column, he had made suggested edits. Jack read through the suggestions, muttered, 'idiot' a couple of times. These were just changes made for the sake of it, nothing more. As they made no material difference to the article, Jack decided not to bother to question them. Instead, he waited an hour, then replied, saying the changes were okay.

At two thirty, he stopped, and reread what he had put down so far. Five and a half thousand words. Not too bad for a morning's work. He would finish off Monday, or over the weekend if he had the opportunity.

As it was Friday, he would be picking up his daughter from school later, so he cleaned up the flat, then phoned Susan. It was outside her lunch hour, so he was not sure if she would be able to talk, but she answered.

'I wasn't sure if you'd be free,' Jack said.

'No, it's okay. This afternoon's pretty quiet. I was just finishing off some paperwork. How was your meeting last night?'

'Er… it was interesting, let's say that.'

'And you're having Cathy this weekend, as usual?'

'Picking her up in an hour or so. Listen – that's partly why I was calling. Will you be around tomorrow?'

'Part of the day. What did you have in mind?'

'I was hoping to arrange for you and Cathy to meet. Nothing heavy; just to meet.'

'I'd like that. Have you told her about me?'

'Not yet. You?'

'No, but I think he suspects something. I'm sure my mother does, and she's bound to ask him.'

'You could come over for lunch?'

'Couldn't we meet somewhere out? To be honest, I'd prefer somewhere neutral for our first meeting. Not that I've ever been to your place anyway.'

'No, you haven't. We need to put that right asap. I need to cook you breakfast.'

'That sounds inviting. What about somewhere like Covent Garden?'

Covent Garden again.

'That's good for me,' Jack said. 'Any particular place in mind?'

'What about *Café Rouge*?'

'Yeah, that sounds fine. One o'clock?'

'That's good for me. Meet you outside?'

They had agreed. One o'clock outside *Café Rouge*, Covent Garden. Jack and his daughter, and his girlfriend. Is that what Susan was now? Maybe she was.

After he picked Cathy up from school, they had the usual conversation about what they were doing that evening. During the drive to Jack's flat, they went through the gamut of meal options: McDonalds, going out somewhere, to a takeaway. Once they had established a takeaway as a preferred option, there was much discussion around the menu. They settled on a Deliveroo Indian.

Tikka Jalapeno, and Lamb Chana.

'We're going out somewhere tomorrow,' Jack said, as they arrived at his flat.

'Yeah? Where?'

'It's a surprise.'

'What kind of surprise?'

'A surprise surprise. That's all I'm going to say, apart from the fact that's it's in the West End.'

'Cool. Can we go shopping?'

Inwardly, Jack groaned. Outwardly, he said, 'That would be nice. We can do some of that while we're out.'

That evening, after they had eaten, Cathy told Jack about a new show on Netflix. Her mother was hooked on it, and she'd like to watch a few episodes. Jack had never heard of it. It was called *Leroy*, and featured a member of the Los Angeles Police Department. Cathy obviously enjoyed the show, as she hardly touched her phone while they watched.

Halfway through their fifth episode, Jack's phone rang. It was Parmar. Curious as to why his informant would be calling on a Friday evening, Jack answered.

'Jack!' his contact said excitedly. 'Have you seen the *Standard*?'

'No, I tend not to look at the competition out of working hours. Why?'

'There's something in it you need to see.'

'You talking about the online edition?'

'I've got the paper copy. Tell you what – I'll send you a photo of what I'm talking about.'

'Okay, fine. I'll check it out.'

Jack hung up, and within a few seconds a message came through with a photograph attached. Jack retrieved the photograph, which was of a small newspaper column. Using the tips of two fingers, he enlarged the image, and read the article.

'Jesus,' he mouthed. The gist of the article was that, at five AM, a body was found under a bench in the gardens of Leicester Square. The body had identification in a pocket.

The person was named Kasim Daramy. His throat had been cut.

CHAPTER FORTY

SATURDAY MORNING, NINE AM, and to say Jack was tired was an understatement. He had probably got around three hours sleep. He could hear Cathy chatting at first, and was on the verge of asking her to be quiet, but she must have stopped and gone to sleep. Then he lay awake for hours thinking about Kasim.

His first thought was how it had been a good call to take Parmar's nephews along with him: had he not done so, it could well have been him lying in Leicester Square with his throat cut.

And then, how did Kasim get to be killed in that way, and by whom? Was it related to their encounter the night before, or some grisly coincidence? The other guy – what was his name? Idi – was unconscious, surely.

*****

Jack turned back to Kasim. 'Tell me how he gets the stuff. Once he's bought it online, how does he take delivery? How does it get to his flat?'

'Guy on a bike.' As he replied, he glanced down at Idi, who was still prone.

'Best keep an eye on him,' Jack said to Samir. 'In case he's shamming.' He turned back. 'So, it arrives by courier. How does that all happen?'

'Kwento knows when it's due to arrive. He waits at the flat, checks it when it's delivered, then puts it in the safe.'

As Jack and Kasim talked, Samir watched, listening, glancing down now and again to make sure Idi was still unconscious. What he failed to see was that Idi's eyes opened momentarily as he came out of unconsciousness, closing again as he listened to the conversation.

Jack nodded. 'And what else do you do for him?'

'That's it. We just drive him around, travel with him if he uses the Tube, stay there in the pub with him, do stuff for him.'

'Errands?'

The guy nodded.

'You're not very loyal,' Jack remarked.

'How'd you make that out?'

'Telling me all this just for a hundred quid.'

'He don't pay much.'

'This flat in Covent Garden; where is it?'

'I didn't say in Covent Garden. Near it. Neal Street. Above Seven Dials.'

'So the flat's in Seven Dials?'

'No, above a shop called Seven Dials. They sell watches.'

'And that's where he lives?'

'No way. He's got some fancy apartment out East. Shoreditch.'

'Very nice, very expensive,' said Deepak.

'Yeah,' Jack agreed. 'Very gentrified out there these days. Are you telling me he keeps his supply of drugs in an empty flat?'

'They're in a safe, and there's loads of security there. Sometimes he or one of us stays over there. He's got it in a different name.'

'So he can't be connected to it if the shit hits the fan,' Jack said. 'Look,' he said, glancing down at the prone body, 'you said he doesn't pay much.' As he spoke, Jack handed over the five twenties. 'There's more where this came from. You up for making this a regular thing?'

'You mean being some kind of informant?'

'Pretty much.'

'It'll take more than a hundred. What do you want?'

'I don't really know yet. Just somebody on the inside I can contact if I need to; or who can contact me if something is about to go down.'

'If the money's right. Two hundred at least.'

Samir and Deepak looked at each other, laughing.

Jack agreed. 'Where's your mobile?'

He reached into his pocket. Deepak grabbed his arm. 'Careful. Just the phone.'

'Unlock it,' Jack said, and send me your number.' He recited his own number, and checked his burner phone after it pinged. 'What's your name?'

'My name is Kasim.'

'Need anything else, Jack?' Samir asked. 'I think he's beginning to come round. Unless you want me to -'

'No, no. I think we're done here.' Kasim's partner was beginning to move about. 'Let's go.'

'Wait,' said Kasim. 'You need to hit me. When Idi comes round, he and Kwento will ask why I wasn't touched. They will get suspicious.'

'If you insist,' said Deepak, lifting up his wood.

'No,' said Jack. 'Not that.' Deepak backed off as Jack stepped towards Kasim. He took a deep breath and swung his right fist, impacting on Kasim's jaw. Kasim flew back, crash-landing on a pile of crates and tied up bin bags. 'I hope nothing's broken. You know what to do.' He turned to Samir and Deepak. 'C'mon guys, let's get out of here.'

Samir kicked the still prone Idi in the ribs for good

measure, and he and Deepak threw their pieces of wood at Kasim and Idi's bodies, and followed Jack, who was already hurrying out of the alley, back onto Frith Street.

Idi remained prone, eyes open now, waiting for the sounds of the men's footsteps to fade away. Then he pretended to come round.

Cathy was awake by ten. She wandered out of her bedroom, still dressed in her night shirt, rubbing her eyes and yawning. She had bed hair.

'Breakfast?' Jack asked. 'I've had mine. Toast?'

'Yeah. Tea and toast,' his daughter grunted.

When she was sitting down eating, Jack said, 'Now. We're going out for lunch today. But first, I have something I need to tell you.'

'Yeah? What?'

Jack told her. Her name, where she lived, how they met. How long he had been seeing her.

Cathy sat there, not moving, not speaking.

'Say something, then,' Jack said, after a few moments of silence.

'About time. It's been ages since Lucy died.'

Jack nodded. 'Eight years.' Lucy Ryder had been Jack's first serious girlfriend since he and Mel, Cathy's mother, split and divorced. Eight years back, Lucy was killed in a tragic case of mistaken identity when Mel's then partner tried to engineer Jack's car to crash, not knowing it was Lucy alone in the car, not Jack.

'So it's time,' Cathy added. 'After all, Mum's had boyfriends off and on.'

'I know,' Jack nodded.

'And she keeps saying you've hardly been a monk.'

Jack cleared his throat. 'Yes; well, we don't need to go down that avenue. So you're okay with this?'

'Of course. Why shouldn't I be?'

'No reason. You can meet her later. That's why we're

going out for lunch. Covent Garden *Café Rouge*.'

'That'll be cool.' She clambered off the stool. 'I'm going to take a shower now.'

Once she had closed the bathroom door, Jack let out a sigh of relief. One, he had finally told her; two, she seemed okay with it; three, she seemed happy for him. He reached for his phone and texted Susan with an update.

She replied quickly. *Wow, relief. Cu 1pm xx*

Later, Jack drove them to the car park at Cockfosters station. As they sat on the train and Cathy got engrossed with her phone, Jack's thoughts returned to what had happened to Kasim last night.

Idi had got to his feet, and helped Kasim to his. 'Come on,' he said. 'We need to tell Kwento what happened. He said he'd be at the flat.'

They both walked to the flat in Neal Street. Kasim rang the bell, and within seconds the lock buzzed and they went inside. The flat was on the second floor. Kwento Usman was in the kitchen drinking a mug of coffee.

'I'm sorry, boss,' Kasim said. 'He wasn't alone. He came with two other guys. Big guys.'

Usman waved a hand to dismiss the apology. 'This fucker's clever, obviously. What did he ask you?'

Idi spoke first. 'I got knocked out,' he said, rubbing the back of his head. 'I was out cold the whole time.' He looked over at Kasim.

'You were out cold too?' Usman asked.

'Almost. They beat me up a bit, and he asked me about you. I told him to go fuck himself, so they beat me up some more. They had kind of baseball bats.'

'So you told him nothing? That's good. Who is this cocksucker, anyway?'

'I asked him who he was and he said he's from a newspaper,' Kasim explained.

'That's right,' Usman muttered, looking down into his

coffee. 'He is. I wonder how much he knows already. I wonder how he knew not to come alone.'

'Maybe he's naturally suspicious, being a reporter,' Idi suggested. 'Maybe he knew it wasn't Taheen texting him.'

Usman nodded, slowly. 'Maybe. Let's worry about him in the morning. Let's get to the pub. It should be a good night. I know at least two are coming.' He downed the last of his coffee, and left the flat, Kasim and Idi following.

It was a lucrative evening: three people made contact, and twice Idi went back to the flat, and once Kasim to pick up the package.

After closing, they stood outside the pub.

'I'm hungry,' Usman said. 'Let's go get something to eat.' They walked across Shaftesbury Avenue, and through the narrow streets to Leicester Square. It was late, and the square was quiet. The movie and theatre goers had long since vacated the area; most of the restaurants and eating places were already closed, or in the process of closing. Usman nodded over to a burger outlet. 'Go get three burgers,' he said to Idi. 'All with fries. We'll be over there.' He pointed over to the gardens in the middle of the square. He and Kasim walked over and sat on a bench, where Idi joined them five minutes later. After they had eaten, Usman looked over to Idi, who then said, 'I need to stretch my legs.'

'You're quiet,' Usman said to Kasim, once Idi had gone.

'Just tired, I guess. My head hurts a bit still.'

Usman nodded. He held out his hand. 'Give me the trash,' he said. He took the wrappings, and looked around. 'There's a bin there.'

'I'll take it,' Kasim said.

'You're cool. I'll do it.' Usman stood and walked round to the bin.

Kasim sat alone on the bench. He noticed Idi standing at the edge of the gardens, smoking.

Suddenly, he was aware of Usman standing behind him. He heard Usman's voice in his ear, whispering. He could feel Usman's breath on him.

'So you want to be an informer, do you, motherfucker?'

He was aware of the sharp pain of the knife across his throat. He was aware of the warm life blood pouring from his throat.

Then he was aware no more.

'Dad! Dad! Wake up. We're here.'

Jack came to, feeling Cathy tugging at his arm. He could see the Covent Garden signs on the wall as the train pulled into the station. He leapt out of his seat and he and Cathy jumped off the train.

'Did you fall asleep?' Cathy asked as they took the lift up to street level.

'No, nothing like that. Just thinking about something. Work.'

She was not convinced. 'Yeah. Right.'

On exiting the station, they walked down James Street, past two living statues, a copper-coloured cowboy and a silver-coloured robot, to the square, and walked round the central mall to *Café Rouge*, where Susan was waiting outside. She was wearing jeans, with black knee-length boots, and a dark blue coat. Somewhat inappropriately as he was with his daughter, he momentarily visualised Susan wearing only the boots.

Susan held out her hand to Cathy. 'Hello, Cathy. How are you? I'm Susan.'

The lunch was going well. They seemed to be getting on. Very well, in fact. There were a couple of awkward silences in the beginning - that was inevitable - but now they were chatting easily, quite animatedly in places. Susan asked Cathy about her school, and Jack learned a few things he had no idea about. Perhaps he had never asked the right questions. Cathy asked if Susan had any children, and Susan began to talk about her son. They both enjoyed shopping, and shared tastes in TV programmes. Susan was also a fan of that cop show Cathy made Jack sit through the night before.

It wasn't intentional, but after a while, Jack's bladder got the best of him. He excused himself, and, whilst standing at the urinal, wondered what the conversation was like in his absence: would there be that awkward silence as he was not there to be the commonality?

He need not have worried. When returned to the table, they were still talking. Susan looked up at him. 'How soon do you guys have to get back?'

Jack shrugged and sat down. 'We've nothing else on today, have we?'

Susan checked her watch. 'I've got until three. How about Cathy and I take a look at some of the shops around here?'

'Please, Dad,' Cathy pleaded.

'Fine by me,' Jack replied.

'You could tag along behind us,' Susan suggested.

'But wait outside the shop,' Cathy added.

'Fine by me,' Jack said again.

After they had left the restaurant, Cathy and Susan began browsing. Not every shop: they both seemed to gravitate towards clothing stores. Jack wandered a few feet behind them, remaining outside the places they visited.

They did a full circuit of the square, and slowly made their way up James Street, again past the living statues, quickly checking them out. Across Shelton Street at the tube station, and onwards. It was then that Jack noticed the name of the street they were on.

Neale Street.

So this was where Kwento Usman had his flat, where he stored God knows how much pure Ecstasy. The street was pedestrianised, and they wandered along in the centre of the road, looking over at the shops either side, sometimes, going closer to the window, sometimes going in for a few minutes.

They paused at one store which seemed to specialise in Harry Potter memorabilia. Jack stayed in the middle of the street, looking around. It was then that he noticed, on the other side, a store called *Seven Dials*. So that was the place. There was a black wooden door next to the shopfront, with a multi-occupancy bell system, with a camera lens. That had to be it.

'We'll just go up to the end,' Susan said, as she and Cathy joined him. He nodded and followed behind. As they passed the shop, Jack heard a noise and turned his head.

The black wooden door slowly opened.

CHAPTER FORTY-ONE

JACK TENSED.

If only they had taken another street out of the market. The last thing he needed right now was to bump in to Kwento Usman, or his associate Idi.

Especially with Cathy and Susan a few feet away.

Tensing had caused him to involuntarily pause and stare at the opening door. To his relief, exiting were a bearded white man in his twenties, followed by a woman of the same age. The man was clutching a London A to Z.

Just a couple from a neighbouring flat.

He turned to look where the others had got to and walked a bit faster to catch up. They followed Neale Street to the end, then took a left down Monmouth Street, as far as Seven Dials. The location, not the shop. Then the side streets back to Covent Garden.

They paused outside the tube station. This is where they would part company: Susan down to Green Park, with a connection up to Willesden Green; Jack and Cathy back up to Cockfosters.

They actually said their goodbyes at platform level, with Jack promising to call the next day. As their train sped through the tunnel, Jack looked down at his daughter.

'Well?' he asked.

'She's nice,' Cathy replied. 'How long have you been seeing her?'

'Not long. Just a few times.'

'Has she been to your place yet?'

'No, not yet,' Jack replied, keeping his fingers crossed that she would not ask him if he and Susan had slept together.

'Why not?'

'She just hasn't yet. We've not being seeing each other long.'

'Have you been to hers? She told me where she lives.'

'Once. Actually twice. No, three times. The first time I had to talk to her about work.'

'Work?'

'Yes. Something going on down her road. I needed to talk to the people living in the street.'

'Yes. She told me that.'

Jack knew that she was expecting him to ask what they talked about while he was in the gents, or while they were in the shops, but decided not to give her the satisfaction.

'You need to,' Cathy said.

'Need to what?'

'You need to ask her round to yours.'

'I will. I will.'

'Have you met her son?'

'Not yet.'

'You need to.'

'You're quite the expert, aren't you,' said Jack, looking down at his daughter, who just shrugged.

Jack said nothing. He resumed staring across the carriage, out of the opposite window. He reflected on the irony of a middle aged man with no little experience being coached on his love life by a daughter who was barely in her teens. It should be the other way round; although he was in no hurry to deal with boyfriend issues. He still had that to come.

That evening, at the time he would normally have prepared something or had something delivered, neither of them was that hungry; still full from lunch. Cathy made them some beans on toast, and they settled down to continue the Netflix cop show. Season 2.

They were halfway into the second episode when Jack's landline rang. Only one person ever used his landline.

'That has to be Aunt Madeline.'

Cathy said nothing; Jack reached over to the phone and picked up. She still said nothing, just watched the show while Jack small-talked with Madeline. She looked up when Jack said, 'Cathy's here tonight.' She cringed.

'You want to say hello to her?' Jack asked his sister. Cathy silently waved a hand and mouthed a no. 'Maddie?' Jack said. 'You've just missed her. I think she's in the shower. Yes, next time.' He mouthed *you owe me* as he listened to what his sister was saying.

After five minutes of chit chat about what she had been doing and about their parents, Madeline said, 'Did you know Amanda's been in hospital?'

Jack straightened up. 'No, I didn't. You never told me that.'

'I didn't know myself,' Madeline replied. 'I spoke to her earlier and she told me.'

'She's still there?'

'No, she's back home.'

'Home? As in with you?'

'No, I mean back at that house she and Ryan share.'

'So what happened then?'

'She was feeling unwell, so Ryan took her to A & E.

They kept her in overnight for observation.'

'Just unwell? In what way?'

'I think she's been overdoing it. She said the hospital said she was suffering from exhaustion and needed rest. Overtired. She said she hasn't been sleeping, finding it difficult to get to sleep at night. She's been getting headaches, and fainted a couple of times.'

'Really? Fainted?'

'Once during a lecture, if you please, and the other time at the house. The second time led Ryan to take her to the hospital. The Royal Kendal Infirmary. I think she just needed rest; all that studying and partying.'

'And you know she's partying all the time?'

'She's a student, isn't she?'

'Maddy, weren't you young once?'

'Yes, but not like that.'

'Are you going up to see her?'

'No need now. She's out of hospital, and better. And *I* didn't find out until it was all over.'

'I would have thought she or Ryan would have called you at the time.'

'Apparently she told Ryan not to.'

'I see. Fair enough.'

'You could give her a call, see how she is. She might tell you more than she does me.'

'Yeah, I might do that. Not tonight though; not Saturday night. I'll call her tomorrow.'

Jack hung up and turned to Cathy. 'She says Amanda's been in hospital.'

Cathy looked up. 'Yeah? What's wrong with her?'

'Just exhaustion, apparently. She's out now.'

'That's good,' Cathy said, before returning to the TV.

'Plenty of cousinly concern,' Jack sighed, sitting back down again.

'Mm?'

'Nothing.' His daughter just didn't get irony.

*****

After another four episodes, Cathy announced she was going to bed.

'You mean you're going to chat with your friends?'

'Why not? I've not spoken to them all day. In any case – aren't you going to call Susan?'

'I said I'd call her tomorrow.'

'Right. I'll say goodnight then.'

Once he was alone, Jack sent Susan a brief text. Did she get back okay, did she enjoy lunch, as he and Cathy did. The reply came back after a couple of minutes with a yes to all three questions. Housework for her tomorrow, as she was back to work Monday. He said he would call her the next day; maybe a video call. Susan replied with a thumbs up emoji.

Jack tossed his phone to one side, leaned back and closed his eyes. He had got over the surprise of his niece being hospitalised, and was glad she was back home okay. Maddie was probably right. Insomnia, headaches, fainting: all signs of overdoing it. Up late drinking, up early for lectures. Probably a longer day than he had.

Then he paused.

'No, no, no,' he said quietly, going over to his table, on which lay the pile of paperwork for work. He sat at the table and leafed through the notes he had made earlier that week. 'No, no, no,' he said again as he read the notes.

Fainting, difficulty sleeping, headaches.

All symptoms of a student who was working late into the night on assignments, who was up early to go for lectures, who probably wasn't eating properly, who was probably drinking too much.

They were also side-effects felt by somebody taking Ecstasy.

CHAPTER FORTY-TWO

ANOTHER DAY, AND another trip back up to Kendal.

This time, Jack left the car at home. He was still getting pressure from Mike Smith to submit more work, and the only way to combine getting that done and going to see Amanda was to take the train. A journey time of just under three hours, at least an hour quicker than the motorway, and he was able to work while travelling. First Class of course, as the paper was paying.

His conversation with Mike the night before went easier than expected. Even though he was going back up there because of his niece, this part of the chain, and the Sun Lee connection, was a genuine part of his investigation.

'After all,' Mike had said, 'who knows what other students are on the books, and where they might be?'

Jack had the feeling that had he contacted Mike during the week, and not late on a Sunday afternoon when he had obviously been drinking, then authorisation might not have been so easy to get. He would have gone up there anyway, but would probably have driven, and if the paper was happy to pay his fare and two nights' accommodation, who was he to argue?

He had booked into the same hotel he had used before: he was familiar with it, it was clean and comfortable and convenient, so there was no reason to change. Jack like familiarity. Once he had got settled, he called Amanda.

'You've been speaking to my mother, haven't you?' she asked. 'You didn't need to come up again. I'm fine now. I probably didn't need to go to the hospital. Ryan panicked.'

'It's not just because of you. Part of the story I'm working on involves what's been going on up here, and I need more information. Are you around this evening?'

'Uncle Jack, it's Monday. Where would anybody go on a Monday evening?'

'Fair point. I don't want to intrude again. I'll eat here, then come over.'

'You can always eat with us.'

'I've already ordered room service. About seven?'

'That's fine. No, make it seven thirty. We'll be done eating by then.'

'Great. See you after seven thirty.'

He hung up and picked up the room service menu. He hadn't already ordered, but he had the feeling things might go a little differently tonight, and it might be better if he didn't eat with them this time.

'Hey, Uncle Jack. I mean, Jack,' Amanda said later as she let him in. 'You come by cab?'

'I came up on the train,' he said, as he followed his niece into the kitchen.

'Really?'

'I can work on the train,' Jack explained, 'and the paper's paying my expenses.'

'So it really is a work visit. Coffee?'

Jack nodded, in answer to both questions. He looked

around. 'The others out?'

Amanda shook her head. 'They're both upstairs. They both have stuff to do for tomorrow.'

'You don't?'

'I got mine done over the weekend. While I was resting, as they say.'

Jack took his cup of coffee. 'So what did happen, then? Your mum told me you'd fainted a couple of times, and hadn't been feeling well.'

She nodded. 'Well, I had. Once during a lecture, which was a bit embarrassing. Ryan wasn't there at the time. I came round straight away, though. The college arranged for me to take a taxi back here. The other time I was here, exactly the same, but Ryan panicked somewhat – he can be like a mother hen sometimes – and threw me into the back of a cab and took me to the Royal Kendal. They did a couple of tests, said I was suffering from exhaustion, recommended I stayed in overnight for observation. Which I did, only to get away from Ryan fussing. He was really worried, poor thing.'

'Anything else?'

'I'd been sick two or three times; don't worry, I'm not pregnant. It must have been something we'd eaten, as Ryan said he didn't feel too good, although no puking.'

'Your mum said you'd not been sleeping.'

'Jesus. Yes, I'd had trouble sleeping. Not being able to get off to sleep when I want to, or waking about two in the morning, and not getting back to sleep again. The hospital – and Mum – said I was burning the candle at both ends.'

'They're probably right.'

'This is why I don't tell her anything. She always overreacts. Thinks I'm about twelve. I'm sure she thinks as we've got our own rooms, we're not sleeping together.'

'I'm sure she doesn't, but rest assured I'm not that naïve. However, that's your business.' Jack nodded at the ceiling. 'Is Ryan in his room? I'll go and say hi.'

'He knows you're coming round. Said he wanted to finish off his assignment. He'll be down soon.'

'I need the loo anyway. I'll just stick my head round the door.'

'Okay. 'Amanda took his empty cup and Jack went upstairs. He did use the bathroom, then knocked on Ryan's door, and went in.

'Hey, Jack.' Ryan looked up from his text book. He was making notes on a pukka pad. 'How you doing? Amanda said you'd be round. I'm nearly done here. I'll be done in a bit.'

Jack stepped into the room and quietly closed the door behind him. 'I just wanted to get you on your own for a minute or so. While Amanda's not in earshot.'

'O-kay,' said Ryan, uncertainly.

Casually, Jack leaned on the wardrobe. It matched the one in Sun Lee's room: maybe the landlord had bought a job lot. 'I just wanted to say thank you for taking her to the hospital the other day.'

Ryan sat back, folding his arms. 'That's okay. What do you expect me to have done, anyway?'

His own arms folded, Jack nodded. 'I know, I know. I'm grateful, anyway. I'm just trying to work out what caused it. Her condition, I mean.'

Ryan's expression changed. Uncomfortable was the word Jack would use to describe it. 'The hospital said exhaustion,' he said, looking down at his textbook. 'Burning the candle at both ends.'

'Yes,' Jack nodded. 'That's what Amanda told me. And her mother.'

Ryan made to turn to his desk, but turned back when Jack spoke.

'I just need to ask you something. I feel a bit embarrassed about asking this, to be honest.'

Ryan looked up at Jack.

'Her mother's so naïve, I'm sure she thinks that as you both have your own rooms, you're not sleeping together,' Jack said, trying to sound disarming. Ryan looked even more uncomfortable. 'What I'm trying to ask you, clumsily, is are the two of you… taking anything when…

you know?'

'I don't know what you mean, Jack.'

'I think you do. Any recreation drugs.'

Ryan swallowed. He stood up and stepped over to the door. 'We're not. Now, I need to -'

'I'm sorry to have to ask, but is that the case? Not even poppers?'

Ryan leaned on the wall, looked up to the ceiling and exhaled. He nodded. 'I have. Just to… you know.'

'But she doesn't?' Jack asked.

'No.'

'Not even without knowing?'

'No. Of course not.'

Jack said nothing. His eyes met Ryan's.

Flustered, Ryan said, 'Why would she? How would she?'

Jack said nothing. His eyes stared into Ryan's.

Eventually, Ryan blurted out, 'Okay, okay. We did use. Only a bit. She didn't know. I found something in Sun's room. Another hiding place.'

'And you gave her some? Spiked her drink?'

'No, nothing like that. I… I don't know why I'm telling you this. When we were in bed, while she was in the bathroom, I put some - a tiny bit, just a sprinkle - on…'

'On what?'

'You want a diagram, Jack? On my dick.'

'And that's how she ingested it.'

'Yes. It seemed to work, so I did it a few times more. Then she got sick.'

Jack grabbed Ryan's neck and pushed him back against the wall. 'You idiot! You could have killed her, you realise that?'

'I know, I know, I know. I stopped when she started passing out. I wouldn't do anything to hurt her, you know that, don't you?'

Jack released Ryan and took a deep breath. 'I don't know what to think. And she doesn't know?'

'No. She thinks it was exhaustion. Jack, you're not

going to tell her, are you?'

Jack pushed Ryan down onto the chair. 'Now, tell me exactly about you, and about Sun Lee. You can start with how you knew where to look for the drugs he left behind.'

'Okay.' Ryan took a deep breath. He was close to tears. 'This is just between us two, isn't it?'

'I'm not going to tell Amanda anything. You might have to, though. Right: I'm all ears.'

'I have been using for a while. Just me; she knows nothing about this.'

'Ecstasy?'

Ryan shook his head. 'No, cocaine. I know Sun was dealing in E, and that time was the only time I've gone anywhere near it.' He looked up, and laughed. 'I don't even know what it tastes like.' Jack gave no reaction. Ryan continued, 'I take a little cocaine now and again. Not from Sun Lee. I used to get my supply from a guy in *West Coast*.'

'*West Coast*? What's that? A bar or something?'

'It a club. In the city centre. A lot of students go there.'

'I bet they do. What's this guy's name?'

'Will.'

'Is the place open Mondays? Will he be there tonight?' Ryan nodded his head weakly. 'Could be.'

Jack pushed himself off the wardrobe. 'Get your coat.'

'Why? What for?'

'You and I are going clubbing.'

CHAPTER FORTY-THREE

JACK AND RYAN got an Uber to *West Coast*.

As they sat in the back of the grey Skoda on the ten minute journey into the city centre, Jack looked over at Ryan.

'Let's get this clear. I'm not going to be spending the night here boogying away. I just want to meet your pal Will, get what I can from him, then leave. You can stay if you want to.'

'It's the same with me,' Ryan said. 'I still have work to finish off.' He paused. 'Do you think Amanda believed us? Maybe we should have said we were going out for a drink.' He paused again. 'But then, she might have insisted on coming with us.'

Jack shrugged his shoulders. Looking straight ahead, he said, 'I don't give a shit whether she believes us or not. As long as she's kept out of all this.'

'Here we are,' Ryan said. Jack paid the driver and they

got out. The club was situated in the city centre, at the periphery of a group of shops. Black double entrance doors sandwiched between a *Poundland* store and a *Pizza Express*. The small neon sign above the double doors had seen better days: part of *Coast* was flashing. It would not be long before the tube needed replacing.

To Jack's amusement, they were granted admission by the doorman, who looked young enough to be his son. Some bouncer, Jack reflected: he was barely growing facial hair.

They walked down the passageway to the main part of the club. Jack estimated there were twenty people here tonight, tops.

'This is the first time I've been here on a Monday night,' Ryan said. 'I always assumed Monday nights would be quiet.'

Jack nodded. Quiet was an understatement. He didn't recognise or like the music that was playing. The only people dancing to the music were two twenty-something girls having a slow dance together. A small group of people was gathered around the tables at the edge of the dance floor, and a similar-sized group was congregating at one end of the bar.

Jack was the oldest person there by a mile. 'Are these all students, then?' he asked Ryan.

'Most likely, though I don't recognise anyone.'

'Is he here? Your pal Will? Can you see him?'

Ryan did a three-sixty, looking around the room. 'I can't see him. I'll go and ask around. If he's not here tonight, somebody else is bound to know where to find him. He may be in the gents. He quite often hands over the coke in there.'

'You got his phone number?' Jack asked.

'No. We never speak on the phone. Only face to face, here.'

Jack said, 'You go and look for him. I'll get a couple of beers.' He strolled over to the bar and bought two bottles of beer. Bud Light – not Jack's drink of choice, but it would suffice. He leaned round to look for Ryan, who he could see the other side of the room talking to the group by the tables. He turned back to his beer, and stared down the neck of the bottle. He wondered if this trip was going to be a waste of time. What else could Will add to what Jack already knew? But this trip was more about checking on Amanda, who seemed to be okay now. Saying the trip was part of his research only served to justify claiming his expenses from the paper, if he was honest. But Mike agreed it, so all was good.

He checked on Ryan again. No sign of him. Maybe he was in the gents looking for Will. This all seemed redolent of what went on in London, carrying out drug transactions in the gents. By the look of some of the individuals in this place, that wasn't the only type of transaction being carried out in the gents.

The girl behind the bar sidled along to the end where Jack was sitting. She smiled at him as she wiped the top of the bar with a tea towel. 'Anything else I can get you?' she asked, pleasantly.

Jack smiled. 'No, thanks. I'm good here. My nephew and I are looking for a guy called Will. Is he here tonight, do you know?'

She frowned. 'I think I've seen him.' She stood on tiptoe and looked around. 'Yeah, Pretty sure. There are so many nooks and crannies and alcoves in this place. It's not always easy to find somebody in the dark. Especially when it's busy.'

'Not busy tonight,' Jack said, taking a mouthful of beer.

She laughed. 'No, it's not. It's very quiet tonight, even for a Monday. Oh, look,' she added, gazing over Jack's shoulder. 'It looks like your nephew's found him.'

Jack swung around on his stool. He saw two figures walking across the floor towards him. In the darkness and the reflections from the disco ball, he could only make out their silhouettes. He recognised Ryan's shape; the other not so.

Until they got nearer.

Ryan said, 'Jack, this is Will. Will, this is Jack.'

Will stopped dead, six feet away from Jack, his mouth agape.

Jack froze also, just momentarily.

He had met Will before.

Only before, he was called Guillaume.

CHAPTER FORTY-FOUR

IT WAS DIFFICULT to tell who was the most surprised.

Jack or Guillaume/Will.

Guillaume/Will made to leave, but Jack reached out and grabbed his arm. 'Not so fast,' he said.

'You two know each other?' Ryan asked.

Guillaume/Will said nothing.

Jack said, 'Remember the guy I went to see at the hall of residence, at the student accommodation? Sun Lee's friend? His friend with benefits? Only then he called himself Guillaume.'

'Guillaume?' said Ryan. 'Isn't that the French word for William?'

Jack nodded. 'Hence Will. Will the drug pusher.'

'Is that right?' Ryan asked. 'You're Sun's friend? You're a student at the university? Why have I never seen you?'

'Because nobody notices me, asshole. Nobody. Only

Sun did. I'm not going to use my real name when I'm selling in here, am I?'

'Let me get this straight,' Jack said. 'Sun Lee was dealing in Ecstasy, but you, his special friend, are selling cocaine? Have I got that right?'

Guillaume's eyes darted around. 'I don't want to talk in here. Outside, on the street.'

'Okay,' Jack said, taking Guillaume's arm. 'I could use some fresh air, anyway.'

Guillaume shook Jack's hand off his arm and led them to the exit.

'No tricks, remember,' Jack cautioned. 'No trying to grow a brain.'

'Going for some air,' Guillaume/Will said as they passed the youthful doorman. 'Back in ten.' The boy nodded.

Out on the street, Jack said, 'You didn't answer my question. Sun Lee was pushing Ecstasy, and you cocaine? Are there two chains of supply, then? Or are you selling both, or more types? You got a catalogue or something?'

'Just Molly,' Guillaume said.

'But you told me it was cocaine,' said Ryan.

Guillaume laughed. 'And you believed me. It was Molly, mixed with powdered milk.'

Ryan opened his mouth to speak, but Jack cut in first. 'But you,' he said, pointing to Ryan, 'were living in the same house as Sun Lee, who was supplying you,' pointing to Guillaume, 'who supplied you,' pointing back at Ryan.

Guillaume confirmed. 'Pretty much, yeah.'

Jack looked at Ryan. 'But you said you got some from Sun's room. The stuff you gave to Amanda.'

Ryan nodded. 'After you found some under his bed, I looked through his room for more. Not sure why, really; just curious, I suppose. I found one more bag, under the carpet, under his wardrobe.'

Guillaume chuckled. 'And you gave some to your girlfriend?'

'Just a little.'

Guillaume laughed. 'Fuck, man. What you took was near a hundred percent. She dead yet?'

Jack pushed Guillaume against the wall and put a hand on his throat. 'No, you piece of shit – she's not dead. If she was, you'd be joining her. You got any on you?'

'Some,' Guillaume croaked, Jack's hand still around his throat.

'Where?'

'Why?' croaked Guillaume, instinctively laying a hand across his coat pocket.

'Get it out,' Jack ordered.

'What?'

Keeping one hand on Guillaume's throat, with the other hand, Jack brushed the boy's hand away and reached inside the pocket. He pulled out three small brown envelopes. He passed them to Ryan, who opened the envelopes. Each contained a small sealable plastic bag of white powder.

'Hey, that's mine!' Guillaume choked.

Jack released him and took the plastic bags from Ryan. He opened each in turn, and tipped the powder out onto the pavement.

'Hey, you can't do that!' Guillaume cried out, his hands flailing around, as if trying to catch the powder as it floated to the wet pavement or blew away in the breeze. 'That that cost me four hundred!'

'Tough shit,' said Jack. 'Any more on you? Any more in your room?'

'No, that's it, that's all.'

'Maybe we should all go back to your room and search it?' Jack said. 'Or maybe the University authorities might want to? What do you think?'

Before Guillaume could answer, the doorman put his head around the corner. Jack had forgotten about him: had he been listening? 'Everything okay here, guys?' he asked.

'Yes, everything's fine here, thanks,' Jack replied. 'We're all good, aren't we?' While Jack and Ryan were momentarily distracted, Guillaume pushed past them, and started to run off. Ryan made to follow, but Jack put a hand on his arm. 'Don't bother. There's no point. He'll do no more dealing tonight.'

Guillaume was now at the corner of the street, around fifty yards away. He paused and turned to shout out, 'Kwento's gonna kill you, you son of a bitch!' He raised a middle finger, and disappeared around the corner.

'We know where he'll be tomorrow. I might give the bursar's office an anonymous call in the morning,' Jack said, scraping his foot on the ground, so there was no powder left.

'What did he say? Kwento's gonna kill you? Who's Kwento?'

'Kwento Usman,' Jack explained, 'is the guy based in London who was Sun Lee's supplier. As far as I can establish, he gets his own supply over the dark web, then sells it on to people like Sun Lee, who sells some on to people like your mate Will, and so on. Somebody to avoid, I think. Down in London last week, I managed to get some information – don't ask how – from one of his minders.'

'Yes? That was good.'

'For me, yes. But that minder was found in Leicester Square the next morning with his throat cut.'

'Fuck.'

'Quite. Come on, let's get back to the house.'

'There's a cab rank just around the corner. There's normally at least half a dozen there. As long as Will isn't there waiting himself.'

'I doubt that. Come on, let's go.'

They began to walk around the corner, then Jack stopped suddenly.

'What is it?' Ryan asked.

'When we were at your house, looking through the Instagram stuff, the pictures. There was a picture of him with Sun Lee, together. You said something like you couldn't place him, but you must have known what he looked like, as you were buying from him.'

Ryan looked down at the ground.

'Well?' Jack asked.

'Yes, I did know him. I just didn't want you and Amanda to find out I was buying from him.'

Jack looked down the street, away from Ryan, and exhaled deeply.

'I'm sorry, Jack. I just…'

'Anything else you've not told me?' Jack asked angrily.

Ryan shook his head and ran a hand through his hair. 'I'm sorry,' he said quietly.

'I'm getting a cab back to the house,' Jack said, walking off. 'You can do what you want.'

Ryan paused a second, then ran to catch up with Jack. There were three taxis waiting, and they got the one in the front of the line. On the way back, Jack was silent. Ryan said, 'Jack…?'

Jack shook his head dismissively. 'Forget it. It is what it is.' He stared out of the window, avoiding looking at Ryan.

When they were almost there, Ryan asked, 'You're coming in, aren't you?'

'I'll come in for a while, just to make sure Amanda's okay, and to say goodbye. Then I'll go back to the hotel.'

'This cab?'

'No. I'm sure Amanda will force feed me another coffee, so I'll just get another Uber. I have their app, I think.'

'When do you head back south?'

'The hotel booking is for two nights, but there's nothing to stop me going back early. It depends when I've done all I came up to do.'

They arrived at the house. Once again, Jack paid the driver, and they turned towards the house. The downstairs and hall lights were on.

'That's odd,' Ryan said as they stood at the foot of the steps leading up to the front door.

'What's odd?'

The front door was six inches ajar.

'We never leave it like that,' Ryan said.
They both looked at each other.
Then they both leapt up the steps and into the house.

CHAPTER FORTY-FIVE

JACK COULD TELL by the way Anji was lying at the foot of the stairs that her neck had been broken.

He quietly knelt and put a hand on her forehead. It was still warm.

He heard Ryan gasp and whisper something like, 'Oh, no,' before running upstairs calling for Amanda.

Jack ran into the kitchen, where Amanda was most likely to be. The kitchen light was on, but it was empty. A pack of spaghetti lay on the counter top, next to the stove, on which a pan of water was boiling.

He turned and ran into the lounge, calling her name. He froze in the doorway. Amanda was sitting in one of the dining chairs, at the table. Her face was white, streaked with tears, her eyes wide open. The expression on her face was one which would remain with Jack for a long time. She opened her mouth to speak, but could make no sound.

Jack immediately took a step forward, but once he had

got over the threshold and was in the room, he felt an unbelievably heavy blow at the back of his head. His vision became hazy as he clutched his head, then he began to see flashing lights as the red and grey rug on the floor rushed up towards him.

He was on the floor, but not quite out. He managed to raise himself so he was on all fours. He turned and looked up and, emerging from behind the door, was the towering form of Kwento Usman. Usman stepped towards Jack, and as he did so, Ryan appeared in the doorway.

'Bastard!' Ryan cried as he vaulted onto Usman's back, his legs around Usman's waist, and his arms around his neck. Usman stepped back against the wall, hard, three times. Each time, Ryan's head and back took the full force of the impact, and after the third blow, Ryan collapsed off Usman and into a pile on the floor. Amanda screamed.

The big man made two strides over to Jack, who was still attempting to get up, and lashed out with his left foot, propelling Jack six feet across the room.

Angry eyes still fixed on Jack, Usman reached to a sheath attached to his belt, and pulled out a knife. At least six inches in length, it was probably the knife that did for his minder.

'You stay the fuck there, *ashiere*,' he spat at Jack. His voice was deep, heavily accented, and had a rasping tone to it.

Jack looked up at Amanda, trying unsuccessfully to reassure her. He had no idea if Ryan was alive or dead, crumpled up in the corner.

Pacing up and down, gesticulating with the knife, Usman said, 'You a newspaper man, right?'

Exhausted, Jack nodded. Blood was dripping from his mouth.

'You writing about me?'

Jack said nothing.

'I know all about you, newspaper man. I know about all the people you have been talking to.'

'And that's how you knew about here?' Jack asked

breathlessly.

'My people can't take a shit without me knowing about it.' He stopped pacing. 'Before I put this to work,' he said, theatrically studying the knife, 'I want you to tell me all you know. What you were going to write. Who you have shared this with.'

'Go fuck yourself,' Jack said, beginning to get his senses back. 'If you're going to put that knife to work anyway, why should I tell you anything, you piece of shit?'

Usman laughed, a deep, throaty snigger. 'I didn't mean on you. Not at first, anyway.' He stepped over to Amanda. 'I mean on your lady friend here. On this *ashawo*.'

'She's not my lady friend, you stupid fuck,' Jack said. 'She's my niece,' he added, coughing blood, realising it would have been better if Usman had not known that.

'Even better. I could cut her. Where shall I cut her, Jack? On her face? Over her body?' As he spoke, he threateningly caressed her face and arms with the tip of the knife. 'Or maybe these?' he leered, running the knife over her breasts. Amanda squirmed, a look of terror on her face.

'All right, all right. You've made your point,' said Jack. 'The police will be here soon.'

Usman looked down at Amanda, caressing her chin with the knife. 'No police coming.'

'Look,' Jack said. 'I'll tell you anything you want to know. I don't care what you do to me. Just let her go. Please.'

'You'll need to do better than that, newspaper man.' Usman strode over to Jack. He lashed out with his foot again, once more sending Jack flying across the room. Jack landed against a cupboard, still conscious, but more dazed. 'I'm in no hurry,' Usman sneered, as he put the knife back in its sheath, and pulled Amanda by her arm off the chair. 'We have time for some fun first.' He dragged her away from the chair, and bent her over the table. She screamed as he kicked her legs apart, held her down with one hand whilst tugging at the back of her jeans with the other.

Jack summoned every ounce of strength he could muster. With a roar, he staggered to his feet and flung himself at Usman, shoulder-charging the bigger man onto the floor. He was now on top of Usman, who was surprised and slightly dazed himself.

Jack tried to climb off Usman and manoeuvre himself out of the way, but Usman was too quick. Jack was back on all fours, and Usman pushed him so he was flat on the floor. Jack was strong, but Usman was stronger, and had Jack pinned down with his knee in the centre of Jack's back. Jack could hear Usman fumbling and prepared himself for the six inch knife.

That was not to be his fate, however; he felt Usman wind a length of wire around his neck, and pull. Usman was pulling so hard, he was lifting Jack's neck and head off the floor. Jack was choking and felt close to blacking out.

Jack managed to get an arm free and tried to pull the wire away from his neck.

Then the screaming began.

A female scream, somehow different from the sound Amanda made minutes earlier. Then a man's scream. Jack did not immediately realise the second shriek came from Usman. As he felt Usman's grip on his neck and back weaken, he felt drops of scalding hot water across the back of his head.

Painfully, he turned and looked up. Amanda was standing in the doorway, clutching the pan which had been on the stove earlier. It was empty. Usman was staggering around, clutching his face with both hands, steam coming off his head. Jack took the pan from his niece, and swung it, impacting with the side of Usman's head. Then a second blow, then a third. After the third, Usman was on the floor, hands still on his face, his legs flailing around. As Jack prepared for a fourth blow, he was aware of a flashing blue light coming from outside.

He dropped the pan to the floor as two police officers

burst into the house and into the room. He staggered back, leaning on the table, wiping the blood off his mouth, and staring down at Usman.

'He's all yours,' he said to the police officers, before he and Amanda collapsed into each other's arms. After a few seconds, Amanda pulled herself away and went over to Ryan. Jack sat at the table, getting his breath back and watched as Usman was handcuffed and led out.

CHAPTER FORTY-SIX

IT WAS EARLY the following morning.

Very early. It was still dark. Dawn was at least three hours away.

Jack and Amanda were sitting in the Accident & Emergency waiting room of the Royal Kendal Infirmary. Where Amanda had been only a few days ago.

After the uniformed police had arrested Kwento Usman, two detectives arrived. They had a brief conversation with Jack and Amanda about what had happened. Ryan had come round, and one of the detectives called for an ambulance to take them to the hospital. Jack protested at first, but eventually Amanda and the detective were able to persuade him to go.

Jack and Amanda had been checked out. No broken bones, although Jack's face did have to be patched up. He was relieved to learn he had not lost any teeth; however the doctor did tell him his ribs and back would ache for a few days, and by then the bruising would have gone. He was prescribed pain killers. Amanda was in good shape, physically at any rate.

The detective accompanying them advised them that Usman would also be attending the hospital to have his face attended to. He had been badly scalded by the hot water Amanda had in the saucepan. He would also need to be checked out for concussion. His eyes would need medication too, as it was salt water that Amanda threw over him. Boiling salt water. For the spaghetti. Jack's new favourite meal. The detective reassured them, especially Amanda, that they would not meet. He would be escorted into another part of the hospital, and would probably be unaware that Jack, Amanda and Ryan were even there. The detective told them Usman would be held in respect of Anji's death as well as assaults on them, and he expected that the Metropolitan Police would be interested in him with regards to the drug ring, and the murder of his associate Kasim. It would be a long, long time before Usman ever saw daylight again.

Anji's body was taken separately to the mortuary.

After they had been seen by the doctors, they both gave preliminary statements to the detective. Now they were sitting waiting for Ryan.

'What sort of scan are they giving him?' Amanda asked, as Jack gave her another paper cup of coffee. 'They did tell me, but it didn't sink in.'

'It's a CT scan,' Jack said, sipping his own coffee and pulling a face. It was disgusting. 'They do it to check for any internal bleeding, or any swelling of the brain. Or to detect a skull fracture.'

'His x-ray showed no broken bones. Is that a good sign?'

'Absolutely. It was his back that took the full force of being banged up against the wall, I think.'

'I take it your x-ray was clear as well?'

Jack rubbed his chest. 'Yes. But lots of bruising.'

'What does CT stand for?'

'I have no idea.'

'Do you think Ryan will be all right?'

'I expect so. He was only dazed, only out for a few seconds.'

'The whole thing was over in a few seconds, wasn't it?'

'It was,' said Jack.

'Poor Anji,' Amanda said. 'I still keep thinking about her.'

Jack nodded. 'I know it's no consolation, but it would have been quick. Instantaneous.'

'She was coming down the stairs when he broke in.'

'Just the wrong place at the wrong time. The door wasn't forced. The detective said it looks like she answered the door, he forced himself in, she tried to run, and he caught her.'

Amanda nodded. 'I did hear a knock.' She rested her coffee on the small table. 'First Sun, then Anji.' She paused, as if something had occurred to her. 'What if you and Ryan hadn't got back when you did?' Her eyes teared up.

'Don't get upset about that. It was me he was after. He wanted to know what I knew.'

She nodded slowly. He was not sure how convinced she was. He certainly wasn't. What would have happened if they hadn't got back did not bear thinking about.

'Thanks, Uncle Jack,' she said, emotionally. 'For everything.'

'Thank Ryan,' Jack replied, a little embarrassed. 'He had the presence of mind to call the police while he was upstairs. Before he leapt on Usman's back.'

Amanda laughed through the tears. 'Yes, he did do good.'

'A regular Errol Flynn,' Jack said.

'A regular what?'

Jack shook his head. 'It doesn't matter. We were also very lucky that a police car was already just around the corner.' He sat quietly for a moment, thinking how differently things could have turned out if the police hadn't been that close.

Amanda looked up. 'It's Ryan!'

Jack turned round as Amanda leapt off her seat and went up to embrace her boyfriend. They both sat down opposite Jack. 'All okay?' he asked Ryan.

Ryan nodded. 'Yes, both the x-ray and CT scan were negative. I'm just a bit sore. They gave me a load of painkillers, and want me to come back on Friday for a check-up.'

'That's good,' said Jack, as Amanda rested her head on Ryan's shoulder.

'So,' Ryan said. 'Are we leaving now?'

Jack picked up his phone. 'I'll get us a cab.'

The police were still at the house when they got back. The spot at the foot of the stairs where Anji was killed was clear, and it looked as if they were almost done in the lounge. The lead detective said they would be able to use the kitchen as it was not part of the crime scene.

'I'll make some coffee,' said Amanda. 'Oh shit!'

'What is it?' Ryan asked.

She stood by the stove. 'It's okay. I don't remember switching this off after I took the water off.'

'You must have done,' said Jack. 'Unless one of the police did it.'

'That would have been good,' said Jack. 'The Fire Brigade here as well as the police.'

At least they were able to laugh.

As Amanda made coffee, Ryan asked, 'What about your story, Jack? What's going to happen about that?'

'It's really done, now Usman's out of the picture. Up here: well, one source has dried up. I'd like to think that's the case in other places, other unis, maybe. I really don't know.'

'And Guillaume? Are you going to shop him to the college?'

'I don't think there's much point. He's lost his source, and his supply. If he did keep any drugs where he lives, there won't be any there now. I might pay him a friendly visit before I leave, just to make sure he stays on the straight and narrow.'

'What about down in London?'

'I expect the Met will want to see everything I have. I'll get the story done and move on to the next assignment. The police will probably raid the pub, and find nothing. Usman kept a supply – I don't know how much – in a flat near Covent Garden. I would imagine somebody would have already cleared that out. He had two minders, assistants, whatever you like to call them. One of them got his throat slit because he spoke to me. The other seemed to be more loyal. He ratted Kasim out. He'll probably store the stuff somewhere else. Usman apparently purchased it over the dark web, using a cryptocurrency. Perhaps if Idi or somebody else gets hold of Usman's ID, password and stuff, they can carry on trading.'

'What about the people you spoke to down in London?'

'Well, I only spoke to two. The police will be contacting them, I would imagine. I don't know how it will be resolved, if at all. It depends on what evidence the police have, and if they decide to prefer charges. I've no idea.'

'What were they like, the ones you spoke to?' asked Amanda.

'Just ordinary kids. One of them lived near the Oval cricket ground. Similar to Guillaume, to Will, in many ways. And to Sun Lee, I'm sure. I felt a bit sorry for them, to be honest. The other one was a supercilious little prat who deserves all he gets.'

'You got on well, then?' Ryan joked.

'Like a house on fire. He even called me an Ethan Hunt.'

'I bet that really endeared him to you,' Ryan said.

Jack nodded, put his cup down. 'What are you two going to do? What are you going to tell your folks?'

Ryan scratched the back of his head. 'I'm not sure yet. I'll tell them something. I assume it'll all come out when the case goes to trial.'

Jack agreed. 'I expect so, whenever that'll be. What about you?' he asked Amanda.

'Oh, God,' Amanda said. 'I really don't know. Same as Ryan. I'd like to think what happened in there stays between the three of us. You won't tell, Mum, will you?'

'All finished here, sirs, ma'am,' said one of the police officers.

'I'll let you out,' Ryan said, and walked them to the door.

'I won't tell her anything. All she knows is, you had a night in the hospital, and are better. I just popped up to check on you, and you are fine. What you tell her is up to you.'

Ryan came back into the kitchen. 'He said somebody will be in touch about a full statement. I said that'll be okay.'

'I just need the bathroom,' Amanda said.

Once she had gone upstairs, Ryan asked, 'You're not going to tell her about me dealing, are you? Or the Instagram thing?'

Jack sighed. So much had happened over the last few hours, he had forgotten about that. 'Has it stopped, the dealing?'

Ryan nodded his head vigorously. 'Definitely.'

'In that case, if she needs to know, it's down to you to tell her. If it's stopped, I don't think she needs to know.'

'Thanks, Jack. I think we ought to ask the college to put us somewhere else, other than here. Too many bad memories. I think she'll agree.'

Jack agreed. 'I think you're right. On both counts. You just need to focus on taking care of each other. Don't give me cause to worry.'

Ryan nodded. 'I will. I love her too, you know.'

Jack looked Ryan in the face. 'I know that.'

'You know what?' Amanda asked, as she returned to the kitchen.

'I know,' said Jack, trying to think of what he did know, 'that I have a lot to do. Oh, shit.' He looked at his phone. Two missed calls and three text messages from Susan.

'What is it?' asked Amanda.

'Missed calls and text messages.'

'From Mum?'

'No. From… It's probably over already now, before it's even begun, but I've been seeing somebody.'

'You have? Who?'

'Her name's Susan, but I'll tell you all about her another time. Look – you don't want me to stay here, do you? Rather than the hotel?'

'No, we'll be okay. He's not going to come back. And we'll keep the doors and windows locked. Does Mum know? About her, I mean?'

'Good God, no. Not yet, anyway. Look, lock and bolt the door after me. I'm going to get a cab back to the hotel. I'll call you this evening.'

'Okay,' said Amanda.

Jack embraced his niece and shook hands with Ryan. Amanda hugged him again at the door, and promised once more to lock and bolt it.

'You're going back to the hotel, then?' she asked.

Jack turned and stood on the middle step as he replied.

'Yes. I'm going back to the hotel. I'm going to get something to eat. I'm going to ring Susan, hoping we're still in a relationship, I'm going to speak to my boss about the story, and tell him what's happened up here. Then I'm going to have a long, hot, soapy bath, then I'm going to lie down on the bed and go to sleep for a week.'

THE END

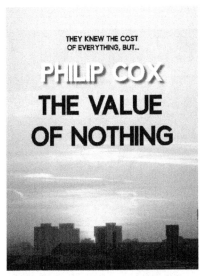

THE VALUE OF NOTHING

A WET AUTUMN NIGHT
Newspaper reporter Jack Richardson lends his coat and car
to a friend

AN ACCIDENT
Within thirty minutes, Jack's car lies in flames

The crash seems suspicious, and Jack wonders if it was an
accident, or murder.

But if it was murder,
Who was the intended victim?

THE ANGEL

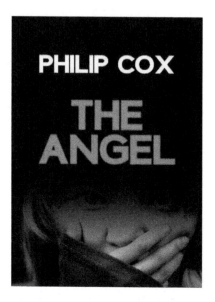

Investigative reporter Jack Richardson is assigned to a story involving sleaze and a prominent Member of Parliament.

During the investigation, Jack receives a call relating to an old case, one involving the murder of a twenty-year-old girl, suggesting that the case might not be as closed as everybody thinks.

Torn between his assigned story, and one where there might have been a terrible miscarriage of justice, Jack must make a choice.

His decision leads him into a dark place he never knew existed, and which puts him in great personal danger…

THE COYOTE

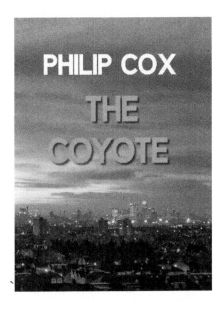

London newspaper reporter Jack Richardson is working on a story when he receives the news that his brother-in-law has been found dead in his car.

Having reservations about the verdict of suicide he starts to probe the circumstances, and finds similarities between his brother-in-law's death and the story he is working on, both connected to a chain of events which began three years earlier, and over a thousand miles away…

INTRODUCING LAPD DETECTIVE SAM LEROY...

LAST TO DIE

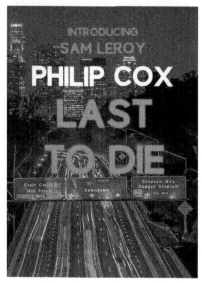

Los Angeles, late September, and the hot Santa Ana winds are blowing, covering the city with a thin layer of dust from the Mojave and Sonoran deserts.

That night, there are three mysterious, unexplained deaths.

The official view is that they are all unrelated. The victims had no connection, and all died in different parts of the city.

However, Police Detective Sam Leroy has other ideas, and begins to widen the investigation. But he meets resistance from the most unexpected quarter, and when his life and that of his loved ones are threatened, he faces a choice: back off, or do what he knows he must do...

SAM LEROY RETURNS IN...

WRONG TIME TO DIE

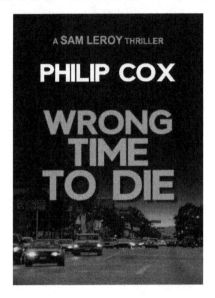

'I don't think I've ever seen so much blood.'

When LAPD Detective Sam Leroy is called to a murder scene, even he is taken aback by the ferocity and savagery of the crime.

Furthermore, there seems to be no motive, which means no obvious suspects.

Believing the two victims themselves hold the key to their own murder, Leroy begins his investigations there, and before long the trail leads him to the island of Catalina, where a terrible secret has remained undiscovered for almost thirty years...

SAM LEROY IS BACK IN

NO PLACE TO DIE

A severed head is found beneath the Hollywood Sign.

Fresh from wrapping his previous case, LAPD Detective Sam Leroy is called to the scene. Now he is tasked with identifying the victim and finding the rest of him.

Not necessarily in that order.

Following up on the few leads they have, Leroy and his partner, Detective Ray Quinn, find themselves unravelling a complex puzzle, one which began two thousand miles from home, and which involves sex, extortion, and ultimately murder.

While Leroy follows the trail, he is feeling himself coming to the end of a relationship, and may possibly be making decisions he might later regret.

SAM LEROY IS BACK IN

ANOTHER WAY TO DIE

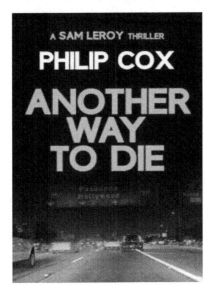

Seven years ago, LAPD Detective Sam Leroy shot and killed Harlan Cordell, and breathed a sigh of relief that the reign of the infamous Pentagram Killer was over.

But now, the killings have begun again. The police believe they are dealing with some fanatical copycat, but these new murders share a small detail with those before, a detail only the police and the killer would know.

How can today's killer know the intimate details of seven years ago?

Or, as he fears, did Leroy kill the wrong man, leaving the real Pentagram Killer to wait and resume his grisly trade on an unsuspecting city?

READY TO DIE

The FIFTH Sam Leroy thriller!

In the middle of the night, a woman reports her husband missing. Soon after, his body is found by the side of Mulholland Drive, killed by a single bullet through the head.

When an adult movie executive is found shot, execution-style, LAPD Detective Sam Leroy and his partner Ray Quinn take on an investigation with minimal clues and no obvious suspects. Statistically, if a murder is not solved within forty-eight hours, it is likely to remain unsolved, and so they are in a race against time to find the killers.

Meanwhile, both men are each facing life-changing events, all of which conspire to make this case all the more challenging…

AFTER THE RAIN

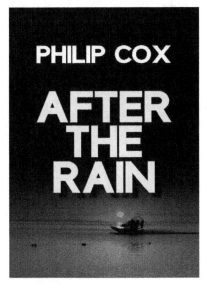

Young, wealthy, handsome - Adam Williams is sitting in a bar in a small town in Florida.

Nobody has seen him since.

With the local police unable to trace Adam, his brother Craig and a workmate, Ben Rook, fly out to find him.

However, nothing could have prepared them for the bizarre cat-and-mouse game into which they are drawn as they seek to pick up Adam's trail and discover what happened to him that night.

DARK EYES OF LONDON

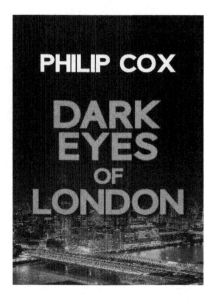

When Tom Raymond receives a call from his ex-wife asking to meet him, he is both surprised and intrigued – maybe she wants a reconciliation?

However, his world is turned upside down when she falls under a tube train on her way to meet him.

Refusing to accept that Lisa jumped, Tom sets out to investigate what happened to her that evening.

Soon, he finds he must get to the truth before some very dangerous people get to him...

SHE'S NOT COMING HOME

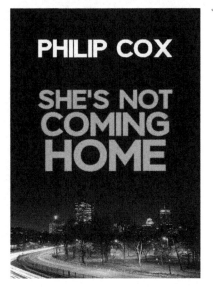

EVERY MORNING
At 8.30 Ruth Gibbons kisses her husband and son
goodbye, and goes to work.

EVERY EVENING
At 5pm she finishes work, texts her husband leaving now,
and begins her walk home.

EVERY NIGHT
At 5.40 she arrives home, kisses her husband and son, and
has dinner with her family

EXCEPT TONIGHT

SHOULD HAVE LOOKED AWAY

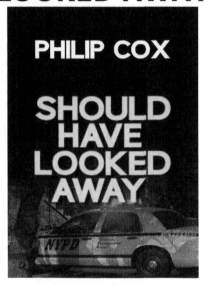

It began on a Sunday. An ordinary Sunday, and a family trip to the mall.

Will Carter takes his five-year old daughter to the bathroom, and there he is witness to a fatal assault on an innocent stranger.

Over the next few days, Will tries to put the experience behind him, but when he sees one of the killers outside his home, he becomes more and more involved, soon passing the point of no return.

Becoming drawn deeper and deeper into something he does not understand, Will feels increasingly out of his depth and is soon asking where this is going and was the victim as innocent as he first thought…

Printed in Great Britain
by Amazon